STEADFAST
HEART

Books by Tracie Peterson

www.traciepeterson.com

BRIDES OF SEATTLE
Steadfast Heart

LONE STAR BRIDES
A Sensible Arrangement
A Moment in Time • *A Matter of Heart*

LAND OF SHINING WATER
The Icecutter's Daughter
The Quarryman's Bride • *The Miner's Lady*

LAND OF THE LONE STAR
Chasing the Sun • *Touching the Sky*
Taming the Wind

BRIDAL VEIL ISLAND**
To Have and To Hold • *To Love and Cherish*
To Honor and Trust

STRIKING A MATCH
Embers of Love • *Hearts Aglow*
Hope Rekindled

SONG OF ALASKA
Dawn's Prelude • *Morning's Refrain*
Twilight's Serenade

ALASKAN QUEST
Summer of the Midnight Sun
Under the Northern Lights
Whispers of Winter • *Alaskan Quest* (3 in 1)

BRIDES OF GALLATIN COUNTY
A Promise to Believe In
A Love to Last Forever
A Dream to Call My Own

THE BROADMOOR LEGACY**
A Daughter's Inheritance
An Unexpected Love • *A Surrendered Heart*

BELLS OF LOWELL**
Daughter of the Loom • *A Fragile Design*
These Tangled Threads

LIGHTS OF LOWELL**
A Tapestry of Hope • *A Love Woven True*
The Pattern of Her Heart

DESERT ROSES
Shadows of the Canyon • *Across the Years*
Beneath a Harvest Sky

HEIRS OF MONTANA
Land of My Heart • *The Coming Storm*
To Dream Anew • *The Hope Within*

LADIES OF LIBERTY
A Lady of High Regard
A Lady of Hidden Intent
A Lady of Secret Devotion

RIBBONS OF STEEL***
Distant Dreams • *A Hope Beyond*
A Promise for Tomorrow

RIBBONS WEST***
Westward the Dream • *Separate Roads*
Ties That Bind

WESTWARD CHRONICLES
A Shelter of Hope • *Hidden in a Whisper*
A Veiled Reflection

YUKON QUEST
Treasures of the North • *Ashes and Ice*
Rivers of Gold

A Slender Thread
All Things Hidden****
House of Secrets
What She Left for Me
Where My Heart Belongs

*with Judith Miller   **with Judith Pella   ***with Kimberley Woodhouse

BRIDES *of* SEATTLE,
BOOK ONE

STEADFAST HEART

TRACIE PETERSON

BETHANYHOUSE

a division of Baker Publishing Group
Minneapolis, Minnesota

Published by Bethany House Publishers
11400 Hampshire Avenue South
Bloomington, Minnesota 55438
www.bethanyhouse.com

Bethany House Publishers is a division of
Baker Publishing Group, Grand Rapids, Michigan

Printed in the United States of America

Library of Congress Cataloging-in-Publication Data
Peterson, Tracie.
    Steadfast heart / Tracie Peterson.
        pages ; cm. — (Brides of Seattle ; book 1)
    Sumary: "In 1880s Seattle, Washington, Lenore Fulcher desires love while so many around her are finding it; when lawyer Kolbein Booth arrives searching for his sister at a finishing school for mail-order brides, he and Lenore face danger and uncertainty amidst their growing attraction"— Provided by publisher.
    ISBN 978-0-7642-1301-4 (hardcover : alk. paper)
    ISBN 978-0-7642-1061-7 (softcover)
    ISBN 978-0-7642-1302-1 (large-print softcover)
    1. First loves—Fiction. 2. Man-woman relationships—Fiction. 3. Seattle (Wash.)—Social life and customs—19th century—Fiction. I. Title.
PS3566.E7717S74 2015
813'.54—dc23   2014031982

Scripture quotations are from the King James Version of the Bible.

Cover design by LOOK Design Studio

15   16   17   18   19   20   21   7   6   5   4   3   2   1

To Abrianna

May you be blessed in the Lord
all the days of your life.

1

Lenore Fulcher swept into her father's offices, feeling like a flower in full bloom. The men who worked for Fulcher's freight brokerage business glanced up to smile and then rose to their feet.

"Mornin', Miss Lenore," one man offered. "What a lovely color you're wearing. That yellow complements your brown hair."

"You're like sunshine" came another comment.

"My, Miss Fulcher, you are more beautiful each time we see you."

Lenore offered a ladylike smile but wanted to giggle. Each one old enough to be her father, these men never failed to fuss and fawn over her as if they were would-be suitors. She gave a nod in acknowledgment of their statements, but a glance at her father caused her to cringe.

"We have freighting matters to see to, or have you forgotten what you do for a living?" Josiah Fulcher roared. Softening his expression, he looked at Lenore. "You always cause such a stir when you come here."

"But, Father, you know as well as I do that you are the one who asked me to be here today." She took hold of his arm and decided it was best not to inquire about the frown crowding his face. "Otherwise I would have gone immediately to see Abrianna. I have some gowns to share with her. After you show me what it is you want me to see, I'm heading upstairs to Mrs. Madison's school." Mrs. Madison owned the building where her father kept his freighting business, but he'd never quite approved of the bridal school being hosted upstairs or of Mrs. Madison's ward, Abrianna Cunningham.

Her father's frown deepened as he escorted her into his office. "I don't know what to think about your friendship with Miss Cunningham or that school. Why, the very thought that Mrs. Madison advertises back east for women to come to Seattle to a school for would-be brides is rather appalling. Isn't she a bit too old to be running such a school? And what of her ward, Miss Cunningham? She seems a bit of a wild and headstrong young woman. And that red hair." He sighed and shook his head. "You know what they say about redheads—they're certain to be challenging. I'm not sure her influence is a good one."

"If they are all so questionable, why rent office space from them?"

"Because it was the only place in close proximity to my own buildings. You know full well that was the only reason. Mrs. Madison is a complete mystery to me, but she lets me have the space at a low rate, so I have no choice. Even so, I retain my concerns about her and the other ladies who work with her. And I believe my worries about Miss Cunningham have been proven over and over."

Lenore laughed and squeezed her father's arm. "Oh, Father, you and Mother watched Abrianna and me grow up! We've been dear friends forever. And we attended and worked for the same church and charities. What is all this newfound worry about? I've turned out quite fine, haven't I?" She released her father's arm and gave a twirl.

"Well, I, for one, think you have" came a male voice.

Lenore turned on her heel so fast that her skirts ballooned in a swoosh of air. One of her father's associates stood in the open doorway with a look of amusement. Heat crept up her neck.

"Come in, James," her father ordered.

James Rybus did as instructed, pausing only long enough to give Lenore a quick bow. Of all the men in her father's office, he was the handsomest and the youngest, even though the man was a widower and pushing forty.

"I do apologize for any discomfort I've caused."

"Nonsense, James," her father replied before Lenore could form words. "Take a seat and let us get right to the heart of this matter."

Lenore worked to calm the rapid beat of her heart with a few deep breaths. Was Mr. Rybus joining them? Why would her father ask her to meet with him and his accountant? Perhaps he had something to share with Lenore about the trust she would inherit when she turned twenty-one. Of course that was still several months away, so it wouldn't be of any importance just yet. Would it?

Father took hold of Lenore's arm and brought her out of her thoughts, moving her to a large leather chair. Lenore settled on the edge of the seat, knowing that should she ease back into the comfort of the chair, her feet would not reach the floor. What an embarrassment that would be. And after her last little spectacle, goodness. Not that it was a shameful thing to stand a mere five feet tall, but with dangling limbs, Lenore would feel more like a child than a regal and fashionable young woman.

Father walked to his desk and picked up a cigar. Crimping the end, he looked to James. "Would you care to begin, or shall I?"

"You are in charge here," Rybus replied, yielding to his superior.

Her father lit the cigar and puffed on it a couple of times before taking his seat at the massive mahogany desk. There was an air of confidence about him, but Lenore could see something in his eyes that suggested worry.

"Lenore, I wanted you to come here today because Mr. Rybus has asked for permission to court you."

A lump formed in Lenore's throat, and for a moment she feared fainting. *Mr. Rybus?* Her immediate thought was to refuse. *Surely Father must be suffering a fever to think such a thing would interest me. The man is very nice looking and has a steady situation, but goodness, how could Father want me to court this old man?*

Yet how could she possibly refuse? Her father would speak for her at least until she married or came of age. She really had nothing to say on the matter—at least nothing she could voice in front of Mr. Rybus.

"I'm certain this comes as a surprise," her father continued, "but I thought perhaps it was time to see you take on a serious beau. After all, your mother is worried that you'll be an old maid."

Mr. Rybus shot her a smile. "I doubt that would ever be possible. One as lovely as you, Miss Fulcher, must have a great many admirers. Even so, I'd be very honored if you would accept my request."

Lenore needed time to think. But she knew it would be impossible to leave the office without offering some kind of commitment. "I don't know what to say," she replied honestly. "I never expected to come here and be presented with such a request. Mother would have palpitations if she knew we were having such an important conversation here—at your place of business, Father."

Her father blanched, and Lenore knew she'd taken the right approach. Even so, she didn't wish to shame her father. She folded her gloved hands together. "I will consider the matter, however. Perhaps we should continue the conversation later this evening if Mr. Rybus could come for dinner."

"A splendid idea," her father replied. "We will dine at six, James. I'm sure you can attend." It was more a command than invitation. "And we always dress for dinner."

"I would be honored." He smiled at Lenore and came to where she sat. He gave a low bow. "Until tonight, Miss Fulcher."

Lenore nodded. "Yes. Until tonight."

"He did what?" Abrianna asked but never gave Lenore time to respond. "Right there in the brokerage office? In front of everyone?"

"Yes. Well, no. It was in Father's private office. Still, I'm sure that everyone knew what was being discussed. I don't know what must have gotten into him. It wasn't like Father at all."

"Perhaps he's suffered a malady of the brain," Abrianna suggested. She tapped her finger to her chin. "I believe Mrs. Madison said that people his age were often given to such things."

"He's had no symptoms," Lenore replied. "But I suppose you could be right."

Abrianna pushed back her curly hair. Dark auburn-red with

gold highlights rippled and caught the sunlight. Lenore had always thought it quite pretty but wished that Abrianna cared more about fashion and propriety. Sometimes her friend was known to do some of the strangest things. Lenore had always hoped that maturity would tone down the risks she took, but instead, it seemed they had increased.

"Has he taken a fall?" Abrianna questioned. "I read that a blow to the head can alter a person's state of mind."

"I'm sure it can, but Father has taken no fall."

"Are you certain?" Abrianna looked most concerned.

"I would have heard it discussed around the house. The servants are always sharing one scandal or another." Lenore plopped onto Abrianna's bed in a most unladylike manner.

"I don't want to court Mr. Rybus. He's handsome and all, but he makes me feel like a child. He's so much older—nearly forty. Goodness, but that's ancient."

Abrianna giggled and put her hand to her mouth. Glancing around as if to make certain no one overheard, she lowered her hands and whispered, "Don't let my aunts hear you say that. There's not a one of them who doesn't long for that age."

"Well, it's all right for aunts to be old, but not suitors."

"I quite agree," Abrianna said.

By the look of her contorted expression, Lenore knew her friend was deep in thought again. Lenore couldn't help but find a small comfort in Abrianna's consideration of her dilemma. The young woman was good at problem solving. Where Lenore always seemed to be focused on the questions of why and how, Abrianna took more interest in the solutions.

"He's to come to supper this evening. It's there that I'm supposed to give him an answer. Fiddlesticks. I don't see how I can possibly refuse."

"Perhaps tell your father there is someone else."

"But there's not," Lenore replied. "Furthermore, Father and Mother know that very well. They oversee all of my activities. You know that. I can't even slip away to see you without having to notify a driver."

Abrianna sat on the opposite side of the bed and lay back to stare at the ceiling. Lenore did likewise from her side and their heads met in the middle. Turning to face her friend, Lenore shrugged. "It's hopeless."

"Never. We just need to figure out how God wants us to resolve the situation—then make it happen."

Lenore wasn't convinced things were done that way, but Abrianna's wisdom bore consideration. She could be quite spiritual in times of trouble.

"I don't suppose it would hurt to allow him to escort me a few times. I could then tell my father that he wasn't a suitable suitor and let him handle dismissing Mr. Rybus."

"I'd like to think he might." Abrianna looked toward Lenore. "However, your father is an educated man."

"Meaning what?"

"Meaning that he has most likely spent a great deal of time analyzing and evaluating this matter. Aunt Selma told me once that her husband was like that. He would spend hours pondering a situation before making a decision. She said that most men were like that." She paused, sat up, and flipped her hair over her shoulder. "It wastes time, if you ask me. I say why not just plunge right into a decision. If it works out, you've saved yourself a great deal of time, and if it doesn't work, then you've still plenty of time to try again."

Lenore considered Abrianna's comment. Her father was a man who liked to weigh his options. No doubt he had considered this idea for some time, even if Lenore was just now hearing about it. And then there was Mother to consider. She had often tried to suggest various acceptable suitors. "Goodness, but sometimes I wish we could go back to short dresses and ribbons in our hair."

"I still wear short dresses," Abrianna declared. "At least short enough to run in. Sometimes I get myself in quite a hurry and I don't have patience for a gown binding my legs."

"*Limbs*, Abrianna. *Legs* are vulgar."

Her friend giggled. "Not if they can run fast."

"Be serious. This weighs heavy on my heart."

A brief knock on the bedroom door was followed by Mrs. Madison's brisk entry into the room. "Abrianna, you have a lesson in baking bread. You're late again and I do not appreciate having to round you up while the other young ladies wait."

"But I have a guest." She dramatically jumped to her feet and put her hand to her breast. "Lenore has just received some troubling news, and we are in deep spiritual thought for an answer."

Mrs. Madison raised her eyebrows and lowered her chin. "I am quite certain you can continue to think deeply while kneading bread. Perhaps Miss Fulcher will wait for you in the parlor. She will find a selection of ladies' magazines there that I'm sure will occupy her time." She gave Lenore a knowing smile. "Or you could spend the time in prayer."

Lenore didn't wish to ire the lady any further. In an instant, she was on her feet. "I will be happy to wait there, Mrs. Madison. Father will be busy until lunchtime, so I really haven't anywhere I need to be. I only wanted to bring some gowns to Abrianna. Might I have our man fetch them?"

"Of course." Mrs. Madison glanced at Abrianna's wrinkled

appearance. "If you can persuade her to dress in a manner more befitting her age, I would be most appreciative."

"Oh, Aunt Miriam," Abrianna sighed. "First bread and now my attire. Must I always suffer such trials and torments of disapproval?"

Mrs. Madison tightened her lips and turned for the door. "Two minutes, Abrianna. Do not give me cause to berate you in front of the other young ladies." With that, she exited the room, leaving Lenore and Abrianna to follow.

"My life is such a chore." Abrianna retucked her blouse into her skirt. She went to the dressing table and began forming her long curls into a knot at her neck. She secured this with a few pins and sighed. "I have no great love of bread, so why must I learn to bake it? Would God not have me do something of greater value? Just look at all the times in the Bible where bread got folks in trouble. The Israelites had to make it without leaven so they could leave quickly, and the disciples always seemed confused about bread."

Lenore couldn't hold back her laughter. "Oh, Abrianna, you do go on. Perhaps the greatest value of your life will be baking bread. Perhaps the Lord has plans for your bread-baking abilities. Just imagine it—you might very well be able to feed thousands by giving your bread like the boy in the Bible with his loaves and fishes."

Her friend gave Lenore a troubled look. "I don't mind feeding the hungry, but why must I be the one to bake their bread? I would be just as content to serve it or even pay for it—if I had riches."

Lenore laughed again and put her arm around Abrianna's shoulders. "Pity you weren't born into a wealthy family."

Abrianna sighed. "It is, Lenore. It is a great pity."

Miriam Madison advertised her school as a place for "practical women who desire to become practical brides." When her husband passed away shortly after coming west to make a new life in Seattle, she found he had left her a small amount of money and this building near the waterfront in Seattle. Taking her situation in hand, Mrs. Madison took on the task of reordering her life, and the idea of the school came to her. With the help of her younger sister, Poisie Holmes, and dear friend and widow Selma Gibson, she turned her misfortune into a way to support not only herself but the other two women, as well. They lived quite comfortably and trained other women to do likewise. Together they had managed the Madison Bridal School for nearly twenty years.

Miriam knew a deep satisfaction at her success. The early years had been difficult, but based on a previous idea tried by a local man named Mercer, Miriam was certain she could make the arrangement work. Mr. Mercer had no doubt failed because he was a man. At least that was her firm belief. After all, what godly woman would want to set sail and leave kith and kin to risk Mr. Mercer's proposal of mail-order brides? The man might just as well be a debaucher of women. For certain he had persuaded a few, but the project never worked as well as he had hoped, and many a bachelor was sorely disappointed. That was, until Miriam took on the project.

"Now, ladies, you must form loaves and put them into the pans to rise." She walked down the center table and nodded in approval at each woman's progress. "This will take several hours. During that time you can work with Mrs. Gibson on crocheting doilies for your hope chests."

Another idea that had come to Miriam. Most of these young women arrived in Seattle with nothing much but the clothes on their backs. The school provided their train ticket to San Francisco and a steamer ticket to Seattle. The girls would earn their keep while attending school by making various things to sell to locals. There was always a wide variety of foods and handwork for sale. Particular favorites were jams and cookies, as well as items of sewing. Work shirts and simple wool blankets often were sold in a frenzy of bidding. Some of their talents were auctioned off at monthly receptions, which serious young men seeking a bride could attend and get to know the young ladies better. Of course, there was an admission fee. That was one of the only ways to prove a man was serious, according to Selma. If a man were to part with some of his hard-earned cash for the right to dress uncomfortably and spend a day attempting to be cultured and socially astute, then the ladies believed them of serious interest.

At the end of the table, Miriam found Abrianna and her attempt at bread making. Her ward was generously sprinkled with flour, as was the floor. In fact, Miriam thought perhaps more flour had made it onto the floor and into Abrianna's hair than into the bread. The tiny lump of dough looked gooey and refused to form up properly.

"What have you here, Abrianna?"

"I think it looks rather disappointing. Don't you, Aunt Miriam?" Abrianna shook her head. "I would not want to be the recipient of bread so obviously wanting. I do not believe I have the talent to make bread. Pity, too, for I would have enjoyed tasting the finished product. You always make such lovely loaves, Auntie, although bread is certainly not my favorite. I'm much more appreciative of your apple pies."

Unwilling to give in to flattery, the older woman merely nodded. "Start again, Abrianna. This time I shall watch you measure out your ingredients. My guess is that you simply put in too much water or perhaps not enough flour. Either way, we shall endeavor together to overcome your *disappointing* dough."

She saw the disappointment on the redhead's face but knew better than to feel sorry for the girl. Abrianna had been her most difficult pupil since the ladies took her as their own. Perhaps it was the trauma of losing a mother so young. It might even have been the desertion or death of her father right after Abrianna was born. They were never quite sure which was the case, although Abrianna's mother was certain to her dying day that he never would have abandoned them. Who knew how such things truly affected one's ability to function—and to make bread. In Abrianna's case, however, Miriam Madison had found her greatest and most frustrating challenge.

2

For Abrianna Cunningham, anything related to cooking was a chore. Nevertheless, days after the "Great Bread Ignominy," as she had come to call it, she found herself making cookies. She liked cookies well enough. In fact, she loved sneaking huge numbers out of the school to give away to all the homeless sailors and orphans she'd befriended. Aunt Miriam was always horrified at this, chiding Abrianna for taking off unaccompanied and befriending old men who were of questionable repute.

Abrianna laughed this off, for since she'd been a child she had sneaked out to visit the docks and surrounding city. Everyone knew her and looked after her like a wayward little sister. And she liked that. It suited her nature to be sister to the entire world. Besides, by slipping out to venture forth on her own, Abrianna had become well acquainted with the city life of Seattle. She knew where she could finagle extra food or a blanket or two for her homeless friends. Abrianna also learned to avoid the more dangerous areas of town, including places where the staunch church matrons might see her. They would only condemn her aunties for such behavior, and Abrianna couldn't bear the thought. Her aunts were good women, and when others questioned their actions or attitudes, Abrianna always found herself feeling overprotective—even unforgiving.

Of course, she always did forgive them in the end. By the time she said her evening prayers, her conscience wouldn't allow her to continue in hard-hearted anger. But it was only after asking God to sear the old biddies' hearts with a desire for mercy and kindness, and to remind them that gossip was a sin, that Abrianna truly repented.

Now as Abrianna juggled two cookie pans into the oven, she tried to focus on why she was there. Aunt Miriam was determined she learn to cook. Aunt Selma was just as determined she become an accomplished seamstress, while Aunt Poisie was less imposing—an amusing play on words that made Abrianna giggle. She often said that Aunt Poisie did not "impoisie" herself on folks. Just as often, Aunt Miriam requested that she keep such thoughts to herself.

"At your age, Abrianna, you should comport yourself in a more ladylike manner," she could hear Aunt Miriam say.

But the trouble was, Abrianna didn't care about being a lady. Nor was she particularly happy about growing up. Growing up brought with it a great many requirements and responsibilities that Abrianna would just as soon not worry about. For instance, it was thought to be quite socially unacceptable for her to visit the docks or even go to see her lifelong friend, Wade Ackerman, at his little shop, much less "mill about town," as Aunt Selma called it. Not only that, but she was expected to wear her hair up and her skirts down—down to her boot tops. And she didn't even want to think about gloves. Couldn't her aunts understand that she would only soil them when visiting Wade's wagon shop or when giving food to one of the hungry?

"You look deep in thought."

Abrianna startled and put her hand to her breast. "Speak of the devil."

"What?" Wade Ackerman asked in confusion. He glanced around as if looking for someone else.

"Oh, not really. I do apologize. That was rather harsh and uncalled for. You aren't at all like the devil. You have morals and values that would make the devil quite uncomfortable." She smiled. "Let me start again. Good afternoon, Wade. What brings you to the Madison Bridal School?"

He laughed and pushed back a strand of brown hair in annoyance. "I don't think my new hair tonic has quite the hold it's been boasting."

"I can't say that I'm surprised," Abrianna declared in a self-assured manner. "What can you expect from a product produced by the Hoggleson Brothers? I mean, the name suggests something less than tidy." She noted his slicked-back hair. Other than the single errant strand, Wade looked quite well groomed. Except that he had a two-, possibly three-day growth of beard.

"Did you lose your razor?"

"What?"

"You need a shave," she said, pointing to his face.

Wade touched his hand to his chin. "I suppose I do. I've been busy." He rubbed his finger along the stubble under his nose. "You do realize mustaches are all the rage now."

"I just don't believe it becomes you. Your appearance isn't enhanced by the hair. You just look . . . well . . . hairy." She shook her head. "I suppose there is nothing to be done about it right now. What are you working on at present?" Abrianna settled herself on a kitchen chair. She liked her casual talks with Wade. Their friendship had survived all sorts of ups and downs, and Wade was very much like the older brother she'd never had but always wanted.

He joined her at the table. "I've been making repairs to the depot wagons. They sure go through a great deal of wear, and I can't say that the workers in charge of them ever think to properly care for them."

"Maybe they're too busy," Abrianna suggested with a raised brow and tilt of her head. She cocked her head to the other side. "Honestly, I'm not sure I can continue to converse with you and that beard. I really find it distracting."

Wade laughed. "You would send me away because I didn't have time to shave? I only stopped by to return some dishes. I set them down over there." He pointed. "You didn't even hear me come in."

"I was preoccupied with collective thoughts of great importance," she defended. "I am not a mindless ninny, Mr. Ackerman. I spend many an hour contemplating."

He grinned and leaned back against the very table where Abrianna had failed at bread making. "And what, pray tell, do you have need to contemplate?"

She was taken aback. Did he not realize she was a woman of deep thinking? Goodness, they'd known each other for most of their lives, and somehow he had missed this point. Were all men so blind? "I contemplate a great many things."

He crossed his arms against his chest. "So give me an example. Tell me what goes through that fiery red head of yours."

"My hair is not fiery. It's a honeyed auburn. At least that's what Aunt Poisie calls it." She wasn't sure if she agreed, since honey had many shades, and who was to say which hue a person might think of when such a remark was made. "Lenore says it's more of a gold-touched cinnamon, but Aunt Poisie is most insistent."

"All right. What goes on in that honeyed-auburn, gold-touched cinnamon head of yours."

"Well, my *head* isn't really colored either one. It's only the hair that could be called by that name."

He shook his head in frustration. "I give up."

"Well, if you must know," Abrianna said, mimicking his exasperation, "I'm still quite undone by the entire Chinese matter."

Wade looked at her a moment and then rubbed his chin as if contemplating a puzzle. "What do you mean?"

"The way they rounded the Chinese up and tried to force them from the city," she replied. "Have you forgotten?"

"That was two years ago, and the matter was somewhat resolved. As I recall, they were allowed to remain."

"Some were, but others had already been sent away. A good number of people of whom I was fond were loaded like cattle onto ships for market."

"I didn't realize you had so many close relationships. I thought you were mostly fond of the Chinese for their food," Wade said with a chuckle.

Abrianna fixed him with a glare. "While I did enjoy their food, I was also quite taken with their culture and traditions. I learned a great deal from our kitchen girl, Liang. She has told me many stories about her life in China. You do remember that her parents and sisters were some of those sent away. Liang thought she and her family would all be killed, but she managed to escape before her family was put on a ship. She was left destitute and betrayed by the very society that should have rallied to her protection."

"But they did rally . . . well, some of them did. Besides, what can you do about it now? Your aunts took in Liang, and she's now safe and well cared for. And her family was able to resettle in San Francisco with relatives. Liang chose to remain here in your aunt's employ. That's hardly destitute or without friends."

"That's true enough." Abrianna shifted against the ladder-backed chair. "But I'm still deeply offended by what happened and by the prejudice that remains. Poor Liang was but twelve. How terrible to be taken from the people you love. And she wasn't the only one, Wade, as you well know.

"This city should answer for what they did. Not only that, but one of the biggest supporters, that Mary Kenworthy—" Abrianna jumped to her feet and began to pace, all the while waving her arms to accentuate her speech in case Wade somehow missed her distress. "She continues her ugly disapproval of the presence of Chinese in Seattle. She believes them to be the cause of so many white men having no work, but you tell me what white man would be caught dead working at the jobs some of the Chinese are doing." She stopped, arms akimbo. "Just tell me."

"Well, I didn't mean to work you up into a lather." He shook his head. "Now I can see why you're preoccupied most of the time. Your mind must never stop churning."

Abrianna sighed. "You have no idea. It's quite a labor to be me."

Wade's face screwed up. "Is that smoke I smell?"

Glancing around the kitchen, Abrianna saw the gray cloud rising from the oven. "Oh, fie. I forgot my cookies. I put the blame on your facial hair." She hurried to the stove and opened the door. Thick smoke caused her to cough, and for a moment rendered her senseless. She reached into the hot oven, but Wade jumped toward her, pushing her aside.

"Move back. Let me get it." Wade took up a dish towel and doubled it twice before pulling the burning cookies from the oven. "You could have seriously burned your hands, Abrianna, reaching into the oven like that. What were you thinking?" He placed the smoldering discs atop the stove and stared at them. "Some of them aren't too bad." He cleared his throat.

Abrianna frowned. With a spatula in hand she flipped one of the cookies over to reveal the burned bottom. "Aunt Miriam will never allow this."

He shrugged and gave her a smile. "She doesn't have to know. I can help you scrape off the bottoms where they're burned."

"She'll smell the smoke. I'm surprised she isn't here already. If she wasn't busy showing her students how to properly dye cloth, I'm sure she'd be wondering what catastrophe I had brought about this time."

Wade quickly went to the windows and opened first one and then another. "The room will air, and since the kitchen door is closed, I doubt the smell went further than right here."

"I suppose we can hope such a miracle will befall us." Abrianna moved the cookies to a plate for cooling. "Goodness, I had such high expectations for this batch." She poked at one of the cookies. "Aunt Miriam says I'm likely to be an old maid for all of my life." Abrianna looked Wade in the eye. "I think she has given up hope for my chances at matrimony, despite running a school for brides." She paused, most contrite. "I am her deepest sorrow."

Wade laughed. "Abrianna, you are no one's sorrow. Now, let's get to scraping those cookies."

They had been working on the cookies for nearly ten minutes when Abrianna heard the unmistakable sound of shoes on the back staircase. "It's Aunt Miriam. She's coming to survey my accomplishments. Hurry and close the windows, or she'll know for sure what a mess I've made."

Wade did as instructed while Abrianna scooped the mess of

blackened crumbs into the garbage pail and quickly covered it with some potato peels she had left over from earlier tasks. They both hurried back to the counter just as Miriam Madison entered the room. For a moment the older woman stood frozen in place, narrowing her eyes. Her expression suggested that she knew something to be amiss but couldn't quite put her finger on it.

"Wade," she finally said with a nod, "it's good to see you again. I have another job for you, if you're of a mind. Oh goodness, are you growing a mustache?"

"Not exactly." He smiled. "Why don't we go out to the parlor and discuss the job you have for me?" He offered his arm in a gentlemanly fashion. "My, don't you look lovely today, Mrs. Madison."

Abrianna barely heard her aunt's reply, but she was most grateful to have avoided a reprimand. Perhaps that would come later. Little ever escaped Aunt Miriam's fine sense of order. She had an uncanny way of knowing when things were amiss. Abrianna smiled and prayed that should her aunt turn back, she would see her ward relaxed and happy. Maybe that would assuage her aunt's concerns.

But it was not to be. Aunt Miriam turned at the door with a look of disappointment. She opened her mouth as if to say something, but then closed it and shook her head. Abrianna had no doubt she knew what had taken place and was deeply grieved.

Oh, bother. I can't seem to do anything right. Sometimes I contemplate whether God made a mistake in making me, but of course God doesn't make mistakes. Still, I can't help but wonder just what He was thinking.

Wade sat waiting for Mrs. Madison's final instructions. Like the former schoolmistress that she was, the woman didn't miss any point.

"I do hope you understand, Wade. It must be done in such a way as to completely eliminate the drafts."

"I believe I can master the repair you need."

The request was for Wade to repair cracks around the windows on the third floor, and Mrs. Madison had even shown him how she perceived the job to be accomplished. Wade was just about to get up and excuse himself when Mrs. Gibson and Miss Poisie Holmes entered the parlor.

"Why, Mr. Ackerman, we hadn't realized you'd come to visit." Miss Poisie sat opposite him. "It's so nice to have a gentleman caller." She looked to her older sister as if she'd made a mistake and added, "On a day other than our normal receiving days." She glanced back to Wade and gave a quick bobbing of the head before lapsing into silence. Miss Poisie was often outdone in conversation by the two older women, and she knew her place.

"What brings you here today?" Mrs. Gibson asked. "Did you have a premonition that we were in need of your skills? You know, God often lays a thought on a person's heart when others are in need."

"That's true," Mrs. Madison murmured.

"Yes," Miss Poisie added, again bobbing her head as if it had come loose at the back of her neck.

"I can't say that I had any premonition, Mrs. Gibson. I actually figured to return your dishes. The food you ladies sent home with me last Sunday was quite substantial, and it saw me through until today."

"I'm so glad that nothing is amiss." Mrs. Gibson waved a handkerchief to her face. "I do worry in these difficult times that there are things amiss for which I have little knowledge." She leaned forward rather conspiratorially and added, "It troubles me deeply."

Wade might have chuckled had the woman not been so serious. The three ladies were sometimes amusing to him in their unfounded frets and concerns. It seemed to Wade that if anyone could create a situation of great apprehension and despair, it was the ladies of the Madison Bridal School.

"So what do you hear around the city?" Mrs. Madison questioned. "I read in the paper that there were problems with the steam pipes at the Spring Hill Water Company. I do hope that matter was resolved."

"Oh dear, yes," Mrs. Gibson said in a most foreboding manner. "A city without water is a frightening thing."

Wade didn't bother to point out that there were other sources of water. Instead, he offered a smile of comfort. "It has been resolved, and water is once again being pumped. I have that on the best authority."

"What a relief," Miss Poisie said, both hands covering her heart. "Bless the Lord for His favor."

"Indeed, Sister," Mrs. Madison replied.

"Mr. Gibson used to find such things quite fascinating," Mrs. Gibson said as she began settling back into her seat. "You know he was a man of science—"

"God rest his soul," Miss Poisie interjected, as she always did when mention was made of the dead.

"Amen," the other women replied in unison.

It was an act Wade was familiar with and had come to expect. He nodded, as if approving their prayer.

"Of course, he dabbled in things he would have been better to leave alone," Mrs. Gibson said in her ominous way. "He read those things written by Robert Chambers and"—again she leaned forward as if to share something that her present company had yet to learn—"that Darwin man."

Miss Poisie gave a shudder.

It was always the same. Wade wasn't annoyed by the repeat performance at all. To the contrary, the consistent presentation amused him and endeared the older women to him more each time.

"I'm certain that it grieved our God in heaven." Mrs. Gibson shook her head.

"Amen," the sisters agreed.

"I hope you will never partake of such things, Mr. Ackerman," Mrs. Gibson lectured.

"No, ma'am. I have no desire for such things."

"That's wise of you. Very wise. Mr. Gibson should have been blessed with such wisdom. He wasn't at all given to reading such nonsense when we first married. I believe in truth it's why he suffered apoplexy—bleeding on the brain, don't you know. It was to my great shame and embarrassment." She looked very much the martyred soul. "He was unable to speak or move in his final months, and I am certain that was visited upon him for his promiscuous affair with such dark sciences as evolution and astronomy. I endeavored to save him for God, however, until the day he passed on."

"God rest his soul," Miss Poisie murmured. She looked as if the sorrow was too great to bear.

"Amen."

Wade found himself murmuring the word in unison. Their conviction that this was a most troubling situation was sincere, and he would never tell them that he questioned some of their beliefs.

"I read the Bible to him every day of his remaining life," Mrs. Gibson said with a look that suggested she'd gotten the upper hand in a game of cards. Not that the old ladies would ever allow for such items in the house, much less to partake of their purposes. "I read the Scriptures from cover to cover until the day I found him passed on to glory. To glory—if God would have him; although I've never been entirely assured God could forgive such grave misjudgments."

"Is anything too difficult for God, Mrs. Gibson?" Wade hadn't meant to ask the question aloud. He certainly had no desire to offend the women.

But rather than be offended, Mrs. Gibson nodded thoughtfully and put her index finger alongside her temple. "That, Mr. Ackerman, is a very good question. I shall endeavor to ponder it for some time to come."

Wade smiled. "I'm glad to have shared your company, ladies, but I really must get back to my work. I'll try to come on Saturday to fix those windows for you." He stood and bowed to each woman.

"We shall look forward to your coming." Mrs. Madison rose from her seat. The other ladies did likewise. "We pray you have an easy labor today."

He nodded, remembering the pile of work that waited. "I pray so, too."

Just then Mrs. Madison turned and sniffed the air. "Do you smell something burning?"

Wade blanched and moved toward the door in a hurry. "Good day, ladies." He hurried down the hall to where he'd left his hat. He chided himself for being a coward, but he had no desire to try to once again distract Mrs. Madison. For all he knew, Abrianna had just burned down the kitchen.

3

Kolbein Booth looked at the address he'd written down. He seemed to be at the right place, but he couldn't imagine that a brothel could reside in this stately looking office building. He entered the main doors and found a small lobby. A sign pointed straight ahead to the freight brokerage firm of one Josiah Fulcher. Another sign to his left pointed up the highly polished wooden stairs. Under this was a small placard reading *The Madison Bridal School*.

These were a brave lot to advertise so freely. Bridal school indeed. He stuffed the slip of paper into his vest pocket and took the stairs two at a time. He reached the second-floor landing to find a single point of entry. The door was closed, but a beveled glass window revealed a tidy entryway and what appeared to be a small sitting room.

He hesitated for a moment, not knowing whether to knock or just barge in. After all, if this establishment was really what he figured it to be, surprise might well be his best weapon. With that in mind, Kolbein turned the handle and opened the door. He heard girlish laughter and wondered if it might be his sister Greta.

"So Mr. Rybus didn't come for dinner?"

"No. Something important came up at the last minute. I was relieved, but then Father rescheduled the dinner for next week."

The second one sounded somewhat like Greta, and Kolbein steeled himself to confront her. However, when two young women rounded the corner, he could see that neither was his sister.

The girl with red curls flying in all directions startled, while the young lady with the fashionably coiffed hair and elegant gown offered him a smile. She was beautiful—the most beautiful woman he'd ever set eyes upon.

"Good morning. Welcome to the Madison Bridal School."

He turned to the redhead, who fixed him with a stare as she studied his face. "Uh, good morning." He pulled his hat from his head and reminded himself he wasn't there for small talk. "No, it's not a good morning. In fact, it's probably one of the most unpleasant I've had to deal with."

"Oh my," the young woman replied. She pushed red curls over her shoulder. "Are you ill? Have you suffered a financial loss? Or perhaps you are as disturbed by the Anti-Chinese League as I am? Goodness, but there are hundreds of problems to lay a person low."

Kolbein hadn't expected such a barrage of questions. "I . . . uh . . . I'm a lawyer from Chicago."

"Oh dear," the redhead replied again. "I've heard nothing good comes out of Chicago. Of course, they said the same of Nazareth, and our Lord clearly lived there, so perhaps my sources of information have been prejudiced by unseemly characters who compromised the experience for them."

"What? What are you going on about?"

At this the fashionable young woman stepped forward and

took his hat. "I'm Miss Fulcher and this is Miss Cunningham. Her aunts are the proprietors of this school. If you have a card we can certainly take it to Mrs. Madison." She handed the hat to Miss Cunningham, who placed it on a receiving table by the door.

He nodded numbly and reached into his pocket. He took a small gold case from his jacket. "I have one here." He handed over a calling card.

"'Mr. Kolbein Booth,'" she read. Looking up, Miss Fulcher smiled, and it very nearly took his breath. "Why don't you take a seat, and we will deliver this."

Kolbein wasn't sure what to say. He had so expected to find debauchery of every sort behind the doors of the school's façade that seeing such refined young ladies—well, at least one of them was refined—came as a surprise.

He softened in her nearness. "Is this . . . I mean . . ." He fell silent and then tried again. "Is this truly a school set up to train brides?"

Miss Cunningham's brows knit together. "What else would it be?"

"I heard a man's voice." An older woman dressed in a starched white nautical-looking blouse and navy skirt joined them.

Miss Fulcher turned first and then Miss Cunningham. "Miss Poisie, this is Mr. Kolbein Booth. I believe he is looking for Mrs. Madison." She looked back over her shoulder and threw him a smile. "Or perhaps you would care to visit with all three ladies, Mr. Booth?"

Kolbein was at a complete loss. All he could do was nod. Every threat, every word he had planned to rail at the management of this establishment, fled his conscious thought at the sight of this petite young lady.

The older woman gave a bob of curtsy and took the calling

card in hand. "I am Miss Poisie Holmes, and you may address me as Miss Holmes or Miss Poisie. Come this way, Mr. Booth. We are taking tea. Girls, you will join us, as well. Miriam sent me to find you, and she's adamant that you come at once."

Kolbein watched the girls fall into obedient step behind Miss Holmes. They appeared content to follow the older woman's instruction and seemed well behaved. Kolbein glanced around at the fine furnishings. They weren't opulent, but neither were they shoddy. The furniture and bric-a-brac had been given the utmost care. He felt almost certain that he could see his reflection in the polished wood floor, but there wasn't time to study it because the ladies were moving right along.

Miss Holmes stopped without warning before a set of pocket doors. Miss Fulcher and Miss Cunningham all but walked right into her.

"What is the purpose of your business, Mr. Booth? Are you here to find a bride? I only ask because our regular receiving day is Saturday. We have a monthly event with refreshment and entertainment, but that isn't for another week."

"I am searching for my sister," Kolbein replied with renewed determination. "Her name is Greta Booth."

Miss Holmes nodded and pushed back the pocket doors. "Sister, Selma, we have a visitor."

They entered a large parlor where two old women sat sipping tea from fine china cups. They looked at him with an expression that suggested he'd just broken protocol in a most unforgivable way. For the first time in years, Kolbein felt rather sheepish.

"Mr. Booth, this is my sister, Mrs. Madison. The school, you might have guessed, is named for her, since the Madison Building was once owned by the dearly departed Mr. Madison. God rest his soul."

"Amen," the other women responded softly.

"And this is Mrs. Gibson. She is one of the instructors here, as am I. My sister also teaches."

Kolbein gave a slight bow. They studied him for a moment and then Mrs. Madison pointed to the chair across from them. "Please sit there." It looked rather like the position of honor one might give a criminal about to be interrogated. Afraid of further offending, Kolbein sat, while Miss Holmes remained standing to one side.

"Would you care for tea? We have Darjeeling today, and it is quite good."

"Poisie, do sit down. We will determine if Mr. Booth is to have tea after we learn of the reason for his coming."

"He's looking for his sister," Miss Holmes offered and then took a seat beside Mrs. Gibson.

"Booth, you say?" Mrs. Gibson interjected. "You aren't at all related to that horrible scoundrel who killed President Lincoln, are you? What a vicious man—a sneak of the worst possible kind. Oh, it was a terrible tragedy. Poor President Lincoln, struck down in the twinkling of an eye."

"God rest his soul," Miss Holmes murmured.

"Amen" came the chorus from the other women.

Kolbein found the entire scene rather disconcerting. "As far as I know, our family is not related to John Wilkes Booth. However, whether we were or not, there is still the subject of my sister."

"I say!" Mrs. Gibson gasped. "It very well matters, for we would never entertain a man or woman related to that cad. You seem quite unconcerned with the company you share."

"He's from Chicago," Miss Cunningham whispered ominously but loud enough that all could hear.

"Well, that explains it." Mrs. Gibson leaned toward Mrs. Madison. "I believe we should put him out."

"Now then, Selma, we must have charity. Perhaps the man could not help his place of residence."

"That's true." Miss Holmes nodded. "Perhaps he was stranded there by circumstances and unable to leave. Such a tragic thing. Much like my dear Captain Richards when his ship broke up at sea. God rest his soul."

"Amen," Mrs. Madison said in a curt manner. "Now, Sister, this man has no time to learn of your lost captain." She turned back to Kolbein. "Mr. Booth, no matter your reason for residing in Chicago, please tell me why you feel your sister has come to be with us."

"She left me a letter before running away. Your school was mentioned as her destination."

"I see. What is your sister's name?"

"Greta. Greta Booth. She's but a child, only nineteen."

Mrs. Madison looked at him in the same fashion his sixth-grade schoolmistress had when he'd forgotten his homework and made up a story about its absence. "Now, Mr. Booth, that is a bit of an exaggeration. Nineteen is hardly the age of a child. Your sister is a young woman of marriageable age."

"But she's too young to run away and make do for herself. And despite what you think, she's also too immature to marry. Her departure from the safety of her home proves that."

"I assure you, Mr. Booth, the laws here allow for a woman as young as eighteen to marry," Mrs. Madison declared. "Therefore, I would venture to say that the territory of Washington thinks her not a child at all."

"I don't care about that or what the territory believes. My sister is young and naïve. She's not been out in the world to know what dangers abide. She grew up sheltered in boarding schools of the highest repute. Now, may I see her?"

"I'm afraid not," Mrs. Madison declared. "She isn't here. I have never met your sister."

Kolbein had prepared himself for the worst, that his sister might have been duped to go west and found herself forced into prostitution. He had prepared himself to find her wounded and beaten for refusing such a position. However, he had never considered that she might not have gone where she claimed to be going.

"I have made inquiries and followed her from Chicago to San Francisco and finally to Seattle. Witnesses along the way declare her to have taken the train west and then came north by ship."

"She may very well have arrived in our fair city, but she did not come here to participate in our school. Of that you are clearly misinformed."

Sitting back hard, Kolbein could only shake his head. "Then where could she be?" The fear he'd shoved down for many weeks now reared its ugly head. What might have become of her? What if he never saw her again?

"I believe now would be a good time for the Darjeeling, Poisie," Mrs. Madison said. "I do apologize, Mr. Kolbein. The tea is from the autumnal flush, which ended in December. However, as you know, Darjeeling tea is not picked from December to March, so we await the spring flush most eagerly."

"We hope to be some of the first to receive it," Miss Holmes added, her head bobbing up and down.

Her sister quickly took over. "It is some of the very finest tea. Personally, the spring flush is my preference."

Kolbein couldn't believe that the women were droning on about tea. His sister was lost somewhere in the city, and they were talking about whether the tea was fresh. Unable to gain further insight, Kolbein knew he had no reason to remain. He stood with abrupt agility.

"If you'll excuse me, I really must go. I need to find my sister."

"We could certainly ask our friends," Miss Holmes declared, looking to her sister and friend for approval.

"That is a good idea, Poisie." Mrs. Madison gave Kolbein another stern look. "Why don't you return here in say a week? We will ask amongst our friends at church. If anyone has heard of your sister, we will make certain they are here to meet you."

This was a turn Kolbein hadn't expected. The old ladies were looking at him with expressions of deep concern. Perhaps he had misjudged them. "I could return next week. Is there a day that would be convenient?"

"Actually, Mr. Booth, if you would desire to come on Saturday, we have a reception where young gentlemen may come to meet our young ladies. There is usually a fee; however, we wouldn't expect that of you. You may take your choice of days. I only offer the Saturday reception as an option."

"No, I wouldn't want to participate in the reception. If it pleases, I'd just as soon return here next Monday."

"Very well. Abrianna, why don't you show Mr. Booth out." She paused and frowned. "Surely you had a hat."

Kolbein could hear the concern in her voice. "I do. Miss Cunningham took it at the door."

"Ah, very good. Abrianna, don't forget to return his hat."

"Yes, Auntie." The redhead got to her feet and motioned him to follow.

Kolbein glanced at Miss Fulcher. He lost himself in her smile. "Miss Fulcher, thank you for your kindness. And, ladies, thank you for your concern." He followed Miss Cunningham from the room.

"I do hope you find your sister," she began. "The city isn't nearly as dangerous as one might think. Not if you know where to go. Of course, your sister won't know where to go, so I suppose that is a concern." She glanced over her shoulder at him as they retraced their steps to the front door.

Kolbein didn't know what to say. Miss Cunningham had a way about her that suggested she was unconcerned with social etiquette. He found her openness rather refreshing, but her manner of chattering on and on was exhausting.

She extended him his hat and smiled. "I do hope you find your sister."

"Yes, you said that."

Miss Cunningham nodded. "So I did. Well then, perhaps I shall merely say farewell . . . until next we meet again."

4

Priam Welby was a man used to making things happen—especially when they involved something that he wanted. He smiled at Miriam Madison, but inside he was seething. He'd just offered the old crone an outrageous sum of money to buy the Madison Building, but she had refused.

"Mr. Welby, you must know that my husband left me this building. It was one of the few things Mr. Madison owned when he passed on."

"God rest his soul," Mrs. Madison's sister declared.

Mrs. Madison nodded. "Amen."

Welby shook his head. "Ladies, I understand sentimental value, but this building is perfect for my import business. It is just beginning to make me a decent profit, and I need this building. You are perfectly situated to the harbor, not residing in the Lava Bed area, where the worst scum and degenerates are to be found along Skid Road, nor far up the hill to that intellectual society of university dwellers. It's a good location for a business such as mine."

"Mr. Welby, while I can appreciate your desire to better your business, I simply cannot help you. This is more than just a building. I house dozens of young women here at any given time. We run a finishing school for potential brides."

Welby knew all about the school. He had thought it rather ridiculous, while others in his circle of peers spoke of finding accomplished brides, who could not only sing and play the piano but comport themselves like women befitting a higher social station. Priam thought it all nonsense and beyond any interest to him. What interested him was his own business and the fact that the demand for imported goods had grown over the last year.

"Mrs. Madison, I am not suggesting you give up your lucrative business. On the contrary, I have a proposition to make. Not only will I pay you the amount I offered for this building, but I also have a beautiful house in the Lower Queen Anne area. It's a palatial estate. There are acres of well-manicured lawns, servants' quarters, a stable, and a carriage house. The main house itself is massive compared to your setup here. The entire third floor comprises a ballroom."

"We have that here, Mr. Welby," Mrs. Madison replied.

"I assure you that my mansion is far better suited than what you have here. I myself found it rather alarming to learn that young women were living in this building. Why, you are in one of the roughest areas of Seattle. There are all manner of hoodlums lurking about. I would think you would want to get away from the waterfront."

"Oh, but we can't!" the younger woman declared without warning. "I could never live without having the sea in view. It would just break my heart. My dear fiancé, Captain Jonathan Richards, God rest his soul, of the fishing vessel *Sea Vixen* and the United States Naval Services prior to that, lost his life at sea. I couldn't be parted from that connection."

"Poisie, take that basket of lemons upstairs to Selma," Mrs.

Madison commanded. "I'm certain she has need of them by now."

The woman who had been introduced to him as Miss Holmes got to her feet, and Priam did likewise, as any good gentleman would. "Good day, Mr. Welby." She gave a little bob of her head and crossed the room to take up the basket of lemons she'd earlier deposited by the door.

Once she was gone, Priam returned to his seat to address Mrs. Madison in earnest. "I realize this place was left to you by your husband. However, as I mentioned before, it is hardly a decent location for the school you operate, much less for a home. You are putting the lives of dozens of young women in danger. Don't you think that a place away from downtown would better serve?"

"Of course not. The men are downtown. They've come to depend on the women being here. Why, right now we're serving tea and lemonade with light refreshments upstairs in the ballroom. Are you married, Mr. Welby?"

"No. I've never had reason to be."

Mrs. Madison looked at him as if he were a child in need of guidance. "*Tsk tsk.* I believe God has a man for every woman and for every woman a man. Why don't you join us upstairs? You can get an understanding of what we do here. And you just might find a bride for yourself."

"Forgive me, but I truly have no interest. A wife would require more attention than I have to give at present. Perhaps one day I will take you up on your offer, but for now I'm quite content with my bachelorhood."

"Nonsense!"

Mrs. Madison's sharp declaration made Priam jump ever so slightly. He had faced down grown men of questionable reputations and dealt with high society kings who thought they knew all the tricks in the book, but never had he felt quite this intimidated. And to think it was an old woman who caused him such discomfort.

"Aunt Miriam," a much younger woman called from the door. Priam got to his feet once again. The stranger stepped into the room with a blaze of untidy red curls and a winning smile. The smile faded just a bit when she noticed Priam. "Excuse me. I didn't know you were still here," she said, staring at him. She seemed to realize how harsh this sounded and proceeded to apologize.

"I hope you won't take offense at my comment, sir. I very often speak before thinking. In fact, Aunt Miriam chides me for it at least six days a week. But never on Sunday. Sunday is the Lord's Day of rest, and Aunt Miriam says that even she must rest from disciplining. Although with so many young ladies, she also says it's hard to rest . . . even on Sunday."

Priam was fascinated by the young woman's chatter. She had a way of going on and on about the silliest things. He'd never seen anything quite like her.

"Abrianna, I will be finished here shortly. I just invited Mr. Welby to join us upstairs."

"I'm afraid that's impossible today," Priam said. "I'm due at another appointment—a luncheon—and the time is already noon."

"Abrianna will show you out. I should get back to the reception. I do hope you aren't overly disappointed, Mr. Welby. I'm certain that upon prayer and reflection God will direct you to another property."

But Priam knew better. He'd already reviewed other properties, and this one suited him in full. But he realized by the set of the woman's face and firmness of tone that she had made up her mind. For this battle, Mrs. Madison could call herself the victor. But winning one battle was not winning the entire war.

The redhead—Abrianna, Mrs. Madison had called her—waited for him. She was a pleasant enough looking young woman, but there was something of the hoyden about her.

"So Mrs. Madison is your aunt?" He made his way beside her.

"In a manner. You see, my mother died when I was quite small and there were no other relatives. She asked the ladies to take charge of me before her death." The woman shocked him by giggling. "Well, of course it was before her death. She could hardly do anything after she died." Abrianna smiled. "It's amazing the things we say, isn't it, Mr. Welby?"

"It is indeed, and you seem at no loss for such things."

She looked embarrassed, but it passed quickly. "I'm afraid I am quite the complex soul. I fear there are so many words that float about my head that I must speak them or they will rupture something." She held his gaze for a moment. "*Rupture* isn't one of those words that we shouldn't mention in mixed company, is it? Goodness, I can never keep all the rules straight. Why, just the other day my dear friend Lenore chided me for saying *legs* when I should have said *limbs*."

Abrianna frowned and shook her head. "There. I suppose I've just said it again. I'm quite hopeless, but my heart is good."

He laughed in spite of himself. "I'm certain you are right, for you seem gentle of spirit despite your enthusiasm for life."

She surprised him by touching his arm. "You are so kind to say so, but I am afraid that I am quite incorrigible. Especially when it comes to talking and speaking my mind. Aunt Miriam said it was a pity that a young woman couldn't earn a living by talking, or I might be wealthy." She looked at him with such an expression of sober contemplation that Priam couldn't help but grin.

"I must say, it has been a pleasure meeting you, Miss . . . ?"

"Cunningham. Abrianna Cunningham. No relationship to the very wealthy Cunninghams of Tacoma, however. I didn't even know they existed until one of the gentlemen who attended our receptions made mention of it."

"Well, Miss Cunningham, I don't believe that matters one whit. You are charming and obviously intelligent. Very pleasant to look at, as well. Now, if you'll be so kind, I'll take my hat and bid you adieu." He gave her a slight bow.

Abrianna handed him the hat. "Good day, Mr. Welby, and do have a pleasant lunch. It looks to rain, so I hope you have an umbrella or maybe a closed carriage."

He chuckled. "I have both. Never fear." She nodded and he took his leave. What a curious creature, so vivacious and unabashed in her ways. He smiled to himself. Perhaps she was the answer to his problems. Perhaps Miss Cunningham—not of the Tacoma Cunninghams—could help convince her adopted aunt that selling to him would be the best thing.

* * *

"I'm so glad your aunts allowed you to accompany me today," Kolbein told Abrianna. He then turned to the beautiful woman between them. "And I'm very grateful for your help."

"Between Lenore and me," Abrianna said, "we know more than half the city's occupants. Surely if your sister is here someone has seen her. Although, if she's trying to disguise her appearance so that no one can find her, it will be more difficult. Do you suppose she is traveling incognito? Perhaps she has taken another name."

"I doubt she would go to such trouble," Kolbein assured her.

"At least the rain has stopped," Lenore commented.

"Yes," Abrianna agreed. "It rained all the time we were in church yesterday, and it made concentration impossible. I wonder if the Lord ever thought about how distracting rain can be when it rivals the words of a preacher teaching on the Beatitudes."

"I'm sure the Lord knows very well what we endure," Lenore told her.

She smiled at Kolbein and he felt his heart beat all the harder. He had never felt this way about a young lady—not even once in his life. Could this be what all the fuss was about? Could this be the same fever his friends had caught? The sickness that led them to the altar?

"Mr. Booth, I wonder how it is that you came to be guardian of your sister."

"Please, call me Kolbein."

She nodded her approval. "I suppose such ways are the latest fashion. But then you must call me Lenore."

"And I'm Abrianna, but of course you already knew that."

Kolbein smiled at both women. "I would very much like to call you by your given names. It makes conversation so much easier, more personal."

"My mother would say it is more intimate, which is why I suppose she would also discourage it," Lenore replied. "However, I'm of a mind that times are changing, and we must also change with it."

"I agree," Kolbein said. But did he really? Most of his life he had lived by a strict set of guidelines and restrictions. It was one of the reasons he enjoyed his legal work. There were laws and regulations to follow, and it was only when someone or some case set a new standard that he felt uneasy. Now, however, he was breaking all of his social restrictions and speaking to these young ladies as if they were brother and sister rather than new acquaintances.

"You asked me about my sister. Our parents died when Greta was still quite young. Being older by twelve years, I was left as her guardian. We had no other family, save an aged uncle in New York, so there seemed no other choice."

"So that means you are thirty-one," Abrianna declared.

"I will be in September," Kolbein replied. "I was twenty-two when we received word of our parents' death. They were killed in a train accident in the Northeast. Greta was devastated. I was just out of college and had taken a job clerking for a judge in Richmond."

"Virginia?" Abrianna asked. "But I thought you were from Chicago."

"We moved there at a later date."

"On purpose?" Abrianna questioned, as though he'd lost his senses.

They crossed the street and Kolbein noted a dress in the window of a clothing store. "That gown . . ." He walked to the window, unconcerned with his companions. "I'm certain that my sister had a gown such as this."

"Maybe we should check within," Lenore suggested. "The proprietor might remember seeing her."

The idea was more than reasonable, and Kolbein opened the door of the shop and ushered his companions inside. The shop seemed dim, despite electrical lighting. A man at the end of the counter stood examining several pairs of gloves as the trio approached.

"I wonder if I might inquire about the gown in the window," Kolbein began.

"Looking to buy it for one of these young ladies?" the man asked. He looked from Abrianna to Lenore and back again. "I think it might fit this one, but not that one." He looked at Lenore and smiled. "The coloring would be good for you, too, miss. However, you're just a tiny mite and would probably need the gown hemmed considerably."

"I'm not looking to buy the gown, but I need to know where it came from. The young lady who sold it to you is my sister, and I'm desperately trying to find her."

The man frowned. "You're not buying, eh?"

Kolbein had seen that look a million times before. "I might be inclined to buy it back for her, if I knew where I could find her."

The man shook his head. "Don't know where she is. She showed up here one day with a young gentleman. They offered the dress and a pair of matching slippers, and I bought them. It's a quality gown, and I gave her more than I would on the normal trade."

"That was gracious of you," Kolbein said, feeling a great sense of frustration. "But you have no knowledge of where she went after she left your store?"

"'Fraid not. I have plenty to keep me busy without worrying about where my clients go after they sell me their wares."

"It's truly important," Lenore offered. "The young lady may be in trouble."

"Wish I could help you," the shopkeeper replied. "But I honestly don't know anything more than I've told you."

Kolbein narrowed his eyes. "Even if I buy the gown back?"

"Even if you buy twenty gowns in this store. I don't know anything about the girl. She was here one moment and gone the next. I'm sorry, mister."

With a heavy sigh, Kolbein nodded. "I understand." He paid

for the gown and slippers. The man wrapped them in paper while Kolbein tried to figure out what to do next.

The proprietor thanked him for the purchase, but Kolbein said nothing in reply. He tucked the package under his arm and made his way outside, barely remembering to wait for Lenore and Abrianna. Greta had been there—so close and yet so far.

"I'm sorry that he couldn't tell you her whereabouts," Lenore said, "however, if she came to this shop might it be reasonable to assume she could live nearby?"

"I suppose so," Kolbein said, feeling more downcast than when they'd begun.

"I think that would be a correct conclusion," Abrianna stated. "Lenore, you are brilliant. Perhaps we should talk to the hotel proprietors in the area. If that doesn't lend us some ideas, then maybe we could branch out and speak to other storekeepers. If she is residing in this area, she must surely shop at one or more of the stores."

"You're both correct," Kolbein said, clearing the clutter from his head. "It's worth a try. At this point, it's all we have."

"Well, we have the Good Lord, too," Abrianna replied, "although sometimes He keeps His thoughts to himself. I've been praying and praying on this matter and still have no clear understanding. That's not unusual, however." She fixed him with an intense gaze. "Are you a praying man, Mr. . . . I mean, Kolbein?"

"I've never really had much time for church as an adult," he replied, feeling most uncomfortable. His parents had always encouraged regular church attendance, but from the time of college until now Kolbein had found little time for God or prayer.

"You aren't an evolutionist, are you?" Abrianna gasped. "Aunt Selma says they're everywhere, and we must avoid them at all costs." She looked to Lenore. "She says that even God's grace can't cover their sins, but I tend to believe God is able to forgive most anything, don't you agree? Why would He be God Almighty if He wasn't able to be mighty over all sins?"

"I'm not an evolutionist," Kolbein assured her. "But neither am I overly religious. I've been very busy with my law practice. I find it consumes most of my time. And given that God is also consumed by laws and such, I suppose I have something of a connection to Him."

They turned down yet another street, and Abrianna seemed to forget all about the condition of his soul and pointed instead at a building. "That's Wade's wagon shop. Why don't we go tell him what we're doing and get his help? If he's too busy, we can speak to him on Sunday over dinner." Abrianna turned to Kolbein. "I'm certain my aunts would approve of having you to Sunday dinner, as well, and I know the other ladies will enjoy your company. They always fuss over Wade and Thane—that's Wade's best friend— whenever they're there. Frankly, I think they're all just man crazy."

Kolbein chuckled and shook his head. "I think you think too much."

Lenore sat at her dressing table unable to forget the way Kolbein Booth had looked and sounded. His image filled her mind, leaving her almost breathless. She found that he captivated her in a way no other man had ever done. Could this be the start of love? Did it happen that way?

She toyed with an emerald necklace. She would have to deal with Mr. Rybus tonight, but her heart was definitely not in it. Mother seemed pleased that he would share dinner with them, but Lenore knew her mother would be less pleased once she learned the truth.

"I do not want to court James Rybus." She discarded the necklace and walked to the window. Darkness hid the details of the Fulcher gardens, but it didn't matter. She wasn't there to see anything in particular.

"I have to convince them that this is a bad idea. That I shouldn't be forced into a relationship for which I have no interest. But how?" Somehow it seemed to help to speak her problem aloud.

Then in a flash an idea formed. *What if I tell them there's someone else?* The image of Kolbein Booth flooded her thoughts.

"Mr. Booth is a perfect solution." She went back to the dressing table and retrieved the necklace. It didn't matter that Mr. Booth had no idea she found him so appealing. It didn't matter that it would be a stretch of the truth.

Lenore fastened the necklace. The glitter of emerald green at her throat completed her ensemble. *I'll tell them there is someone else—that my heart has been captivated and I wish to court another.*

But what if they demanded a name? What if her father insisted on having her court James Rybus until this other suitor made himself known? Oh, it was all so complicated.

"If I have to lie, I'll lie," Lenore whispered. Her mind whirred with thoughts of how the evening might play out. With any luck at all, she would convince them of another suitor's interest. Then the only problem would be to convince Mr. Booth.

5

Lenore glanced across the table to her father and then to
Mr. Rybus. Her mother looked uncertain about the entire
situation and for once kept her opinion to herself. Lenore wished
her mother would have spoken up, but since she refused, Lenore
knew she would have to speak her mind or lose any chance of
courting Kolbein Booth. She pushed aside her uneaten dessert
and cleared her throat.

"I realize that this is hardly a conversation we would usually
have at the dinner table; however, I cannot in good faith keep Mr.
Rybus guessing my answer regarding his desire to court me."
She saw that she had their devoted attention and continued. "I
have given this a great deal of thought, but the fact is," Lenore
said, hesitating a moment, "I have feelings for another man."

"Another man?" her father asked. "No one else has come to
ask me to court you. Who is this other man?"

Mother gave her a startled look. "What man? You've said
nothing."

"He's a gentleman who showed up at the bridal school looking for his sister. He's a lawyer from Chicago, and . . . well . . .
I would like to give my attention and affection to him." She

looked at James Rybus and smiled. "Please don't take this as an insult to you, Mr. Rybus. I am honored that you would even consider me. I know what a great woman your wife was and how honored she was in the community because of you."

Mr. Rybus lost his shocked expression and nodded. "Eleanor was beloved by many."

Lenore nodded thoughtfully. "She was truly a remarkable woman. She gave a great deal of time to charities and the beautification of the city."

"That's hardly the point," Father interrupted. "I don't know this other man and—"

Mother put her arm on Father's hand. "Josiah, we agreed that Lenore could choose to court whomever she desired. Why not give her young man a chance?"

"Because he hasn't the decency to approach me directly." Her father fixed her with a hard stare. "Why wouldn't an honorable young man seek me out?"

Lenore knew better than to suggest that Kolbein had not yet made any declaration of interest. Instead, she chose a safer route. "His sister is missing. She left their home and headed to Seattle and hasn't been heard from since. Mr. Booth is half sick with worry and came to the bridal school because he had reason to believe his sister would be there. She wasn't, but everyone at the school is trying to get word out to find her. I feel certain that when the situation is resolved, Mr. Booth will seek you out." At least she hoped so.

"Well, while I sympathize, I do not believe it's fair to keep James dangling on a hook. I will give your young suitor exactly one month from today to seek a courtship. In the meanwhile, I hardly think it can hurt if you were to accompany James on a few social outings. Isn't that right, Monica?"

Mother looked to Lenore. "I would say that entirely depends on Lenore, as well as Mr. Rybus. Since he already knows her to be interested in someone else, perhaps he would rather not spend his time trying to woo our daughter."

"Nonsense," Mr. Rybus replied, much to Lenore's disappointment. "I would be honored to escort your daughter. Perhaps if she gives me a chance, her affection might grow." He smiled and settled his dark-eyed gaze upon Lenore. "Would it be acceptable for me to take you to the opera and perhaps a musical concert and dinner sometime?"

Lenore didn't know what to say. On one hand her mind was quite fixed on her father's one-month deadline. How could she encourage Mr. Booth to fall in love with her in such quick fashion? However, she realized that Father might have refused her altogether. She didn't want to shame him in front of his associate.

"I would be honored, Mr. Rybus. So long as you know my heart on the matter, I do not feel that I would be leading you on."

"Thank you, Miss Fulcher. I look forward for a chance to compete for your affection."

His study of her face left Lenore feeling a bit confused. He was a very pleasant sort of man, and while he was nearly twenty years her senior, he hardly seemed that old. Perhaps her feelings for Kolbein Booth were merely a momentary attraction. If Kolbein didn't share her affection, maybe she could reassign her affection on Mr. Rybus.

"Wonderful. If you aren't busy this Friday, I should very much like to accompany you to the opera."

Lenore looked to her mother. To her surprise, Mother frowned. "We have plans to sail for San Francisco on Saturday next. We hadn't yet announced this to Lenore, but she will accompany us."

Lowering her head so that Mother couldn't see her expression, Lenore felt more concern about leaving Mr. Booth than accepting an outing with Mr. Rybus. Why hadn't her parents said anything before now? They knew how much she hated their last-minute plans, especially when they involved her. She wanted to ask why it was so important that she accompany them, but already Mr. Rybus was assuring Mother that they could simply do an early dinner. This seemed to meet with the approval of her parents, and then all eyes were turned to her.

She pasted on what she hoped was a sweet smile. "Of course. I will be glad to accompany you to dinner."

"Wonderful!" Rybus sounded like a man who had just had his fondest desire granted. "I will make reservations for us. Would six be early enough?" He looked to her father.

"I would think so. So long as you have Lenore home by eight-thirty so that she can finish directing the servants with her packing and see to anything else she needs to attend."

Mr. Rybus nodded and Mother rose from her chair. "If you'll excuse us, gentlemen, Lenore and I have some plans to make."

The men stood and Mr. Rybus even hurried to assist Lenore from her chair. He was a very thoughtful man and his manners were impeccable. Perhaps courtship with him wouldn't be so bad. After all, Kolbein Booth might not even care for her. And there was that pesky problem of his hailing from Chicago.

"Then Mother announced out of the clear blue that we are traveling to San Francisco on Saturday."

"Saturday?" Abrianna didn't like the announcement at all. "However long will you be gone?"

"I haven't any idea. Father has business there and Mother

wishes me to accompany her shopping. You know how she hates to let any of the latest fashions escape her perusal."

Abrianna frowned. "I cannot imagine being a slave to such a thing. Aunt Miriam says that idols take many forms. Have you ever thought to suggest to your mother that fashion may well be an idol?"

"I wouldn't dare," Lenore said, shaking her head. "Mother may be shallow in her faith, but it isn't up to me to point that out."

Abrianna considered that a moment. Perhaps Lenore was right. It might seem offensive if a daughter were to reveal her mother's sin. "So you mentioned having a task for me," Abrianna began. "What might that be and how soon will I need to perform it?"

"I want you to endorse me to Mr. Booth."

"In what way?" Abrianna asked in confusion. "What might this endorsement entail?"

Lenore gave a heavy sigh. "Honestly, Abrianna, for a woman of your age, you really should know more about men and women. Haven't you noticed that I have feelings for Kolbein . . . Mr. Booth?"

She couldn't have been more surprised had Lenore suggested that they attempt to walk on water. "You have feelings for him? But you just met him. Aunt Miriam always says that while love at first sight can certainly happen, it is rare and must be evaluated at every turn." She leaned closer to Lenore. "Have you given it such evaluation?"

"I have, Abrianna. I can't help how I feel. I haven't been able to think of anything or anyone but Mr. Booth since first meeting him. I thought perhaps it was just a momentary fascination, but it's more."

"How can that be?"

Lenore shrugged. "I don't know. I just know that I have a deep desire to know him better. I might even call it a longing."

"A longing?" Abrianna couldn't begin to understand. "That sounds most serious."

"It feels very serious," Lenore admitted. "What worries me, however, is that he will find his sister while I'm gone and never know of my . . . affection. I'm so afraid that he'll return to his home and I'll never see him again."

Abrianna looked around the sitting room for a moment. What exactly did Lenore want her to do if he found his sister and headed back to Chicago? What if his sister turned up sick or even dead? He wouldn't care at all about Lenore in that case.

Finally Abrianna looked back to her friend. "I can hardly tie him to a chair. Do you want me to tell him how you feel?"

"Certainly not!" Lenore toyed with the lace on her cuff and, though clearly vexed, did not raise her voice. "I merely want you to keep my name before him. I want you to speak in a glowing manner of my abilities and personal traits."

"I suppose I can do that," Abrianna replied. "Although I don't really know much about such things."

"Goodness, Abrianna. You've grown up in a bridal school. How can you be so clueless about romance and the sharing of affections?"

Abrianna shrugged. "I suppose because I've done my level best to avoid such things. God has better things for me to do. I believe I'm to be about the business of loving all mankind rather than one man. Surely you don't fault me for that."

"No, of course not. Although sneaking around town to take food and blankets to the homeless or to visit the old sailors on the docks seems a most unsettling pastime for a young woman."

"I don't expect you to understand." She shook her head. "I'm not sure that I understand . . . completely. All I know is that my parents were poor folk who could barely keep food on the table. My father left and most likely died shortly thereafter, and my mother had no choice but to seek out the help of her church. She knew that she was sick and wouldn't live long, but she had a child to care for. Such things stir in me the desire to help others. Perhaps I shall be like a Joan of Arc."

"And lead your people to war?" Lenore asked with a giggle.

"Well, then maybe a Florence Nightingale."

"So now you plan to become a nurse?"

Abrianna straightened. "If that's what God wills for me. However I can best help the people is what I want to do. Nevertheless, I will do what I can to see that Mr. Booth remembers you well. Daily—at least if I see him daily—I will endeavor to draw him into conversations that speak of your traits."

Lenore giggled. "Tell him only the good things. I'm afraid the bad will speak for itself."

"You have no bad traits." Abrianna plopped into the closest chair. "I'm the one who has all of those." She heaved a sigh. "I burn more things than I manage to cook. I can sew a straight line, but forget singing or playing the piano. I'm a most uncomely dancer, and my red hair is far too shocking a color to call me fashionable."

"You can be fashionable, Abrianna. And I've seen you dance. You do quite well. Your hair would fit expectations if you were to pin it up all of the time instead of just on Sunday."

"I only pin it up then because my aunts insist. I like having the wind in my hair. Not only that—this mess is difficult to keep pinned in place." She leaned forward. "Sometimes I give serious consideration to cutting it short like a boy."

"Never do that, Abrianna. My father would forbid us any further meetings if you were to do something so questionable."

"I know that full well. It is a terrible burden to carry," Abrianna said with yet another sigh.

Lenore sat down beside her on the settee. "Abrianna, you could do much to improve the way people see you. I believe you to be one of the kindest and most honest people I've ever met. When I look at you, I know that you are authentic through and through. There isn't even a hint of pretense in your mannerisms."

"I know I'm supposed to give the impression of being a well-trained young lady, but the things taught here at the school rarely interest me. I love politics and causes. I fear for the Chinese in the days to come. After all, if the mobs would round them up once, they will be inclined to try again. I am troubled by the hatred people have for those who are different. I want homes and warmth for the cold and weary. I pray for food and healing for those who wander the streets of Seattle. If I had a big building like this, I wouldn't run a bridal school, I'd have a home for the friendless."

"Goodness, that would be a shocking position for a young single woman to take on. You'd be better to carry on the work of your aunts."

"I hardly think so. Eventually there will be more than enough women in the West and thus no longer a need for such a place."

Lenore folded her hands. "Having young women in town is one thing. Teaching them to be acceptable wives and mothers is an entirely different matter."

"Then you can train them, and I shall find homes for those who have nowhere to go." She sat up, realizing this was the very seed of a desire she didn't even know she had. She had long taken goods to the old seafarers who were too old to go to sea but had no other place to call home. Abrianna had given blankets to those poor souls on the streets, shared money and food with the street urchins, and had even taken hot soup to ladies of the evening who were suffering maladies. She knew her aunts thought it all very scandalous, but Abrianna knew it to be a calling.

"We have completely digressed," Lenore declared. "I want only to know that you will hold up my memory to Mr. Booth and encourage a deeper understanding between us."

Abrianna nodded with a weak smile. "I shall endeavor to do my best for you."

The Monday following Lenore's departure, Abrianna hoped to have a chance to help her friend as promised.

"I have cookies and sweet cakes just like you asked." Liang pointed to a cloth-covered tray as Abrianna entered the kitchen. The small Chinese servant threw her a toothy smile. "I take roast meat and put with bread, too. You like?"

"Oh, I like it very much, and the boys will like it even more. Thank you, Liang. You don't think they'll be missed, do you?" Abrianna began loading the food into a basket.

The dark-haired girl shook her head. "You take and help the poor. I will make sure no one worries."

Abrianna loved this tiny girl. Liang made Abrianna want to fight all the harder for the Chinese. Why couldn't they all share Seattle—America, for that matter—and live in harmony?

"Mr. Booth, he wait in the dining room," Liang announced as if Abrianna might have forgotten that he was coming.

"I'll be going now. If my aunts worry overmuch about where I've gone just tell them I'm looking for Greta Booth with Mr. Booth." Abrianna tucked a cloth over the food.

The fourteen-year-old gave her a nod. "I tell them."

Abrianna swept into the dining room. Kolbein stood at the window, his back toward the room. Tapping him on the shoulder, Abrianna spoke in a soft tone. "I'm ready to go if you are."

He turned and smiled. "I am. Thank you for doing this. Here, let me take that." He reached out for her basket.

Keeping her voice hushed, she stepped closer and handed him the basket. "I would like to help you find your sister, and I think I have a pretty good plan."

He appeared to contemplate her statement. Finally he asked, "And what would that plan entail?"

Abrianna put a finger to her lips and motioned him outside. "I need to keep my aunts from knowing what I'm about. They won't worry as much if I'm escorted by you. Although they might think it inappropriate for us to be alone. They often think things to be inappropriate when I see no harm."

"Then why all this secrecy and whispering?"

She hesitated, hoping that Kolbein wouldn't refuse her or, worse yet, report her. "I have friends who live on the streets. I've called upon them for such help more than once."

"I can't imagine how you might have need of them." Kolbein frowned. "You are a most unconventional young woman, Abrianna."

"I'll take that as a compliment. Now, if you'll just accompany me, we can meet up with them and put them to work looking for your sister."

"But I've already hired a private investigator," Kolbein protested, but she was already heading down the street. "Abrianna, your aunts would never want you to take such a chance."

"I know that," she replied, glancing sideways, "but I must do what I must do. The street folks are people just like you and me, but most haven't the same benefits of education or a loving family. Others are old or very young and considered useless by society. I mean to prove that these people are just as valuable as any other. God has put a calling on my life, and I intend to help them."

Kolbein's eyes narrowed. "How do you know it's God and not the devil himself?"

She grinned. "Because I know God. He has been a constant source of comfort to me. Believe me, Kolbein, I've been a mess most of my life, and only through God's grace have I amounted to anything."

"Who told you that? Surely your aunts would not be so cruel."

Abrianna waited until they'd crossed the busy street before replying. "They are never against me. They chide and cajole and do their best to raise me right, but I am a stiff-necked woman. Of course, I am trying to correct that mistake. I do not tell it to you in order to revel in it. The fact is, I'm most ashamed. I just find it so hard to be good—like Lenore," she added, remembering her promise to promote her friend.

"Lenore is always in perfect accord with her elders and the obligations society has put upon her. She never grieves her parents, except when she comes to spend time with me."

"I find that hard to believe, Abrianna. You are charming, and better still, you are smart. I've not ever met a young woman who knew her mind so well. You are well read and capable of handling people in a way that never leaves them feeling belittled or undermined." He paused. "However, your assessment of Miss Fulcher does seem accurate. She is a lovely young woman. How is it that the two of you became friends?"

"Church. We met at church while doing charitable service. We were just girls but found that our contemplations were similar.

We both found it important to be honest and loyal, as well as trustworthy. Lenore has always been good to keep my secrets."

Kolbein cocked his head to the side. "And what of you? Have you kept Miss Fulcher's secrets?"

"Of course," Abrianna replied. She thought of Lenore's interest in knowing Kolbein Booth better. "However, Lenore doesn't have that much to hide."

"And you do?"

Abrianna cocked her head to one side and grinned. "If I did, I wouldn't admit to it. Besides, I'd much rather talk about Lenore."

"I can't say that it is an unpleasant topic. In fact, since you are good at keeping secrets, I will share one. I find myself quite often thinking of Miss Fulcher."

"You do?" Abrianna grinned. "That's wonderful."

A group of boys approached from the end of the alleyway. Abrianna felt Kolbein tense at her side. She knew the boys looked like trouble and were purposely intimidating in their behavior so as to be left alone by anyone who might seek to return them to orphanage living.

He shoved the basket into her hands and pushed her back. "Get behind me. We may have trouble."

She giggled. "No, Kolbein. These are some of my friends." She gave a wave to the boys with one hand while balancing the basket with the other. As they approached, she said, "I knew I would find you here. It is, after all, Monday. Did Mr. Brindle have any old bread for you?"

They nodded in unison, and Bobby, the youngest, held up his loaf. "He was real good to us. Let us have a cup of milk to share."

Abrianna nodded. "Milk is a wondrous thing. What about

you, Toby?" He was the oldest and as such had become their unofficial leader. "Were you able to get the leftovers I arranged for you from Steinman's?"

"I did. We shared them for our supper last night. We had some fried fish and some apple pie. It was good, some of the best we've had in a long time."

"I'm glad. Mr. Steinman said you could see him each Saturday night after nine. He will endeavor to save what he can for you. Sometimes people leave a great deal of food behind on their plates, and he promised to set it aside for you.

"Now, I have someone to introduce to you." She saw the look of apprehension in their eyes. Especially Toby's. He was used to being harassed and kicked around by authorities and probably figured Kolbein to be no different.

"Is he gonna send us to jail?" twelve-year-old Seth asked.

"Goodness, no," Abrianna replied. "He is a lawyer from Chicago, but he isn't here to cause you problems. He has lost his sister. She ran away and came to Seattle."

"She ran away from a rich family?" Toby asked in disbelief. "Why would she do that?"

"Mr. Booth isn't rich. He's just a hard worker who earns his keep. His sister most likely ran off because she wanted an adventure." Abrianna didn't wish to put Kolbein in a bad light, though he had mentioned once that his sister thought him a tyrant. Given some of his comments, Abrianna could understand why she'd take on that thought, but she also considered that perhaps Kolbein had learned his lesson.

"The problem is, she is quite young and unescorted and knows nothing of being on her own. Not like you boys. You know everything about life on the streets, and that's why we've come to you. I'm certain you can learn information by asking around and watching out for her. Kolbein . . . Mr. Booth will show you her picture, and that will get you started."

Kolbein reached into his vest pocket and produced a small photograph. Each of the boys took a moment to study the picture before returning their eyes to Abrianna.

"Sure, we can keep a look out for her. What should we do if we find her?" Toby crossed his arms over his scrawny chest.

"Follow her and learn where she's living," Kolbein said before Abrianna could reply. "Don't give yourself away, or she might seek to flee once again."

"We can do that," Toby said, answering again for the group.

"Thank you, boys. I knew I could count on you." Abrianna held up a basket. "I have some treats here you might enjoy. The cookies and cakes were left over from Saturday's reception. And Liang thought to put in some roast beef and bread for sandwiches."

The boys were used to this routine on Mondays and eagerly dug into the basket to retrieve all that Abrianna had brought. Meanwhile, she turned to Kolbein. "Do you have any walking money?"

He looked at her oddly. "Of course."

"Might you spare two dollars?"

He raised a brow but otherwise only nodded and reached into his pocket. Within a moment he had produced the sum and handed it to Abrianna. She in turn handed it to Toby. "Make certain you use this wisely. I would suggest you each get a new pair of shoes at the secondhand store. You look to be all but barefooted."

Toby laughed. "Well, summer is comin', and we won't need shoes."

"It's not coming soon enough." Abrianna glanced overhead

at the cloudy sky. "You will find yourself down sick, what with the rain and the chill. Spring is always a dangerous time. Please just do as I ask."

Toby sobered and nodded. "We will, Miss Abrianna. I promise." The other boys nodded in unison.

She smiled and touched each boy's cheek. There was no telling the last time they'd had a human touch of kindness. If she wagered, Abrianna would bet it to be the last time she'd met up with the boys. "I'll see you soon." She turned to go but whirled back around.

"By the way, are you continuing to pray each day?"

"Yes, ma'am," the boys replied.

"And we're readin' the Bible you gave us," Toby added. "I'm trying to teach them to read, just like my granny did for me."

Abrianna couldn't contain her pleasure at this news. "You are all wonderful. Keep working hard. I will bring you some pencils and butcher paper when I can. Then you can practice writing what you read. You'll be amazed how wonderful it is to read and write. It will open the world wide to you. If you prove yourself capable with numbers and words, you may very well be able to get a better class of job."

With that, she moved away and Kolbein kept easy step with her. Abrianna considered the boys' plights and wondered what more she could do. Surely there might be someone who could help the boys without forcing them to go back to the orphanage.

"You're truly a remarkable woman, Abrianna," Kolbein murmured.

She shook her head. "Nonsense. I'm just being mindful of those who are poor and sick, just as the Bible encourages us to do."

"And do you offer such encouragements to others on the street?"

"Of course." Abrianna giggled. "Aunt Miriam cannot understand why I am always losing my Bible, but I think she's finally guessed after all this time. She is hardly a dense woman."

"No, not in the least."

Abrianna shrugged. "If she has figured it out, she must think it a good cause."

"Why do you believe that?"

She smiled. "Because Aunt Miriam ordered an entire crate of Bibles to be delivered to the school."

6

It's always so nice to have you walk with us to church and back," Mrs. Madison told Wade.

"Especially when you are clean-shaven," Abrianna added with a grin.

Mrs. Madison looked confused for a moment, then continued to speak. "And what a beautiful day. Don't you think so, ladies?" Everyone murmured an approval.

Wade glanced back at the line of young women who followed after them like ducklings following their mother. Mrs. Gibson and Miss Holmes walked behind the long line of ladies to ensure that no onlookers took liberties. The murmurs and giggles from the young women always amused Wade. Sometimes the ladies were captivated by someone who'd come to the Saturday receptions. Other times they chattered about upcoming events. Today they were concerned with what fashions and accessories they would need for Easter Sunday, which would fall on the first of April, just two weeks away.

Abrianna seemed to be the only one not caught up in the nonsense. She had come abreast of Wade and Mrs. Madison.

"Wade, have you seen Charlie lately?" she asked. She searched the sides of the streets.

"I saw him day before yesterday. Looked like he was getting along pretty well. Said his rheumatism wasn't bothering him nearly so much." Charlie was one of Abrianna's "lost souls," and on Sundays he usually met up with the ladies somewhere along the way home from church. Abrianna always brought a little paper-wrapped bundle of food to give him.

Wade admired her heart. She cared for the souls that no one else seemed to even notice. She met them on their level, despite the unconventional situation it created. She didn't ask permission of anyone. She never had. She had been doing this since they'd been young and often convinced Wade to join her on her exploits. But today Charlie was absent.

Mrs. Madison pointed toward the Madison Building and smiled. "Don't you think it looks beautiful on this bright day?"

"I do, Mrs. Madison. It looks very nice." He knew she desired such a response, and Wade didn't mind offering it. Indeed, today the edifice of brick and wood did look quite regal amidst the neighboring structures. They made their way across the street, careful to avoid a passing carriage.

This had become their Sunday routine. Wade would rise early, eat a light breakfast, dress in his best clothes, and arrive at the bridal school by eight-thirty. He would walk the ladies to church, sit apart from them in order to observe propriety, and then walk them home at noon.

Mrs. Madison insisted that for such gallantry, Wade should stay and partake of the Sunday meal. He couldn't refuse the delicious food created not only by the young ladies training to be brides, but also by the older ladies themselves and Liang, who was becoming a good cook in her own right.

Most of the meal was prepared Saturday evening, but Liang would finish up on Sunday if there was anything left to do. Mrs. Madison kept the Chinese girl hidden behind the doors of the school, lest any Anti-Chinese League member tried to force Liang to leave Seattle. The ladies thought this choice their only wise one, but with Liang unable to attend church, they saw to her spiritual feeding. Abrianna had told him more than once that her aunts preached longer sermons than the pastor did at their church.

Wade couldn't help but smile at the comparison. Abrianna was given to exaggeration, but this time he had a feeling she had merely related the facts as they were.

"I believe, ladies, that if it is this pleasant on Friday, we will set up our baked goods in the park and sell them to passersby." This was one way Mrs. Madison funded the school. The young ladies were never charged to attend the school. They generally came and stayed a year. At the end of that year, the men who desired to marry them paid a bridal fee. Wade knew for a fact it wasn't cheap. He'd heard many a man complain about it. However, as Mrs. Madison said, "Any man could save a goodly sum in a year's time if he devoted himself to such a project." And, of course, the men did just that.

Wade opened the door for the ladies but hesitated. An uneasy feeling fell over him, and the hairs on his neck tingled. He stiffened and stopped in midstep to cast a quick glance around the shadowed lobby and staircase. He felt the presence of another man before he actually saw him. Kolbein Booth stepped from the shadows and tipped his hat.

"Good day, ladies. I hope I'm not too early."

"Your timing is perfect, Mr. Booth," Mrs. Madison declared. "I'm so glad you could join us."

71

Wade relaxed a bit. Abrianna had introduced him to Kolbein Booth in passing, but the two men had not had a chance to get acquainted.

"Ladies, to your places and don't forget your aprons. I don't want you staining your Sunday clothes while you set the table and help Liang bring the meal." The older woman turned to seek out her sister.

"Poisie, please oversee the table preparations and see that we have enough places set." Her sister nodded and left to quickly follow after the brides-to-be. Now only Wade, Mrs. Madison, Abrianna, and Mrs. Gibson remained to greet Mr. Booth.

"Mr. Booth, we are most happy to receive you today. I'm delighted you could join us for our luncheon. I want to hear all about your search for Miss Booth," Mrs. Madison declared.

Mrs. Gibson couldn't help but offer her comments. "And you must take time to speak to the young ladies. You never know, you might find a spark of interest, and it only takes a spark to start a fire." She paused only momentarily for breath. "Mr. Gibson always said, 'The relationship between a man and woman is a wondrous thing.' He believed it was written somewhere in the stars; however, we know it's all God's arrangement." She shook her head. "Poor man. I just pray he's made it through the gates of heaven to seek God's mercy."

Wade said nothing, though he felt almost obligated to add Miss Poisie's usual "God rest his soul." Instead, he turned to Kolbein Booth. "Nice to see you again, Booth."

The man seemed most preoccupied but managed to return the greeting. "Thank you. You're Wade Ackerman, correct?"

"You've a good memory."

"Years of legal training have required such."

Wade couldn't help but wonder about this man's story. Was he who he said he was, or was all of this a confidence game to take advantage of the women? It was certain he dressed like a lawyer, and Abrianna said he held intellectual conversations without difficulty. Still, they knew nothing about the man, and it made Wade most uncomfortable that the old ladies and Abrianna had so quickly taken on his cause. It wasn't at all like Mrs. Madison to allow a stranger such latitude.

The women climbed the stairs, allowing the men to follow. Wade grew more uncomfortable with each step they climbed. The other man could be an escaped murderer or a thug looking for something to steal. He could imagine the man being many things, and it bothered him that Booth had managed to get so close to the women, for whom Wade felt responsible.

"You work as a wainwright," Booth said as they reached the landing and handed their hats to Abrianna.

"Please wait in the small sitting room, gentlemen. We will call you when luncheon is served." She smiled at each man and leaned in as if to share a secret. "Don't discuss President Cleveland. He's a Democrat, you know, and he held a staunch disregard for President Lincoln, whom my aunts dearly loved. If you don't want to stir their ire, you'll avoid Mr. Cleveland altogether."

"You have my word," Kolbein said with a wink, to which Abrianna smiled.

"We'll keep in mind all of the topics of discussion which trouble the ladies." Wade wasn't sure he liked the man winking at Abrianna. "Come. I'll show you the way."

"I already know it," Kolbein replied. His tone made it clear that he wasn't to be made second man to any.

Wade nodded and allowed him to lead the way. Once they were seated, Wade lost little time. "I am a wainwright. I learned at an early age to build wagons and make repairs to them. Abrianna tells me you're a lawyer from Chicago."

Kolbein Booth chuckled. "Yes, I am. I hope you don't hold Chicago in the same contempt as the ladies."

This made Wade smile. The women were very opinionated about a great many things besides the president. The safety and acceptability of various cities was something of which they often spoke, basing their opinions on newspaper articles and Sunday gossip. Chicago garnered no good thoughts from that trio.

"As I recall," Wade replied, "they believe Chicago to be a den of no-good men who take advantage of women and children. Seems their opinion has something to do with the senselessness of a people who would allow a cow to set the town ablaze."

"I'm not entirely certain that the cow alone bears blame," Booth said good-naturedly. "I do not believe she brought the lantern which set the blaze." He shrugged. "I also don't imagine Chicago to be much worse than any large city. I know this place has dealt with fires of its own," Booth countered. "What do you believe?"

"About cows setting fires?" Wade couldn't help but smile. Against his will he was actually enjoying this man's company.

"How do you feel about Chicago?"

Wade rubbed his thighs. "I don't have an opinion one way or the other. I've never been to the place and don't plan to visit there in the future. I like it here just fine."

Booth nodded. "I can understand. Seattle is a fine city. It appears to rain a great deal, but the days of sun are quite pleasant. I am impressed that so many entertainments are available. I was afraid I'd be coming into uncivilized territory. However, reading the newspaper and walking about the town have opened my eyes. Even so, this city, like most, has its fair share of problems, from what I've read."

"That's true enough. We have ranching and mining, much like other western towns. We also have the sea. Earning a living off the water teaches one not to take things for granted. The sea is unforgiving and the men who sail her know that full well. Fishing is a big industry here, as well as logging and shipping. We are quite a complex city."

"I can well imagine. You have a good harbor and good products to offer. I imagine that larger towns desire your lumber, since there's quite a bit of building going on around America. Some have fully recovered from the crash of '73 and are starting to invest in their comforts again. However, I don't see our economy as stable yet. The rich are spending in abundance to further the railroads and financial systems, but in my mind extravagance and excess always lead to problems."

"Gentlemen, we are ready to sit down to lunch," Abrianna announced from the open doorway.

Wade motioned Booth to go first, and the man didn't have to be encouraged.

In one smooth movement the man joined Abrianna and offered her his arm. "Milady, might I escort you?"

Abrianna laughed. "But of course, my good sir." She took his arm, and they led the way.

The large dining table had been arranged with the twelve bridal students placed six on one side and six on the other, with Miss Poisie taking up the end position.

At the opposite end of the table, Mrs. Madison took her place at the head with Mrs. Gibson at her right and Abrianna at her left. Booth quickly took the empty chair beside Abrianna, leaving Wade no choice but the seat to the right of Mrs. Gibson.

Wade watched them for a moment and became aware of something he'd hesitated to notice before. Abrianna had grown into a woman. No doubt some men would seek to take advantage of her. In a protective brotherly fashion, Wade began to plan how he might help to keep her safe. After all, this was a bridal school, and there would be plenty of men at the receptions. Abrianna might find herself in a difficult situation, and Wade wanted to make sure she didn't make a mistake in running off with the first fellow who asked her. Perhaps he should speak to Mrs. Madison about the matter. One couldn't be too safe in these situations, could they?

The meal was wonderful as usual, and Wade couldn't help but enjoy the company of all the young ladies. At this time of the year, many of them had found interested suitors and were in the latter stages of their time with the school. They spoke of this man and that one, sharing what they did for a living and their plans for the future. In June, Mrs. Madison and her companions would stage their annual bridal ball, and many a bachelor turned out. The dance would go on until midnight, and by then many of the girls would be spoken for, if not married that very night, thanks to a special arrangement Mrs. Madison had with a local judge.

The only concern about his entire day had been the appearance of Kolbein Booth. Wade was surprised to see how Booth and Abrianna conversed with ease, and when Booth asked Abrianna to accompany him to a particular place where he'd heard rumors of a young woman matching his sister's description, she agreed to help. Wade was even more surprised to find Abrianna's aunts so receptive. Did they not see that Abrianna was no longer a child? Miss Poisie further stunned Wade by suggesting she and some of the other young ladies might accompany them, but then dismissed the idea when Mrs. Gibson reminded her of other plans they had for the afternoon.

Wade didn't like the idea of Abrianna going alone with Booth. They knew so little about him. For all Wade knew, the man might not even have a sister. What if this was just a huge scam—a means of getting into the middle of the school in order to cause problems. But to what purpose?

"We shouldn't be gone long," Abrianna declared, "unless it starts raining or the streetcars stop running or there's some other sort of disaster." She looked at Booth. "One Sunday there was a small fire near the dock, and the fire horses were spooked and ran away. It was quite the excitement, and we watched most of it from upstairs. Didn't we?" Abrianna looked to the other females. They all nodded and murmured comments about the excitement.

"Oh goodness, I do remember that. Thankfully no one was killed!" Poisie dabbed her neck with a lacy handkerchief.

"Well, there most likely won't be a repeat of that," Mrs. Madison replied. "Abrianna, I shall want you back by four o'clock. No excuses or protests," she added as the young woman opened her mouth.

"I wasn't going to offer either," Abrianna said and crossed her arms. "I merely wanted to inquire as to whether you needed anything while we were out."

"We do not shop on the Sabbath," Mrs. Gibson declared. "And we would not, even if shops were open. It would be an affront to the Lord. I'm not even sure that searching for Mr. Booth's sister doesn't violate the law."

"It's true," Poisie added with a stern face. "Remember that all of Israel and Judah were taken captive for ignoring the seventh year Sabbath rest of the fields. How much more will He punish those who dishonor the weekly Sabbath."

Abrianna shook her head. "I hardly think that the Good

Lord would condemn us to Hades should we happen to need something on the Sabbath. Even Jesus worked miracles on that day. And I wasn't suggesting a day of shopping, only that if you had need of an errand I could take care of it."

"It's true, Selma," Mrs. Madison said, looking to Mrs. Gibson. "Our Savior faced great condemnation from the teachers of the day when he drove out demons and healed the sick on the day of rest. I believe I can see the point Abrianna is making. A steadfast heart seeks God's desires, and if that is best served in helping someone, then who are we to say it's wrong?"

Before the conversation could reach a theological fervor, Wade stood. "Why don't I go along, too?" Not waiting for an answer, he looked Booth in the eye. "Show me the picture of your sister, and I'll help with the search. After all, three sets of eyes are better than two."

"See, Kolbein?" Abrianna said. "I told you that Wade would be more than happy to help us. He's a good man and he cares a lot about people." She looked to Wade. "I am so pleased that you would choose to help in this. There are so many people in the world who just walk by when seeing the needs of others and do nothing."

Wade nodded. "Like those who ignore the plight of the Chinese?"

"Exactly so. I'm glad you understand." Abrianna turned to Kolbein. "I'll be right back. Let me change my clothes. I have no desire to parade around like this. My friends out there might not even recognize me."

Wade frowned. He liked the way Abrianna had dressed for church. She looked quite innocent and unspoiled in the pale lavender gown that had once belonged to Lenore. Frankly, he thought the color looked a lot better against Abrianna's red hair and freckled fair skin than it had against Lenore's brown hair and olive complexion. Wade grimaced at the feminine thought. What man worried about the color of gowns and hair? Maybe he was spending too much time with the ladies.

True to her word, Abrianna was gone only a few minutes. She came back in a state of partial undress, tucking her blouse into the waistband of her dark blue skirt. She had left her hair pinned up, but Wade wouldn't be surprised at all if those pins came out as the trio made their way through the city. Seeing that he was watching her, Abrianna threw him a smile and glanced around.

"I'm glad my aunts are busy. I know it's unseemly for me to act this way, but gracious, you know what a rapscallion I can be, and I didn't want to waste more time. Furthermore, it's not like I'm showing my chemise or petticoats, although I will tell you that once Miss Poisie showed a fair amount of her pantalets when crossing Front Street in a downpour, but don't tell her I mentioned it."

Wade laughed aloud as Booth led the way down the stairs and out the building. Thankfully, it wasn't raining, but Wade and Abrianna had taken up umbrellas just in case. Booth seemed unmindful of such matters. Should he choose to stay in the city for long, however, he'd soon learn the value of staying dry.

They had gone only a couple of blocks, talking about a variety of things, when Booth made Wade most uncomfortable by complimenting Abrianna's faithfulness to assist him. To his surprise, however, Abrianna changed the subject and began speaking in great detail about Lenore Fulcher.

"She is the most beautiful woman in Seattle," Abrianna declared. "Of course, I don't usually make such generalities, but in this case I'm confident that my assessment is accurate. She looks very much like Lily Langtry, don't you think, Wade?" She didn't wait for his reply but hurried on. "I suppose Lenore is shorter than Miss Langtry. I don't believe I've ever been told for sure how tall the actress is. However, Lenore is quite talented, even if she isn't very tall. I have never seen anyone with her gift of organization and consideration. I've seen her contemplate many a problem with me and not give up until she has the matter completely sorted. She's a wonder."

"So are you, Abrianna," Kolbein declared. "And you are just as beautiful."

Abrianna laughed. "Nonsense. I have it on good authority that redheads can never be considered truly beautiful. Especially redheads with curly hair. We might be handsome or comely but not beautiful, and in most cases we are only passable."

"I disagree," Booth countered, stopping in midstep. "Your sources are very wrong. I personally have a great fondness for red hair. I like the difference it offers from blond hair and brown."

"Well, appreciating is one thing. My hair has always gotten me into trouble," Abrianna stated with absolute conviction. "Aunt Miriam says it's the temperament that goes along with red hair, but I'm certain to be troublesome no matter what."

"I would never accuse a lady of lying or speaking lunacy, but you are stretching my limits," Booth replied. "You mustn't let others tell you that you aren't beautiful just because of the color of your hair."

"Oh goodness no," Abrianna said. "It's not just because of my hair. I'm not beautiful for many reasons. I have freckles and dimples, my nose is a bit crooked, and I'm not dainty like Lenore."

Wade shook his head and sighed. "You might as well give up, Booth. I've tried on many occasions to tell Abrianna she's a lovely girl—young woman," he corrected. "She never believes me, and she won't believe you, either."

Booth looked at Abrianna, and for just a moment Wade thought he appeared to be considering the matter as a challenge. Wade could almost see the cogs turning in Booth's mind. But instead of arguing or suggesting he could prove it, Booth fell silent.

"I'm glad you can see reason," Abrianna said, giving Wade a playful nudge with her elbow. "Wade tells me such things because we've been the best of friends since childhood, but we both know the truth. Redheads are a strange lot, and we simply do not fit in."

"Maybe not fitting into someone else's preconceived mold is a good thing," Wade suggested and Booth agreed.

"It would be a very boring world if everyone were alike," Booth said.

"You two are quite dear," Abrianna said. "But we have a task before us. Let us focus on Kolbein's sister instead of me. I'm certain she is far more deserving and in need of our consideration."

7

Easter Sunday dawned bright and clear, much to the amazement of the citizens of Seattle. It seemed God had smiled upon them, and they were happy to take advantage of the moment. The ladies of Madison Bridal School had long planned an Easter celebration. It was to be held at a local park if the weather was pleasant and at the school should it be foul. The day was chilly but otherwise perfect, and Wade had talked his friend Thane into accompanying him with the ladies to church and then to the park. With the promise of food and the company of unmarried females, Wade didn't have to do a whole lot of convincing.

Wade and Thane ended up in charge of transporting the food. Wade brought his wagon, and together he and Thane managed to load up plates and bowls full of delightful treats. And, of course, there were dozens of colorful hard-boiled eggs, thanks to the ladies of the school and their charges. Plans were made for couples to hunt for the Easter eggs, with a prize to be given to the couple who found the most. Several very special eggs were also going to be hidden, and these, too, would bring a prize.

Once the party was in full swing, Wade and Thane made

their way through the crowd. There were still several girls who hadn't yet paired off with a suitor, and Thane asked Wade to make the introductions so he could meet them.

"I think that's something we should leave to Abrianna or one of the ladies," Wade countered, spying his dear friend. "Abrianna, can you help us?"

She hadn't heard him, so they crossed the distance between them to find Abrianna quite intent on a book. "You are a strange one," Wade declared. "Reading away when you might actually do some good."

Abrianna looked at him in confusion. "Do some good? What are you talking about?"

"Thane would like very much to meet the girls, the young ladies who are yet without a suitor."

"I suppose I can make the introductions," Abrianna said, getting to her feet and putting the book aside. She smiled at them both. "After all, we redheads should stick together, isn't that true?"

Thane chuckled and touched his hand to his red hair. "Indeed. I'll come under any excuse if it gets me into the company of the young ladies."

Wade shook his head and smiled. "Let us be about it, then."

Abrianna introduced Thane to the four young women who were yet to find suitors. Wade allowed himself to greet each one, as well, but he had no interest in getting to know them. He moved away from the gathering as Thane began to regale the ladies with stories of his volunteer firefighting job.

"Don't you want to visit with the girls?" Abrianna asked.

"Not really. I thought I'd come and speak with you. Most of the time those girls don't have a clue as to what's going on in the world."

"That's because their world is confined to the school," Abrianna said. "They spend very little time in the world during their training. But it serves them well. Most can cook, clean, sew, and sing by this time, and from now on it's all down the hill, as they say."

"Except for those four?" he questioned.

Abrianna glanced toward the ladies and nodded. "Those four are still struggling. Even so, they are much better at such things than I am."

"I'm sure you are able," Wade said. "God has given you talents, as well."

"Not where the kitchen is concerned." Abrianna's sorrow was evident in her tone. "I am a grave disappointment there. Aunt Miriam said yesterday that she sometimes doubts her ability to teach when she considers my inability to learn."

"So what did you burn yesterday?" he teased.

"Eggs," Abrianna replied. "I forgot I was boiling eggs and, well, the pan went dry and the scorching began. It wasn't pleasant. The smell was even worse. Did you know that burnt eggs have a tendency to explode?"

"I didn't realize boiled eggs could be burned."

Abrianna gave a sad little nod. "If there's a way to burn something, I'm sure to figure it out. Apparently it comes quite naturally. On the positive side, I'm learning to be a most expert cleaning woman; otherwise I'm rather a challenge."

"I would think after all these years of the ladies working to train you, something would have rubbed off," Wade said.

She seemed to think about this a moment before answering. "Considering that for the first dozen years I was so intent on book studies and helping with various church charities, I was excused to a degree. Then as I approached these latter years . . .

well . . . it's my own fault that I've remained a failure. I have no interest in cooking or playing the piano. And don't get me started on dainty embroidering." She looked most forlorn. "It's not the aunts' fault. God knows they have labored long to teach me. I suppose if I put my mind to it, I might do better."

"So why don't you?"

Abrianna shrugged. "I'm just an obstinate burner of food."

Wade laughed. "And none of the others ever burn anything?" he asked, looking back to where Thane continued to entertain the four suitorless women. "You have to look at the entire group, Abrianna."

"Well, there is Militine. She doesn't burn as much as she damages. She tends to be rather awkward, or maladroit, as Aunt Selma says. Aunt Miriam says it's because her hands and feet are big, but I think she's wrong. I think Militine is just scared."

"Scared of what?" Wade asked, curious at this insightful declaration.

"Of most everything. Look at the way she is around Thane."

Wade noticed the young woman was standing away from the others. At one point she backed up when Thane spoke to her, and she would have fallen onto the ground had he not reached out to steady her. "I see what you mean."

"If you watch her for long, you would swear she's making jest. I've never seen anyone stumble, bump into things, or otherwise break objects like Militine does. I believe it's all about her uneasiness with people."

"You may very well be right, Abrianna. She certainly seems a likable enough young woman."

"Oh, she is," Abrianna declared. "I think she is more down to earth and less pretentious than just about anyone in the world. I've really enjoyed Militine's company, perhaps because we suffer some of the same woes in household duties. But her heart is good. If I were to pick out a dear friend among the ladies, it would be Militine."

"Because she makes you feel less conspicuous?"

Abrianna thought for a moment. "I suppose that could be a part of it. We do tend to surround ourselves with people who make us feel better about ourselves, or at least safe. Yes, that's it. I feel very safe with Militine. I know she will not judge me with harsh condemnation."

"I know I appreciate when someone does that for me," Wade agreed. "It's why you and I have so long been friends. You never judge me unfairly, and that causes me to enjoy your company."

"I never thought of it that way, but I see the truth in it. Even so, Militine is a fine person, and I believe if she can overcome her shyness, she'll do well. Her consideration of others is one of her best qualities. Why, she's even gone with Kolbein and me to look for his sister."

"How is that hunt coming along?"

Abrianna shrugged. "Like King Arthur's search for the grail. A worthy cause that has become a most vexing trial."

"In other words like trying to find a needle in a haystack?"

"Exactly so. But Kolbein won't give up. He's much too devoted for that. He dearly loves his sister, and whether it takes a year or ten, I believe he will endeavor to find her. Men like him tend to be that way."

"Men like him?"

"Lawyers, solicitors, and such. They are driven to find the truth. That's what Kolbein is doing, no matter how much it delays his own life and interests."

"But what about his position in Chicago? I wouldn't think he could up and leave his law practice and clients."

"Well, he tells me that he's part of a large firm. They dole out things to him and he handles them. It's all very organized, so he doesn't need to go drumming up business. Not that he wouldn't have it if he wanted it," Abrianna added. "He's very intelligent, and I have to say he knows a great deal about the world. Not only that, but he and his sister lost their parents, just as I have. Although I must say the circumstances were quite different."

"And how was that?"

"A train accident in the Northeast somewhere. Train went right off a bridge, and everyone was killed. I think Kolbein was twenty-two and his sister ten. He took on the role of man of the family and finished raising Greta. Wasn't that admirable?"

Wade didn't care for the way Abrianna seemed to be taken in by Booth. There wasn't time to say as much, however, because Abrianna was speaking again.

"Aunt Miriam has invited the poor man to dine with us on Sundays whenever it fits his plans. Aunt Selma is still worried that he might be related to John Wilkes Booth," she said with a grin, "but Aunt Poisie reminded her that we must extend charity rather than judgment.

"Oh, look," she interjected. "It's time for the egg rolling. Aunt Miriam has a nice prize for the winner—it's a basket of oranges. Isn't that marvelous?" She started off in the direction of where the others were lining up.

"Are you going to compete?" Wade called after her.

"Not at all," she replied. "I just want a better vantage point to watch." She turned and threw him another smile. "Aren't you coming? It's so much fun to watch folks be silly."

Wade laughed. Her girlish charm amused and endeared. "I'm coming, only I'm not sure who I'll be more compelled to watch. Them or you."

Lenore sat picking at her strawberry mousse. Easter Sunday had compelled her parents to spend the morning in church services before heading to one of the finest restaurants in San Francisco for a special luncheon.

If we were in Seattle I might be able to enjoy the day with Abrianna. She knew they would celebrate as they did every year, weather permitting, with egg hunts and camaraderie. Here, away from her best friend, Lenore felt lonelier than she ever had before.

"Are you unwell?" Mother asked.

Lenore shook her head. "I just miss being home."

"Miss the rain and chill?" Father questioned. He pointed to her plate. "Do you plan to finish that?"

She scooted the plate in his direction. "No. Please have it." Father didn't have to be asked twice.

Mother sipped her tea and seemed unconcerned with Lenore's desires for home. Mother loved California, and San Francisco appealed to her for its many diversions. But Lenore was consumed with other thoughts—in particular, thoughts of Kolbein Booth.

Why does he haunt me so? As a test she had tried to force the images of Kolbein from her mind just to see if her feelings were true. Lenore found it impossible to let go of her growing desire to know Mr. Booth better.

But it is impossible to know him better while I sit in San Francisco and he searches for his sister in Seattle.

What if he'd already found her and returned to Chicago? What if he had someone he cared for at home? Perhaps her feelings were for naught and no matter how Abrianna promoted her, Mr. Booth would have no more interest in Lenore than he might for a distant relative.

"I don't believe you are paying any attention to your father," Mother said, touching Lenore's lacy sleeve.

"I'm sorry. My thoughts have been elsewhere. I will try to do better." Lenore straightened a bit in her chair. "What did you wish to say, Father?"

"I was merely explaining that your mother and I have been asked to spend the evening with a business associate and his wife. I wanted to make certain that you would be comfortable remaining at the hotel alone."

"Oh." She thought for a moment and shrugged. "I am sure to be fine. I have a book I can read and perhaps I'll even go to bed early."

"Are you sure you aren't feeling ill?" Mother asked. "I do worry about you. You haven't been yourself since we left Seattle."

Lenore thought it would be the perfect opportunity to reintroduce the subject of Kolbein Booth. Not by name, of course. "If you'll recall, I did not wish to make this trip." Her words were spoken respectfully but with emphasis. "I had hoped to further my relationship with . . . a certain gentleman."

"Bah, that's completely unimportant right now," her father insisted. "We will be home soon enough. For now, there are other matters that need my attention." He dabbed his mouth with a linen napkin, then signaled the waiter. When the man approached, he motioned to the table. "We're finished here."

Lenore sighed. If only that were true of their trip to San Francisco.

Abrianna had thought the day perfect until Priam Welby decided to join the affair. She stood alone to one side of the food tables and watched as couples skittered about looking for

Easter eggs. One of the single young ladies had snagged Wade for her partner and was even now making him rustle through blackberry bushes to seek wayward eggs. Abrianna was hoping for a few quiet moments to herself, but it was not to be.

"You look quite beautiful today, Miss Cunningham."

She felt certain he was only trying to entice her for some personal benefit. "I didn't recall Aunt Miriam saying anything about your coming today, Mr. Welby. Are you lost?"

He chuckled. "Perhaps your aunt said nothing because she did not know." His dark-eyed gaze traveled the full length of her and back in a flash. He smiled broadly, revealing perfect white teeth. Pity his ears were rather large, or he might have been handsome.

"Well, I suppose she would tell you to enjoy yourself. There's plenty of food. She and my aunts will be returning here as soon as the egg hunt is concluded."

"Surely they aren't scouting for eggs themselves."

"No, but they are overseeing the couples who are. You'd be amazed at how fast those couples can get lost."

Mr. Welby gave an uproarious laugh. "I can very well imagine. I was once young myself and quite adept at disappearing with a beautiful young lady at my side."

Abrianna said nothing and instead handed him a plate. "You might as well get started."

"I'd just as soon remain here and talk with you. You are a charming young woman. How did you come to be with Mrs. Madison and the others?"

"It's a tale of great sadness. My folks died. At least my mother did. We were never sure about my father, but since he never showed back up, we're pretty sure he died, too. Of course," she said, growing thoughtful, "I've often wondered if he might have been struck with amnesia. Are you familiar with that term?" She didn't wait for him to answer.

"My father was a man of many trades, and I think it is possible that he was wounded in a terrible accident and perhaps suffered a blow to the head, only to forget everything. I suppose we shall never know." She shrugged and placed the plate back on the table.

"And you came to live with the old ladies because he left?"

"No. My mother grew ill. She knew it wasn't boding well for her, and she knew these ladies were good, godly women. They attended church together, you see. Before Mother died . . ." Abrianna giggled. "Of course it was before she died. It would be most impossible to do it afterwards. Honestly, I have a terrible habit of making such a statement, and yet I know it to be completely preposterous." She shrugged and continued. "Anyway, my mother persuaded the ladies to care for me. Of course they had no idea what they were in for," she said, shaking her head. "My hair should have warned them, for even then it was red."

"And a lovely shade it is. Like burnt copper or perhaps cinnamon."

"Be that as it may, it's not exactly a color that most women desire."

"I can't imagine why not," Mr. Welby said in his appealing manner. "It suits you well. The freckles, too."

Abrianna wasn't sure why, but her hand went automatically to the bridge of her nose. She'd never liked her freckles. Other young ladies had beautiful milky skin. Even Lenore's olive coloring was free from such blemishes, and she often brought Abrianna jars of cream that were designed to bleach out just such marring features.

Mr. Welby reached out and took hold of her hand and lowered

her arm. "You needn't be ashamed of them. They only serve to enhance your beauty."

Abrianna wasn't used to such flattery. She felt her cheeks flush hot and turned away. "If you aren't hungry, we have cider and tea to drink. Aunt Miriam tried to get in her regular shipment of lemons, but something happened to delay them."

Welby stepped closer, still holding her hand. "Miss Cunningham, I find you to be an absolute delight. Nay, I would venture to say I find you to be the most appealing woman I've yet to meet. You speak freely and are of obvious intelligence and great imagination. No doubt you are well-read and educated."

"No doubt," she agreed, pulling her hand from his grasp. "My aunts schooled me at home, and it was like having three taskmasters. Even so, I had a great love of learning and took to books and issues of faith quite easily. I'm afraid it's other things like cooking and sewing that I'm not so good at."

"Well, that is easily remedied."

Abrianna fought to regain her composure. She tried to appear disinterested, but it was possible he had a secret to success that she knew nothing about. "And how is that?"

"By marrying well and having servants, of course." He grinned and gave her a wink.

Goodness, but he is a most forward man. If Aunt Miriam saw his performance, she'd force his exit sooner rather than later. Desiring nothing more than to escape, Abrianna pointed to her approaching aunts.

"It would appear the egg search is over." Abrianna stepped forward. "Mr. Welby decided to join us," she told the three women. "I believe he wishes to speak with you." She took that moment to hurry off in the direction of Wade's wagon. At least there she might be able to escape notice.

Priam Welby watched the animated redhead make her departure. She had a fine figure, and the seed of an idea planted itself in his brain. He had originally hoped to catch her off guard at the party and trick her into giving him answers related to the old ladies. But now, a different plan formed.

"Mr. Welby, I'm surprised to see you here today," Mrs. Madison commented. "You haven't come to speak to me about selling my building again, have you?"

"Not at all." He smiled. "I am here on more amorous endeavors."

Mrs. Gibson perked up at this. "Oh, you've come to meet the young ladies."

"Not exactly," Priam said, looking back in the direction Abrianna had gone. "I've come to discuss the possibility of courting one particular young lady."

Miriam Madison met his gaze without blinking. "And who might that be?"

"Why, your ward, Miss Cunningham. I find her delightful. In fact, I have been able to think of little else since making her acquaintance. If she is not otherwise promised to someone, I should very much like to woo her."

"I see." Mrs. Madison considered his proposal, but Priam could tell she wasn't enthusiastic to agree. She continued to study him for several moments. "You are a man of how many years?"

"Eight and thirty," he replied.

"And how is it that you are employed?"

"I built an import business from very little. I have nurtured the business over the years and now boast a sizable annual profit.

I have a good standing in the community and donate regularly to the charities."

"I see." Mrs. Madison seemed to be thinking of what else to ask him when her sister chimed in.

"And what of your faith, Mr. Welby? Are you a man of God?"

"Are we not all of God?" he challenged. "Did God not create each of us?"

"Indeed," Miss Holmes replied. "But how is it with your soul and God?"

Priam thought to continue toying with the woman but decided against it. If he could convince the ladies to let him court and possibly propose marriage to their ward, he would have a much easier time securing the Madison Building for himself. After all, he had it on good authority that Mrs. Madison's ward was to one day inherit her estate.

"It is well with my soul and God," he lied. "Very well. I was raised in a Christian home and heard the Scriptures read to me daily as a young man." At least that much was true. "As I grew into adulthood, my parents encouraged me to attend seminary back east. I did so and soon realized that God was not calling me to the ministry, but rather to business. For you see, God needs businessmen on His side as well as preachers."

Although his remark might be perceived as flippant, Priam didn't expect them to question him. These ladies weren't the quickest of mind nor the most knowledgeable despite their schooling of Abrianna. No, they were women, and as such were weak and inconsistent. They would be easily swayed once he convinced Abrianna that he loved her and that she loved him. It would take some work on his part, but it would be a pleasant enough task. Abrianna might even make a very enticing companion. Who could say?

"Mr. Welby, we will discuss this matter, and of course we'll consult with Abrianna. We will pray on your proposal and let you know whether we can approve your request."

"And when might you have an answer for me?"

"After we speak to Abrianna and pray," Mrs. Madison said in a tone that suggested he should have known from her earlier statement.

"Very well. I will check back with you." He gave a low sweeping bow. "Until then, my dear ladies."

8

Abrianna couldn't imagine where Charlie might have disappeared to. She had searched the regular places, but the old man was nowhere to be found. Worry flooded her that he might have found someone to fund his drinking. Charlie was fond of the bottle, and there was no telling how low he might stoop to satisfy his need for drink.

"Oh, Charlie, please don't be drinking." She looked up to the rain clouds and worried that despite the warm days they'd enjoyed, perhaps Charlie was sick. Of course! That was a greater possibility than the drinking, for Abrianna knew that Charlie was trying his best to stay away from the bottle.

She slipped down the alleyway and hurried to Wade's wagon shop. It was always possible he might know something. After all, she and Wade had befriended Charlie together. Nearly five years earlier they had come across Charlie drunk and sick, lying in the gutter. Liquor had all but done the man in. Wade had taken him home and, with Abrianna's help, had nursed the old man back to health. But it hadn't been easy.

"Wade?" Abrianna called as she entered the back door of the shop.

It took only a second for her friend to appear. He beamed at her, but Abrianna did not return the smile. "Wade, have you seen Charlie?"

"No, I guess I haven't seen him for two weeks at least. Why?"

"He hasn't been around at all. I keep hoping he'll stop by the school, but I haven't seen him." She tried not to betray her fear, but it was impossible. Charlie was just as precious to her as anyone else in her life. The old sailor had shown her nothing but kindness since his recovery and had become something of a grandfather figure to Abrianna.

"Do you suppose he's in some kind of trouble? Perhaps sick?" she asked.

"It's always possible." Wade gave her a compassionate smile. "Did you pray about this?"

"I did, but I fear what with the various days of focus on our Lord for Easter, maybe our Father in heaven is just a bit busy. You know folks always seem to pray more around religious holidays."

Wade laughed. "Oh, Abrianna, do you really suppose that God is too inundated with prayer and unable to handle the onslaught? He's God and capable of all things."

She nodded. "I suppose you are right. I needed that correction to my thinking. Even so, why doesn't God show me where Charlie is? So if he's sick we can attend him, and if he's in trouble we can assist him."

"I'm certain that God knows what Charlie needs and will provide. Even so, I will ask around the docks and see if anyone has seen him."

"Thank you, Wade." She gave him a hurried hug. "I have to get back to the school. My aunts have informed me that we are to have a private discussion before lunch. If I'm not quick about it, I will be late. And you know how that always bodes ill for me."

"Be careful, Abrianna. You know traveling this area is a questionable thing for you to do by yourself. There are those out there who would seek to take liberties or harm you."

She threw him a smile over her shoulder. "Ever the loving and worried brother. I often wish my aunts would adopt you, as well. Then we might sit together in the evening and talk about things long into the night. I'm certain you would come up with many deep thoughts at late hours."

With that she left the shop and picked up speed. She hiked her skirts, noting that this caused her to reveal a good portion of her black wool stockings. It really didn't matter. Time was what was important, and her aunts hated for her to be late.

Abrianna made it back to the school with only a few minutes to spare. She hurried up the back stairs and paused long enough in the kitchen to look at her reflection in the beveled glass of one of the cupboards.

Liang was moving around in silence tending to lunch, but Abrianna knew the girl had noted what a mess she was.

"I look like an unkempt urchin."

The Chinese girl put a hand to her mouth and giggled. "You look like you pull hair out in madness."

"Well, very nearly," Abrianna said, taking the ribbon from her hair. The auburn curls flared out around her. "I'd best get it in order before the aunts see me." She worked with lacking skill to amass the hair into order. Never in her life had she been one to show great talent in this area.

Liang came up from behind her. "You sit. I make right."

Abrianna did as instructed and handed the ribbon to Liang. "Thank you. I fear I will only make things worse, and I have so little time to set it right."

The girl worked with seeming ease, first pulling the curls from one side to another. She combed through Abrianna's hair with her fingers and separated the mass into three equal parts. Next she plaited it down her back and tied the braid with Abrianna's ribbon.

"There. You look like lady again." Liang stepped back just as Abrianna jumped to her feet.

She took a quick glance at her reflection. "And none too soon. I have to hurry, though. Thanks, Liang. You are most amazing."

Abrianna entered her aunts' private sitting room just as the clock struck eleven. She let out the breath she'd been holding and gave each woman a smile. "Good day, Aunties."

"Good day, Abrianna. Thank you for being prompt," Aunt Miriam said, motioning her to a chair. "Please, come have a seat. We have an important discussion to hold."

Abrianna couldn't imagine what it might be. Were they going to reprimand her for burning a pie the day before? Maybe Aunt Selma had seen the mess she'd made of her embroidery and they were going to berate her for not taking enough time and care. Goodness, she prayed it wouldn't be that discussion about their raising her up to take over the school.

"I know this may come as a surprise, but a suitor has asked to court you," Aunt Miriam said, jumping right into the subject at hand.

A blow to her stomach couldn't have surprised Abrianna more. "A suitor? For me? Goodness, but that is something I did not pray for. Who is he?"

"Mr. Welby."

Her eyes widened at the memory of the man who'd pursued her at the Easter gathering. He had tried his best to appeal to her by offering compliments and praise, but such things had never interested Abrianna.

"I have no desire to court Mr. Welby or any suitor. You know that I feel called to help the poor and downtrodden. I can hardly do that with a husband who expects me to make a nice home and cook his meals." She held up her hand before her aunts could protest.

"I know what you've often said. The right man would aid my cause and come alongside me to offer help. But you must understand that I consider this God's work, and I want to be faithful to Him—not a husband."

"Abrianna, Mr. Welby is a much respected man who gives generously to charities. He might honor your concerns, as well."

"Mr. Welby is a man with a social bearing to consider, and as such," Abrianna countered, "he will have certain expectations of a wife. I doubt he would allow his spouse to frequent the docks and poorer parts of town."

"It has never been our desire that you do so, either, and yet you do," Aunt Miriam declared. "I'm afraid that no matter whom you marry, you will go on doing just as you wish."

"You are most likely right about that. Still, we know nothing of him, and while he might be generous in his charities," Abrianna said, hoping to figure a way to discourage the discussion, "he was quite ruthless when he came here to try to purchase the building from you."

"It's true. But the man did offer a measure of regret. He told me of his great frustration in being thwarted time and again from purchases of prime property for his business. So you see, he is a man of honor. He merely needs to find the right real estate."

Abrianna knew this was getting her nowhere. She'd told them of her need to work for God, had questioned Mr. Welby's integrity, and had shown her own disinterest. What else could she say or do to reason with them?

"Why not have Abrianna and Mr. Welby simply meet at the receptions rather than court?" Aunt Poisie offered. "There we can supervise the couple, and they can get to know each other better while under our guarded watch."

Aunt Miriam bristled. "Well, I never intended to allow Abrianna to accompany Mr. Welby without one of us in attendance. She has never courted, and a chaperone is definitely in order. There may be all sorts of newfangled courting procedures that allow for men and women to be more intimate, but we will not allow that in our house."

Knowing she needed time to figure out how she might dissuade her aunts or discourage Mr. Welby, Abrianna spoke up. "I would be willing to get to know him at the school receptions, but only there. I feel quite guarded in giving my heart to anyone—just as you taught me." She looked to each aunt as if to emphasize their wisdom. "You have raised me to know that God has specific mates for most people, while others are destined to remain single. I trust in Him for direction to know which I might be. I'll definitely need time to pray about Mr. Welby."

"That's a wise path," Aunt Selma replied. "Goodness knows, a man might seem to be honorable and godly, but then without even realizing what has happened, you could find him studying astronomy."

Poisie nodded her head quickly. "And you don't want that to happen to poor Abrianna, Sister."

"Indeed, I do not," Aunt Miriam said. "Nor will I stand for anything less than a man who loves God and proves such love—as well as love for Abrianna."

Abrianna awoke to pouring rain the next morning. The day seemed to match her heart and mood. Not only was Charlie missing, but now she had this nonsense with Mr. Welby to deal with. How she wished Lenore would return. She supposed her friend was having great fun in San Francisco, but Abrianna missed her dearly and needed her counsel.

Making her way downstairs, Abrianna was surprised by the relative quiet of the house. She heard people stirring, but it seemed much more subdued than a typical morning. Abrianna searched throughout the building for her aunts and finally found Militine straining to look out a window.

"Where is everyone?"

"There was a tragedy," Militine told Abrianna in a reverent hush. "We were told to remain in the upstairs drawing room for breakfast rather than come here to the dining room. I'm afraid I had to come, however, for the view is better. If you want to eat, Liang is getting ready to serve."

Abrianna shook her head. "What kind of tragedy?"

"Someone was killed," Militine confided. "Your aunts didn't say so, but I overheard a policeman declare it to be murder."

"Murder!" she gasped. "Who was it?"

Militine shook her head. "I don't know."

"Very well. I shall have to investigate it for myself." Abrianna hurried to the kitchen and found Liang loading up a tea cart. "Where is Aunt Miriam?"

"She down the stairs talking to a policeman. Your other aunties, they there, too." Liang looked most sober. Her black hair had been pulled back tight in a most severe knot, making the girl look years older.

Abrianna took hold of Liang's arm as she turned to go. "Do you know who was killed?"

"No. I do not see. I know it is a man, but no more."

Abrianna tarried no longer. She made her way down the back stairs and hoped that Aunt Miriam might tell her what had happened. It was most unusual to have a murder take place at their door, and the entire situation intrigued Abrianna. Wade had told her how dangerous the area was becoming, and she had doubted him.

I suppose I shall owe him an apology and tell him his concern was merited. But if I do that, will he insist on my staying at home? Worse still, will he speak to my aunts?

She spied her aunt speaking with the policeman. Abrianna hurried forward. "What has happened? Militine told me someone was killed. Who was it?"

"We don't know, miss," the officer said. "Just some poor old sailor who'd met up with bad company."

"A sailor?" The words almost stuck in her throat. "May I see him?"

"Oh, miss, that wouldn't be appropriate," he replied.

"But I know many of these old men. I care for them, give them food and clothes. I've been unable to locate one particular man who was quite faithful to visit me. It might be him."

The officer looked to Aunt Miriam as if for permission. The older woman nodded. "It's most irregular but perhaps necessary. It won't be easy, Abrianna. The man was beaten about the head. It was terribly severe."

"I understand." Abrianna drew in a deep breath and bolstered her courage. "Take me to him."

Wade had just completed securing a new felloe to the spokes of a wagon wheel when Abrianna burst into the room in sobs.

She ran to him and threw herself into his arms before Wade could even put the wooden mallet down.

"What's wrong? Is it one of the aunts?"

She shook her head and continued to cry. Wade was at a loss. She had wrapped her arms around him and clung to him as if she were a drowning woman. Uncertain what else to do, Wade patted her shoulder and then hugged her close.

"It's going to be all right, Abrianna. Don't cry. Just tell me what's happened."

She straightened and fixed her teary gaze on Wade. "It's . . . it's Charlie."

"You found him? Is he sick?"

"No." She barely got the word out before another round of tears took hold.

Wade was now fearful of what she would say. Abrianna had the strength to endure most anything. He had seen her cry only a handful of times, and always it had been something most grave.

"Is he dead?" Wade forced himself to ask.

She nodded, never moving her gaze. "Someone . . . they . . . beat him. Oh, Wade, someone killed Charlie."

Knowing that he would have to get Abrianna to calm down before he could know the full story, Wade moved her to a chair and made her sit. He retrieved a cup of water for her and held it to her lips. She drank only a little, but it seemed to help. Next Wade handed her his handkerchief, and Abrianna dried her eyes and cheeks. Little by little Wade could see her regain her composure. When at last she was breathing normally and the tears had stopped, Wade felt he could press her for answers.

"What happened, Abrianna?"

She squared her shoulders. "Someone killed Charlie."

"How do you know this?"

"It happened in our alleyway at the school. Mrs. Madison said one of the men downstairs discovered him. Someone . . ." She paused and seemed to fight to keep from crying again. Her lip quivered and she bit down on it momentarily before continuing.

"He was beaten and left for dead." She shook her head. "They didn't know who he was, but I did. I just had a feeling it was him." Her eyes welled with tears, but she didn't break down. "The policeman had me identify him."

Wade frowned, unable to reason the sense in letting an innocent girl view a dead body. "That must have been terrible for you. I wish they could have spared you."

"I thought I had known sadness and pain before now, but I was wrong. Poor Charlie. He never did anything to hurt anyone."

"Do they think someone meant to rob him?" Wade asked. The idea of someone setting out to deliberately kill the old man seemed unlikely.

"Charlie had nothing to steal."

"Someone might have thought he did," Wade replied. "I'm sure there are men desperate enough to rob even an old sailor. Then again, he may have annoyed someone and gotten himself into a fight. Perhaps he made his way afterward to the Madison Building, knowing he could get help, but it was too late."

"It makes no sense," she said. "Charlie was a good man. He was kind to everyone. He did nothing to deserve this."

"Folks seldom do anything to deserve that kind of a death." Wade wanted so much to comfort Abrianna, but he knew she had to process this pain, and that would take time. "Do they have any clues at all?"

Abrianna shook her head slowly. "They have no idea. No one heard or saw anything."

This disturbed Wade even more. "So we have a killer roaming the streets of Seattle."

"Apparently so." Her face changed from pain to anger. "I won't rest until I know who is responsible."

"You can hardly involve yourself in this." Wade knew his words were most likely futile. He might as well try to convince his wooden mallet. Even so, the dangers were much too great to ignore. "I don't want you to be out by yourself anymore, especially not in coming here. Do you understand?"

"I do not," she answered. "Charlie was our friend. We can't just sit around and do nothing."

"Abrianna, whoever did this is dangerous and will most likely stop at nothing. If he'd kill an old man, he'd probably kill a woman just as well. You can't risk your life. Charlie wouldn't want it that way, and you know it."

To his surprise Abrianna hiked up her skirt to reveal the lower portion of her stocking-clad legs. Wade looked away quickly but not before he saw the flash of metal.

"I have a knife," she declared, and Wade couldn't help but look back. Abrianna pointed to where she'd strapped a knife to her slender calf. "I can take care of myself. If this murderer attacks me, he won't find me as helpless as he did Charlie."

"Abrianna, you cannot fight off a killer."

"I can, and if necessary I will," she said, jumping to her feet, knife in hand. "See how quick I can move?"

Wade could think of only one way to prove his point. With the speed of a cat, he lunged at her, knocking the knife from her hand. In no more than a moment he had her encircled with his arms and pinned her backward against him even as she fought his hold.

He easily put his hand to her throat. "Do you see what I'm

talking about? A desperate man would do more than this. You can't risk getting hurt or killed. It would break Charlie's heart . . . and mine."

She stopped fighting and her shoulders slumped in defeat. Wade released her. "I'm sorry I was so rough."

"I hate being a woman. Women are always at the mercy of men."

Wade hoped she would now talk rationally with him about the matter. Instead, she headed for the door without another word.

"Abrianna, wait a minute. Talk to me."

She turned with a look he'd never seen on her face. It appeared to be bitterness, almost contempt—but for whom he didn't know.

"You've already shown me I have nothing I can do. I don't want to talk about it anymore. There's nothing to be gained by such a discussion."

9

Kolbein Booth stood in the room watching the young ladies of the bridal school perform as a choir at the Saturday reception. They sang several hymns while one of the girls played the piano and another the flute. The melodious sound was pleasant enough, but Kolbein couldn't ease his mind no matter how hard he tried.

Somewhere, his sister was lost among the masses of people in Seattle. At least he hoped most fervently that she was still in the city. He hadn't allowed himself to even contemplate otherwise. The song ended and the girls took their seats while Mrs. Madison walked to the front of the room.

"As you ladies already know, we have received some new bridal prospects into the school." She motioned three young ladies to stand. "This is Iona, Ruth, and Catherine. I hope you will make them welcome. And gentlemen, I hope you will get to know these three today."

Kolbein found the entire situation rather silly. Couldn't people meet each other without the help of a matchmaker? Although he knew from things he'd read that west of the Mississippi women were still less in number than their male counterparts, the cities were by no means deplete. Even so, Mrs. Madison apparently provided a needed service, for the school had served to support her and the others for some years. Perhaps it was the idea that getting a wife who was well trained in the social graces as well as in keeping a house in proper order was worth the money men paid to participate in Mrs. Madison's receptions and bridal ball.

"You look deep in thought," Abrianna said, coming alongside him. "Are you thinking about Greta?"

"I scarce can think of anyone else. I fear for her, Abrianna. I cannot lie. The murder of your friend set my heart to even deeper concern." Her expression looked pained, and he immediately apologized. "I'm sorry. I shouldn't have reminded you of your loss."

"No one needs to remind me. I suppose it's especially difficult because it's the first loss of a friend. Well, really my first close death. I was too young to remember my mother dying."

"I can understand how hard this must be. Losing people you care about is difficult on many levels."

"Just like losing Greta?"

"Exactly so." Kolbein pulled out his pocket watch. He longed to go searching for his sister, but it almost seemed futile. He had people watching for her all over the city, and he hoped that she would be wise enough to stay away from the worst areas of the town, where a woman was certain to be assaulted, if not killed.

"I know you're not a rich man," Abrianna began, "but perhaps if you offered a reward someone might come forward with news. I fear the police in this town are somewhat remiss at times. There have been occasions when our police forces were less than honorable. Not only that, but I find that people generally respond better with an incentive than without, and money always seems to be the one thing that motivates. Of course, that isn't the way I think things should be done, but no one ever consults me on such matters." She barely paused for breath, and again Kolbein found himself amazed at how her thoughts just jumped from one to another without any kind of barrier.

"A reward would show people that this was a serious situation, because when money is involved, people tend to get very serious. Perhaps because of the burden it presents either in its presence or its lack. But if I've spoken out of turn, forgive me. I didn't mean to further your burden."

Kolbein didn't find his financial state to be troublesome, but he didn't attempt to set the young woman straight. He had long hidden the fact that he and Greta had inherited a vast sum upon their parents' death. The only real sign of luxury he had allowed himself was to send Greta to boarding school, and he'd done that out of selfish desire.

"I had never really thought of a reward, but you are right. We could post flyers about the town, and maybe someone who would otherwise not look for her would seek her for the money."

"It's possible. It's also possible that people might treat her better if she's fallen in with the wrong crowd or taken a position . . . somewhere." Abrianna put her hand to her mouth and then dropped it down again. "I'm sorry. I spoke amiss. Mrs. Madison said I've always been this way. One of my earliest entanglements was to berate a man at church. Mrs. Madison said I was only three and a half and didn't like the man's cologne, so I proceeded to tell him he smelled bad." Abrianna sighed. "As you can see, I am always saying things that would be best left unsaid."

Kolbein had already worried about the positions his sister might have taken in order to care for her needs. He had made himself sick over the possibility. "I know you meant no harm. Believe me, you can't possibly suggest a fate that I haven't already considered."

Abrianna touched his coat sleeve. "I've been praying about it considerably. I want very much for you to find Greta. I find prayer to be the best way to ease the worried soul."

"I've not prayed in years," Kolbein admitted. "I don't imagine God would listen to me. After all, I've not been good to heed His promptings."

Before Abrianna could say another word, a gentleman approached Kolbein. "Mr. Booth, please excuse the interruption. I wondered if I might have a word."

Kolbein looked to Abrianna, but her gaze was fixed across the room and she shook her head. "Oh dear. I see Mr. Welby has appeared. I'm afraid I shall have to spend some time with him. Please excuse me."

Watching Abrianna make her way to where Welby stood was akin to watching a lamb be led to slaughter. The young woman's displeasure seemed acute, and he couldn't imagine why she'd throw herself into the man's company if she hated it so. Kolbein didn't have time to contemplate it for long, however. His companion seemed most eager to speak.

"My name is Heatherstone. Cyrus Heatherstone. I was told by Mrs. Madison that you are a lawyer who works with corporate and government cases, among other types of law."

"I do," Kolbein replied.

"I wonder if you are considering a permanent arrangement here in Seattle? Mrs. Madison said you were from Chicago but are here seeking to find your sister."

"I am." Kolbein eyed the man with serious intent. "What are you proposing, Mr. Heatherstone?"

The man smiled. "My firm is Heatherstone, Heatherstone, and Blunt. My father and I started the firm, and Mr. Blunt joined us just last year. However, we find ourselves inundated with work. In particular, some problems for several of the larger businesses in town. We are in need of someone who understands the workings of patent issues, the abolition of protective taxes, fishing rights, and such. I would very much like to speak with you about the possibility of your coming to work for us. Mrs. Madison has spoken highly of your character, and I'm certain that should you be interested in accepting, we can retrieve letters of reference from your employer and can compensate you in accordance."

Kolbein considered the offer for a moment. "I am unable to say for certain at this time, but I would be open to discussing the possibility with you and your partners. I have considered a prolonged stay in the area, but there's really no telling how long that might entail."

"No matter, Mr. Booth. Here's my card. Come to this address on Thursday, if that is convenient to you."

Kolbein nodded. "I have no pressing appointments. What time would work well for you and the others?"

"Shall we say eight o'clock in the morning? We have some court appointments in the late morning and afternoon."

"I will be there," Kolbein said, giving the man a slight bow.

Heatherstone walked away, leaving Kolbein curious about this turn of events. Abrianna had spoken of praying for answers, as had Mrs. Madison. Kolbein hadn't been much involved with religious matters since he'd been a young man. The last time he had attended services in a church had been at the funeral rites given for his parents. Abrianna had suggested he pray to find his sister. She'd suggested this on many occasions, but

Kolbein hadn't really given it much consideration until now. With Heatherstone's proposal, Kolbein found several of his concerns mastered. If he were to remain in Seattle and take up a position with their firm, it would expand his circle of acquaintances and friends. Having the ear of the public officials just might be the connection he needed. And once he found Greta, they could decide for themselves whether to remain in Seattle or return to Chicago.

Just then another young woman's image came to mind. Kolbein could almost see her there in the room with the others. Her brown eyes always seemed to take in everything at once, and her mind was quick. He'd experienced that in conversation with the young woman. But why should she come to mind just now?

Kolbein frowned. *I don't want to return to Chicago. I want to find Greta and then win Miss Fulcher's heart.* The thought startled him. How could he feel something so deep—so permanent—for one whom he'd just met and knew very little about? It went against everything he stood for. His very nature demanded a detailed knowledge of the things in which he found interest. Of course, Abrianna had told him a good deal about Miss Fulcher, so perhaps he knew enough. Even so, he hadn't thought himself the marrying type . . . until now.

Lenore stood by the hotel window and sighed. How she longed for home and the company of Kolbein Booth. The longer they were separated, the more she thought of him. He even haunted her dreams, and now she felt more certain than ever that they were meant to be together.

She could clearly see the future in her imagination. A grand house, beautiful furnishings, children, and servants. They would move among the socialites and be ever so devoted to Seattle's betterment. She shook her head, knowing that none of it would matter one whit if Kolbein Booth wasn't a part of it. James Rybus was a nice enough man, but her heart and thoughts were with Kolbein.

She toyed with the drapery and watched the heavy flow of traffic on the street below. Was he thinking of her just as much as she was of him? She knew Abrianna would be doing her best to convince Kolbein of her virtues—at least Lenore hoped so. Her friend could be most inconveniently distracted at times.

"What are you looking at?" Father asked as he came into the common area of the hotel suite.

"Nothing in particular," Lenore replied, turning to face him. "I was just contemplating several matters."

"Such as?" He fixed her with a look that let Lenore know he expected an answer.

"I long for home."

"We won't be detained too much longer. I'm sorry that my business here was complicated and extended our stay; however, my attention to the details was critical."

Lenore smiled and went to her father's side. "I'm sure that it was, Father. I'm sorry if I troubled you with my desires."

He returned her smile. "Not at all."

"I suppose it does worry me as to how a man might ask to court me if we are not even in the city to receive him."

"Your young man, eh?"

"Yes. You gave us only a month to work with, and for most of that time we've not even been in Seattle."

"Very well," Father said. "If that has you vexed, I will reset the time to be one month from our return. I'm not, after all, an ogre who would see his only child miserable. James Rybus was

115

only a suggestion because . . . well, because he's been a loyal worker and good friend. I have to admit, I've been concerned that you marry well. I'm afraid a great many men will only be interested in your fortune. Upon my death you'll not only have the trust left to you by your grandparents, but you and your mother will also inherit my vast holdings."

"I know that, Father, but I'm not without my standards and values. I would never allow a man to form his opinion of me based on my financial situation. Mr. Booth isn't like that at all. He makes a good living as a lawyer in Chicago." She had no idea if he did or not, but Lenore assumed it to be true and figured it best to suggest that it was.

"So you would break our hearts by leaving Seattle should this relationship grow serious and lead to marriage?"

Lenore had never really considered that before now. "I can't say. Perhaps Mr. Booth would enjoy living in Seattle. I believe anything is possible, and I am continuing to pray that God will give me wisdom in all things."

Mother swept into the room, all but floating across the floor as she always did. Lenore had worked to mimic her grace since she was just a little girl. "You two look rather glum and serious." She smiled. "I thought we were to go to the theatre tonight, and here neither of you are dressed for the occasion. Lenore, hurry and change. Get the maid to help you with your hair."

Without arguing, Lenore made her way to her bedroom suite. Her mother had insisted that they attend one affair or another night after night, and Lenore was exhausted and bored. It wasn't that a play or concert, or even the occasional party, wasn't to her liking, but her heart was elsewhere.

How did I fall in love with this man? I hardly know him and he hardly knows me. What will I do if he doesn't return my affections? Lenore frowned and began to unbutton her skirt. What if she returned home to find Kolbein gone? The thought troubled her greatly.

Abrianna opened the envelope from Lenore. How she missed her friend!

Dearest Abrianna,

How I long for home. I pray you are well and that this letter will explain our delay in returning. Father has been quite busy with various business negotiations but assures me we won't remain here much longer.

I pray you have kept your promise to speak of me to Mr. Booth. I am counting on you to offer your very best efforts.

"Goodness," Abrianna said, setting the letter aside. "I have no idea if my efforts are my best or not. I haven't been overly thoughtful of the matter lately." She was speaking to no one but the empty room. She cringed a little at the thought. Had she been selfish and remiss in helping her friend?

I find myself thinking of Mr. Booth—dare I say Kolbein?—so often. I suppose that might sound strange to some, given we've only met and have had little time to know each other. However, I believe my heart has assigned itself to this man. I have heard of such things—people falling in love upon the first glance. I don't want to say for certain that this is the case, but I do feel a strange longing to know him better.

I miss you dearly. Please pray that we will soon be on our way home.

With great affection,
Lenore

"Oh, I have been far too focused on the dead rather than the living." She put the letter aside. "But there must be time for both. Charlie was a good man and he deserves my help in finding his killer."

Grief over Charlie had taken a good deal of her attention. There had been a small service, and some of his former mates arranged a burial at sea. Of course Abrianna couldn't attend either one, what with the funeral having been held in the worst section of the town—Skid Road. Efforts had been made on many occasions to clean up the Lava Bed, as some called it, but even Abrianna knew better than to venture there—even to honor Charlie. For the burial at sea she had climbed to the rooftop and looked out toward the harbor. She imagined the boat carrying Charlie maneuvering through the sound and making its way out and around the various islands to reach the open ocean. Charlie would be happy they were doing this for him, but Abrianna couldn't help but feel a deep sadness. Charlie was only one of the many old and forgotten souls, yet his absence left Abrianna confused and angry.

"Who would kill an innocent old man?" she murmured.

Realizing she was focusing on the death of her friend and not the promotion of Lenore to Kolbein, Abrianna forced the thoughts from her mind. She must do better on Lenore's behalf. She hurried to finish buttoning her boots and was nearly done when she heard a commotion outside her door.

Without thought of her boots, Abrianna hurried to see what had caused the disturbance. Outside the door Aunt Poisie was racing down the hall with Aunt Selma close behind, carrying armfuls of towels toward the back staircase. What in the world was going on?

Abrianna hurried after them. "Aunt Poisie, what has happened?"

"Oh, it's terrible," Poisie replied. "Just terrible. A pipe in the kitchen has sprung a leak, and the spring rains and thaws of the mountain snows are sure to cause the sewers to back up. We need to work fast or the leaky pipe might overflow the kitchen with sewage."

"How could the sewage back up all the way to the kitchen? We're on the second floor." She knew there had been trouble with the sewers for as long as they'd been in the place, and while some of the backups had been quite extensive and smelly, they had faired the problem well enough until now.

"I believe," she said, continuing to follow her aunts, "that the pipe in the kitchen is part of the water system and not the sewer system. Although I can't say for certain. Wade would know best."

"Sister has sent for Wade. He should be here shortly to lend us aid."

Aunt Selma nodded. "It is a severe testing to be certain."

In the kitchen, Liang was already mopping up water as fast as she could, and Aunt Miriam was down on her hands and knees trying to figure out something under the sink. Several of the students were hurriedly moving objects from one side of the kitchen to the other. It seemed there was no end to the activity.

"Can I be of assistance?" a male voice sounded.

Abrianna turned to find Kolbein Booth rather than Wade.

"Apparently the pipe is leaking and we are in danger of another situation to match Noah and his ark." Her voice was only loud enough for him to hear.

He grinned. "Well, we cannot have that." He strode across the kitchen and, in a matter of minutes, had the water turned off and the leak temporarily stopped.

"All might have been lost had you not appeared," Poisie declared.

Abrianna suppressed a smile. She wasn't sure how all could be lost because of one leaky pipe, but she wasn't about to question her aunt.

Wade walked in, toolbox in hand, as the last of the food items were moved from one countertop to another. "I see you managed to get here before I did," Wade said to Kolbein.

"We are most grateful that anyone would come in our hour of need," Selma told the men. "It was a frightful thing to watch everything become soaked in water."

"I'll do what I can to get it fixed up for you," Wade said, going closer to see the problem. He tinkered with things for a few minutes, then opened his toolbox and went to work.

Kolbein remained at his side, offering whatever help he could while Abrianna's aunts guided the young ladies to another task. Within a matter of minutes, Wade had the job in hand. Apparently the leak was coming from a loose joint or some such thing. Abrianna wasn't all that concerned. Already she was trying to formulate what she would say regarding her dear friend.

When Kolbein stepped back to give Wade room to put away his tools, Abrianna decided to use the time to speak to Kolbein about Lenore.

"I had a small note from Lenore. She wants very much to come home. She misses us."

Kolbein smiled. "And she is missed, as well. I can tell you are half beside yourself awaiting her return, and I shall be glad to hear her tales of San Francisco."

"I do miss her," Abrianna admitted. "She's a dear friend. I think you would be wise to note her grand qualities. She is quite an amazing find."

He laughed at this. "You sound as though she were a rare diamond found in the heart of darkest Africa."

"She's more valuable than that," Abrianna replied. "I'm sure even the angels are blessed by her example. She is a great beauty, and I know of none her equal."

Kolbein shrugged. "Well, it seems that I know of one. One particular red-headed creature whose loyalty to her friend knows no bounds. However, I must admit that you've caused me to be intrigued, and I find myself pondering the idea of knowing her better."

Abrianna put her hand to her breast. "I am so relieved to hear you say so. I know that would please Lenore."

"Oh? And why would that be?" he asked, his right brow arched.

"Ah, well . . ." She couldn't very well tell him the truth. "Lenore enjoys making friends. I'm certain she would cherish knowing you better, as well."

He seemed to consider this for a moment and smiled. "Then we must hope for Miss Fulcher's swift return."

Feeling satisfied with his comment, Abrianna decided to let the matter rest for the time being. She had done her duty to Lenore, and now she could eat her breakfast with a clear conscience.

10

Days later as Kolbein walked along the wharfs, he spied Wade Ackerman's wagon shop across the street. For reasons he didn't completely understand, Kolbein decided to pay the man a visit. Maybe in talking to another man, Kolbein could sort through some of the thoughts that were going through his mind. Up until now, the influence had mostly been female, and God himself knew that men and women did *not* think alike.

Arriving inside the small building, Kolbein let his eyes adjust to the dim lighting. The shop was full of woody scents and the sound of hammering. Kolbein followed the sounds and found Wade working to build what looked like a wooden box.

"I hope I'm not intruding," he said, announcing his presence.

Wade looked up, surprised. "Not at all. But I will say that I never expected to see you here."

Kolbein nodded. He'd been thinking over some things Abrianna had said about God, and suddenly his visit seemed preordained. "You're a man of God, aren't you?"

Wade put down the hammer and wiped his hands on the leather apron that protected his clothes. "I am. Why do you ask?"

"I realize we don't know each other very well, but I guess . . . I have some questions—man to man."

Wade appeared to consider this for a moment. Then without ceremony he pulled off his leather apron. "Why don't we have a cup of coffee together? I'm ready for a break."

Kolbein agreed and followed Wade into yet another portion of the shop. It wasn't much—a ten-by-ten-foot room at the most, and in it was what appeared to be Wade's entire home. A table for two and a small woodstove occupied one end of the room. Lifting the coffeepot from the stove, Wade motioned for Kolbein to take a seat.

This gave him the opportunity to study the entire room as Wade poured hot coffee into first one mug and then another. A small bed stood opposite the impromptu kitchen, and in between were a couple of bookcases, a reading chair, and a chest of drawers. The top of the chest was covered with a variety of objects, but otherwise the little room was fairly well maintained.

"So you actually live here?" Kolbein asked, uncertain what else to say.

"I do. I know it's not much, but I don't need much. I figure it's better to save money." Wade took a seat. "I didn't think to ask—do you take sugar? I don't have any cream, but I do have sugar."

"Black is fine." Kolbein took a sip of the coffee. It was good and strong. "It's perfect."

Wade smiled and took a slow sip. "Hotter than I expected. I figured it'd be pretty cooled down by now. Guess I stoked that fire up a bit more than I thought."

Kolbein nodded. "What with the rain I can't say as I blame you. I've been walking amongst the street vendors and asking about my sister. It chilled me through."

"I can build up the fire more if you'd like."

"No. I didn't come here to impose." Kolbein fidgeted with his coffee cup. "Fact is, I didn't figure to come here at all, but I found myself standing out front and thought you might be able to help me."

"With what?" Wade looked confused.

"Well, this isn't exactly easy to say, but I know Abrianna puts a lot of trust in you, and she seems to have a deep regard for the Bible and spiritual matters."

Wade gave a nod. "That she does. I've been attending church with her nearly since she was born."

"She seems really knowledgeable about a lot of things, I must say." Kolbein chuckled. "I've never met up with a more opinionated woman in my life."

"Abrianna is that," Wade admitted hesitantly. "But . . . well, you have to consider how she's been raised. Those aunts of hers aren't exactly the demure and silent type. They are more educated than most women. Mrs. Madison was a teacher before she married, and her sister graduated from a women's college. I believe her focus was music. Mrs. Gibson was a preacher's daughter. Her father insisted she study the Bible every day and learn about various views of theology. Then she married an educated man and grew quite opinionated about his love of"—he lowered his voice—"science."

Chuckling, Kolbein rubbed the top of the wood table as if checking for snags. "The cad."

Wade laughed. "She has a definite opinion of what is acceptable regarding issues of faith and what is not."

Kolbein sobered and reconsidered his situation. Why had he come here? Ackerman hardly knew him. How could he ask the man about spiritual matters when they were barely friends?

"You seem really troubled. Is it your sister?" Wade asked. "Or something more?"

"I am continually worried about Greta, but I actually came here with another thought in mind. You see, I grew up respecting God and figured myself to be a good Christian, even though I don't attend church very often. However, I find myself feeling at a loss these days where God is concerned."

He stopped and toyed with the rim of the mug. "I'm sorry. This is probably something you'd rather I take to a minister or priest."

Wade's expression softened. "Not at all. If your spirit is troubled, I want to do what I can to help. God calls us to bear one another's burdens, and many a good man has done the same for me."

Kolbein heard the sincerity in Wade's voice. There was no condemnation. No judgment. Just genuine respect and interest.

"Abrianna is always telling me to trust in the Lord. She tells me to pray about Greta and tells me that she's praying for me and for her. I'm sorry to say that the words just seem hollow to me. Not that I don't believe God exists or that He controls all things, but I don't feel connected to such spiritual matters. I suppose I'm not a good Christian because I have doubts and haven't been attending church."

"Fellowship and learning are important in order to know God better," Wade replied. "But being at the church doesn't make you a Christian any more than being in a wagon shop makes you a wainwright. Being a man of God has to do with knowing Him and seeking Him for direction and answers. However, it starts with accepting that Jesus died for your sins and repenting of them."

"I did that as a child," Kolbein told him. "I remember a time in Sunday school when the teacher had all of us pray and ask Jesus into our hearts." He smiled. "I was only nine, but the teacher was adamant that we all pray together."

Wade shook his head. "Accepting Jesus is a personal experience. You can't force a group of folks into salvation. Did you understand what you were saying when you prayed that prayer?"

"No, I suppose I didn't understand the full implications," Kolbein admitted. "Not like I do now."

"So maybe now is the time you should pray for real." Wade took a drink of coffee and then set the mug down. "I could pray with you . . . if you'd like."

"Here? Now?"

"Sure. God doesn't require us to be in a church to get our hearts right."

"I guess I've always thought of God as the great judge in the sky—out there somewhere waiting to mete out His punishments."

"That's the lawyer side of you," Wade said, grinning. "I tend to think more of Jesus being from a carpenter family. That's because it's what's familiar to me. I think folks need to see something personal that connects them to God."

Kolbein considered this. "I remember a sermon in which the pastor said none of us were good enough to get into heaven. That made me angry. If God made us, then He could have made us 'good enough.'"

"My personal thought is that He did make us good enough, but then man took things into his own hands and made some really bad choices. Did God know that would happen? I think so."

"Then why bother?"

Wade shrugged. "I can't say for sure I know the answer to that. Over the years, I've studied the Bible and prayed to have understanding, only to realize that God's ways are not my ways and we won't always know why. And I suppose knowing why wouldn't change a thing."

"Forgive me for asking all these questions, but why do you say that?" Kolbein found that he longed to know the answer more than anything.

"Well, it seems to me that a lot of folks worry about the *why*s of life when they ought to focus more on the *who*."

This comment only served to further confuse Kolbein. "The who?"

"Exactly. Whose plan is it? Mine or God's? If it's mine then I probably already know some of the whys and realize that they aren't worth a hill of beans. Most of the time we do things out of selfish ambition or personal comfort. If you look at the sinful choices we make, I think you'll find they are all prideful choices. Look at Eve in the Garden of Eden. She listened to the snake and made a choice because the food looked good and was pleasing to her eye, and because her pride longed to know what God knew."

"So the who was Eve?"

"Exactly. God had told Adam and Eve what they could and couldn't do, and they chose their own way. I don't think it took God by surprise, but I also don't know why He would tolerate such blatant disobedience. On the other hand, I'm glad He gives grace and mercy for such actions, because I've been disobedient enough myself. If I'd been in the garden, I've no doubt my choices would have been just as poor."

"As a man of the law, the reason or motive for action is always examined," Kolbein admitted, "but I think I'm getting the point of what you're saying. God gives instruction and our job is to obey."

"In faith," Wade added. "And that's what makes it difficult, maybe more so for men than for women. Trust comes hard for me. It's taken a lifetime of seeing God at work to know my faith is well placed."

"I see where I've fallen short. My faith has been mostly in myself." Kolbein shook his head. He felt sadder than he had in years. "That was certainly not a good place to put it."

"You don't have to leave it there," Wade said, smiling. "The nice thing is that God is always willing to hear us repent and put our trust in Him."

"I can see what you're saying. I guess . . . if you don't mind, I'd like to do that."

Wade nodded in a knowing manner. "I don't mind at all."

"How can another man be dead just steps from our building?" Aunt Selma asked, wringing her hands together. "Oh, this is bad. Very bad, indeed."

Abrianna could see the expression on Selma's face matched that of her other two aunts. They were horrified that their neighborhood had been compromised by such indecency and malice.

"The police said the poor soul probably has no family and will be buried in a county plot. God rest his soul."

"Amen," the women replied in unison.

"What is this world coming to?" Aunt Miriam's tone held a hint of fear. Not something Abrianna heard often from the stoic woman. Her aunt continued. "I would expect this from Skid Road, but not from our area. Another killing . . ."

Another killing—another man that few if any would miss. Abrianna didn't know this one. He was much younger than Charlie, but he'd been killed in the same manner. At least that's what she'd heard the police officer share. Other than that, he'd conveyed very little. He believed the case would go unresolved for lack of evidence. In fact, he said there would be very little investigation into either murder.

The attitude of this man irritated Abrianna to no end, and she would have given him a piece of her mind had Aunt Miriam not rushed her back up the stairs to their home. Now they were gathered in the private sitting room, and Aunt Miriam was most grave.

"It would seem that the neighborhood is taking on a baser nature. Perhaps the people who frequent this area are less inclined to care about human life." She shook her head. "I wonder if perhaps we need to do something more to ensure our safety."

"We could purchase a gun," Aunt Selma suggested. "Mr. Gibson always had firearms in the house."

"Do you know how to handle one?" Aunt Miriam asked.

Selma shook her head. "I'm afraid Mr. Gibson thought it unseemly for a woman to learn such operations."

"My beloved captain, God rest his soul"— Poisie paused momentarily for her companions' *amen*—"he carried a gun."

"And did he teach you to fire it?" her sister asked.

"No, but he said it was an important part of keeping himself safe."

"Well, I do not know how to handle such a weapon, either," Aunt Miriam replied.

Abrianna felt the need to interject at this point. "It can't be all that hard. You point one end at the threat and pull the trigger at the other end. Goodness, we needn't make such a simple thing difficult." Then a thought came to her. "I suppose we might not know how to care for a gun or how to load one, but I'm certain Wade or even Kolbein might teach us."

"And could you truly take the life of a man?" Aunt Miriam questioned.

Thinking on this for a moment, Abrianna frowned. "No. You are right to question that. I don't suppose I could. However, the threat alone might cause the assailant to flee."

"And if it doesn't?" her aunt pressed. "What if the attacker simply disarms you and then kills you with your own weapon? Or flees, now armed to kill in a manner even easier than beating a man to death?"

"Yes, you are right," Abrianna said, remembering Wade's demonstration of her weakness.

"Perhaps, Sister," Poisie began softly, "it is time to consider a relocation."

"Move from here?" Aunt Miriam asked, as if the thought had never occurred to her.

"Not too far," Poisie replied. "Perhaps on the hill. I wouldn't want to move away from the water and not be able to at least see it."

Aunt Selma nodded. "You know yourself that this building is in the perfect location for a variety of businesses. Why, Mr. Fulcher himself might wish to obtain it. And then, of course, there's Mr. Welby."

Aunt Miriam got up and moved toward the window. "I must say the same idea has been brewing in my mind. I can't imagine selling this building. It would be akin to losing Mr. Madison all over again."

"But it doesn't need to be that way, Sister. After all, your husband never intended this to be your home."

"But it became that because it worked out so perfectly with our business." She turned to face them, and Abrianna could see the sadness in her eyes. "Perhaps our days are numbered.

Maybe this is God's way of telling us it's time to put an end to our matchmaking."

"No!" Poisie declared adamantly.

"The sale of the building would bring in a most satisfactory sum. And that, along with our investments, would keep us for as long as we live if we used it wisely."

Abrianna had never wanted to take over her aunts' bridal school and saw this as the perfect time to delay it again. "I think that would be the best solution. Just imagine . . . you could sell this building to Mr. Welby. He's always talking at the receptions about how much he likes it and how perfect it would be for his import business. Sell to him, and we can buy a little house on the hill where I can take care of you as you get older and . . . learn all that you desire me to learn about housekeeping and cooking." She threw the latter in hoping it might tip the scales in favor of the move. She didn't so much want to leave this building as she wanted to put an end to her aunts' desire to have Abrianna take over the school.

"We'd be farther from Wade and Thane," she pondered aloud, "but they wouldn't mind the extra walk to visit on Sundays." Abrianna thought about her various causes: the poor old sailors who barely kept clothes on their backs and a blanket in their keeping. The orphans would still be close enough, as they moved around and would no doubt seek Abrianna out if she didn't look for them. As for the ladies of the evening who plied their trade in the Lava Bed, Abrianna would simply have to figure something else out. Perhaps if they had a carriage . . .

"I suppose it is something to consider." Aunt Miriam looked first to her sister and then to Aunt Selma.

"Perhaps we could grow vegetables to sell," Poisie said. "Or maybe get a cow and sell milk."

Aunt Miriam didn't so much as acknowledge that comment. "Do you suppose I should discuss the matter again with Mr. Welby?"

"I do, Sister."

"But do not be too eager, lest he reduce the price he's willing to pay," Selma cautioned.

Abrianna thought this would be as good a time as any to discuss her desire to no longer attend the receptions. She had the distinct feeling that Mr. Welby's biggest interest was the building; otherwise, why should he ask so many questions about it.

"He plans to attend the reception on Saturday," she told her aunts. "That would be a good time to take Mr. Welby aside and discuss the subject. Of course, you might want to have Mr. Fulcher present, but I don't know when they plan to return from San Francisco. Lenore thought it would be right away."

"I shall take it under consideration," Aunt Miriam said, brushing a piece of lint from her dark blue dress. "And we should all pray about this."

A knock at the door sent Abrianna flying down the hall. She was glad for the excuse to leave the meeting. Goodness, but it seemed to take forever for her aunts to make even the smallest decision.

This really isn't a small decision, she admitted to herself. *But it is just one simple decision. Either they should sell the building or they shouldn't. It really is just that easy.* She opened the door to find Kolbein Booth. He was smiling and seemed most at peace.

"Good day, Abrianna," he said. "Do you feel up to a bit of searching?"

"I do. Let me tell Aunt Miriam our plan." She stepped back so he could enter the room. "Just hang on to your hat," she added. "This needn't take long."

At least that was her hope. Since the killing of yet another person, Abrianna had thought of nothing but warning the orphan boys. "While we're out," she said, looking back at Kolbein as she led the way down the hall, "I have something to attend to, as well."

Abrianna hurried to secure a flour sack and load it with food for the boys. She had just put in a couple dozen cookies—ones she'd managed to bake without burning—when Aunt Miriam came into the kitchen with Militine.

"I told Mr. Booth that you could go searching with him, but I want you to take Militine along. It would hardly look right for the two of you to always be seen alone."

"I don't really care what anyone thinks," Abrianna replied, "but I certainly don't mind Militine's company." She looked down at the sack in her hands and then met her aunt's questioning gaze. "I thought we might . . . well, we could meet up with someone who's hungry."

Aunt Miriam's expression didn't change, but she gave the briefest nod. "Very well." She turned and left the room, leaving the girls to conspire.

Abrianna hurried to finish loading the sack and then motioned to Militine. "Let's find Kolbein and get out of here before anyone changes their mind. Are you sure you don't mind accompanying us?"

"I am so happy to have a day away from lessons," Militine exclaimed as they took up their shawls by the front door. "I would work at just about anything else."

"Surely your lessons aren't that arduous," Kolbein said, joining them. "Sorry, I couldn't help but overhear."

Militine Scott smiled. "I don't mind. The lessons aren't so arduous. Well, the French is. I don't think I'm meant to speak

another language. But the constant messes I make are most arduous. She understands." She looked to Abrianna. "Don't you?"

"I do indeed. However, I know it's best that we discuss such
matters on our way. Aunt Miriam may reconsider our excursion
as she ponders yet another murder in the area."

"I just heard about that," Kolbein said. "Did you know him?"

"No. He was much younger than the old men I care for,"
Abrianna said as they headed downstairs and out of the building.
"And a wee bit old to be considered an orphan boy. Even so, it's
a terrible thing. Aunt Miriam is finally considering concluding
her work as a matchmaker in order to move us elsewhere."

"I'm certain she will need some solid legal advice," Kolbein
said, thoughtfully. "That's another reason I came today. I wanted
to let you know that I've accepted a position with a local law firm."

"You're moving here?" Abrianna asked, unable to contain
her excitement. "Lenore will be so happy."

Kolbein raised a brow and laughed. "Only Lenore? And here
I thought we were friends."

"Well, she's the only one who matters in this," Abrianna
assured him. "She wants very much to . . . to know you better."

"And I hope to give her that opportunity. However, I won't
close out my house in Chicago just yet. I will find a place to
rent here or continue living at the hotel until I am able to locate
Greta. After that, I will decide what to do."

Abrianna took them down one street and then another. There
were a great many people moving about the town, and the streets
were filled with carriages, wagons, and horses. At the overbearing smell of sewage, Abrianna thought that the sewers were
backed up once again, just as her aunts had predicted.

Within half an hour, Abrianna managed to locate the boys.
She couldn't help but smile at the sight of them, all wearing

"new" shoes. She handed Toby the flour sack of food. "Just keep it. I'm sure we have plenty. Aunt Miriam has us turning the sacks into dish towels, so there must be an abundance. Of course, it could be that we've simply worn the others out and are in true need of dish towels, but that really doesn't affect you, does it?" She paused and collected her thoughts.

"There's another, more pressing, reason we've come today. News most grave."

Toby handed the sack back to one of the other boys. "What's wrong?"

"There's been another murder near our building."

"Murders happen all the time," Toby said, shrugging. "Especially in Skid Road."

"Yes, but we aren't in Skid Road," Abrianna countered. "We're close to the docks, true enough, but our location was, until late, a very decent area of businesses. Now my aunts are considering selling the building and moving us to a small house on the hill."

Toby looked at the other boys. "Well, if you're worried about us, don't be. We can defend ourselves, and we all just got jobs."

"Jobs? Truly?" Abrianna asked.

"What kind of job, boys?" Kolbein asked. "Nothing illegal, I hope."

Toby still appeared uncertain of Kolbein. "No, sir, nothing illegal. We're cleaning up at the theatre. It's the one over by Marley's Hotel and that bunch of eating places on the north side. Owner has a new troupe in and said he'd pay us each twenty cents a week to come in and clean up after the shows." The other boys nodded.

"And he said that if we didn't make trouble, he'd let us sleep in the room where they keep the things they use in the play," eleven-year-old Bobby declared.

Toby nodded in affirmation. "It's like God is answering your prayers, Miss Abrianna."

"God is good to do that," she replied. "I'm so glad that you boys have somewhere safe to stay at night. I worried about you, what with a killer loose on the streets."

Toby smiled. "Like I said—we can take care of ourselves." He turned toward Kolbein. "We been askin' around about your sister. Lookin' for her, too."

"I appreciate that." Kolbein's expression betrayed his worry. "Have you had any leads?"

"Not a one," Toby said. "But we're gonna keep lookin'."

"Thank you. I really am grateful."

They didn't stick around long to chat, and Abrianna felt a sense of relief as they turned their attention to looking for Greta.

"I'm so glad God is watching out for them. They're only a few of the many who need homes and help."

"You can't save the world, Abrianna," Militine said, squeezing her arm. "But I do so admire that you are able to care for even these few."

"One day," Abrianna said, "perhaps I will have a place with nothing but beds and a kitchen. Oh, and bathing facilities, of course, and maybe a place for reading. And an infirmary where a doctor can come and treat injuries and sickness. One day I would like to have a place where I can feed as many as are hungry and then let them bed down for the night in safety."

"You have a big heart, Abrianna," Kolbein interjected, "but that's hardly acceptable work for a woman. Especially a single young woman."

"So everyone tells me, but I feel it is God's calling on my life. I am here to help the poor, just as I was helped."

"But how will you finance such an endeavor?" he asked.

Abrianna smiled. "That's the easy part. God will provide what we need. I just have to be willing to work."

"Speaking of God," Kolbein said with a grin, "I had a long talk with that friend of yours, Wade, and I finally feel that I am able to pray and God will hear me. I needed to make things right with Him, and Wade helped me see how to do it."

Abrianna clapped her hands. "I'm so happy for you. I know that must be a tremendous weight off your shoulders. Or maybe your soul." She shook her head. "It doesn't matter, does it? I'm sure it was a great relief, either way."

He laughed. "Indeed it was."

"I don't know what God's calling is on my life," Militine said, as if Kolbein hadn't said anything at all. "Do you suppose everyone gets a calling? I don't know if God even remembers I'm here."

"Of course, Militine," Abrianna replied, surprised by the young woman's question. "God has a calling for each and every person. It starts with our honoring Him and listening to His direction. After that, who can say where God will lead. I once heard the pastor say that God put a calling on his life to dig for the railroad back east. He said he was able to share the gospel with many an anguished soul." She put her hand to her breast. "I marveled at that. Just imagine having all those rough and rowdy railroad workers listening to the Word of God and changing their lives. I can't help but think it would make their hard labors seem much easier. Don't you?" She looked to Kolbein.

"I don't know that anything could make railroad work easy, but I'm certain they were relieved to have their consciences clear before the Lord, just as I am."

Abrianna nodded thoughtfully. "As am I." She smiled at Kolbein. "I'm so glad you have made peace with God. It will make things much easier for us now."

"Why do you say that?"

She shrugged. "Now God will hear prayers from both of us. . . . Well, I know we won't be the only ones praying. Goodness, but Aunt Selma announced it at church the other day when the pastor asked for prayer requests. I imagine there are hundreds of people praying by now. But I digress." She looked to his smiling face. "I just know that having you pray, as well, will make things easier."

"Things?" Kolbein asked. "You sound like there is something we should be praying for besides Greta's return."

"Well, there is Lenore's safe return."

His expression looked as if he'd just realized the answer to a puzzle. "I will most assuredly pray for that. Have you heard anything more about their return?"

"No, but I expect they will arrive soon. Lenore's father has businesses to run. I wouldn't think it prudent to stay away."

"No, it wouldn't be wise," he admitted.

"You know, her parents want Lenore to marry soon." Abrianna paused, wondering if she'd been too bold. "I suppose they worry about her being an old maid, but I hardly think that's possible."

"Neither do I." He looked both uncomfortable and yet somewhat eager to hear more.

Abrianna shrugged. "I think if the right man asks, Lenore would probably say yes." *There,* she thought. *I've made her need quite clear.*

⁓

Priam Welby took the delicate china cup and saucer offered him and nodded approval at the coffee he was served. The old women certainly knew how to make a good cup of coffee and how to cook. He had never eaten so well as when attending one of the receptions. Even though it wasn't a full meal by any means, there was every imaginable type of finger food available—all homemade by Mrs. Madison and her young ladies.

Abrianna Cunningham approached him looking quite wary. He would have laughed had she not been a serious part of his plan. She had dressed in a salmon-colored gown trimmed in a sheer white fabric. It was quite fetching on her and one of the latest styles.

"You look beautiful. That color suits you well."

Abrianna nodded. "Thank you. Aunt Miriam said as much—regarding the color, of course." She seemed nervous, and Priam knew it was important to put her at ease.

Abrianna stared off toward the other reception attendees. She seemed most determined to avoid his gaze. She was always quite opinionated, so perhaps he should speak his mind and clear the air between them. "You don't like me, do you?"

Her eyes widened at this. "I never said that."

He chuckled and sipped his coffee. Putting the cup back on the saucer, he shook his head. "You don't have to. I can see it in your eyes."

"Maybe you just see my frustration at having to be here, but it's not got much to do with you." She frowned and seemed to reconsider her words. "I hope that didn't sound offensive. What I'm trying to say is that it wouldn't matter if it were you or someone else. I have no desire to be here."

"Don't you plan to court and take a husband?"

"No. I have a calling on my life to do work amongst the poor. I doubt a husband would allow for that."

Priam cocked his head to one side. "Why would you think

that? My heart is quite burdened for the indigent. I was once among their number until I managed to work my way out. Their needs are many, and Seattle has more than its fair share of the impoverished."

"It's true," Abrianna replied, "and I apologize, as I did not know your heart was burdened. Most people pass right by the poor and think nothing more of their plight."

He nodded. "I have seen the same. I think I would very much admire a wife who wanted to see to the betterment of such folks."

"Perhaps you would agree to have her sit in a committee formed to address the matter," Abrianna replied. "Dressed in fine clothes and acting socially acceptable with other women who also felt burdened for the poor, but who wanted nothing to do with them physically."

"I'm not sure I understand. Do you mean that you would want to work amongst the poor?"

"Yes. Why not? I'm not afraid of hard work nor of getting my hands dirty, if need be. I'm not all that good at sewing and cooking, as a wife ought to be, but I'm very good at soliciting donations for the poor and organizing their distribution."

"And this is the kind of thing you, how did you say it, feel called to?"

"It is," Abrianna replied. "They need someone to fight for them—someone to care. God has given me that job, and I take it seriously. So you see, Mr. Welby, it has nothing at all to do with you."

"I suppose I should be relieved," he said, grinning. "I feared I had lost my charm."

She looked him in the eye at this comment. "No. You are a most charming man, and as Aunt Miriam pointed out, you are handsome and well tailored."

He nearly burst out laughing. "You needed your aunt to point out that I was handsome. Do you not think me handsome?"

Abrianna looked stunned by his openness. *Good*, he thought, *let her take a dose of her own medicine.* However, he wasn't prepared for her reply.

"I suppose there are those who would think that you're handsome," she began. "Perhaps someone closer to your own age. I've never really cared for eyes as dark as yours, and they are set a little far apart, don't you think? Also, your ears are rather large. I suppose that could be good for hearing, but again, they don't appeal to me. Then there's your height. You're only a little taller than I am, and I always figured that if I were to marry, I would marry a tall man. That way he could get things down from the high cupboards for me."

Priam barely kept his mouth from dropping open at her assessment. He'd never met anyone who so clearly spoke their mind.

"Are you two enjoying the social?" Aunt Miriam asked as she joined them.

"We were having quite an enlightening conversation," Priam replied. "Abrianna was just pointing out a few things to me." The young woman didn't even have the goodness to blush. Welby salved his wounded pride with thoughts of how he could even the score. He smiled at Mrs. Madison. "I don't suppose you have reconsidered my offer to buy your building." He prepared himself for the woman's offense.

"As a matter of fact, I have been doing exactly that."

Her words surprised him more than he could hide. "I . . . well . . . you haven't come to a conclusion, have you?"

"Not yet, but I am in discussion with Mr. Booth about it— he's a lawyer, you know."

"No, I didn't know that," Priam replied. He had hoped to avoid any legal entanglements. "I'm sure there's no need of a lawyer, however. I am a good businessman with perfectly legitimate contracts to offer. I would pay you far more than the building would garner on the regular real estate market, and I would move you to the house I mentioned without your having to lift a finger or disrupt your business. No lawyer could negotiate better for you."

"Perhaps not, but it comforts me to know his thoughts on the matter."

Priam nodded and forced a smile. "I am glad to know that you are even thinking on my request."

"I hope you will enjoy the rest of the festivities. The ladies plan to recite some poetry in a few minutes." Mrs. Madison took her leave and crossed the room to greet another couple.

Priam turned to ask Abrianna if she was to participate, but she was already gone. No doubt she had taken her aunt's appearance as an opportunity to slip away. Well, that was all right. If the old woman would sell him the building outright, he wouldn't need to tie himself up in a courtship and marriage just to inherit the place. Perhaps things were changing for the better.

He touched a hand to his ear. Big ears? No one before this redheaded hoyden had ever thought to say he had big ears.

11

"Y ou are to wear your very best gown this evening," Mother told Lenore. "The Montgomerys are a well-established family and respected for their influence in San Francisco."

"Oh, Mother, I can't imagine that it will matter to anyone what I'm wearing."

Her mother looked at her aghast. "Of course it matters. It's a reflection on your father and on me. Don't you care what other people say?"

"I used to care. But honestly, over the years I've come to see life differently. I think I've been worried about the wrong things. Abrianna says—"

"If this is about her, then I'm certain it will not meet with my approval. I don't mind that the two of you are friends. You have attempted to make her a better woman, and that's an act of charity. However, I can hardly accept that she is guiding your choices. Now, please do as I say. This dinner is important."

"Why must I go?" Lenore asked. She was more than a little homesick and felt her chances with Kolbein were slipping away by the minute. Why didn't Abrianna write and let her know how things were progressing?

Mother looked confused. "Your father feels it is important,

and that is enough. We must present ourselves as his support, and I believe it will also do us good to know the family a little better. After all, they are buying your father's business and all holdings related to freighting."

"I don't know why Father has chosen now to sell. It doesn't make any sense to me." Lenore went to the wardrobe and pulled out the only dress she hadn't yet worn. "Will this do?" She held up the magnificent creation, knowing that her mother would overwhelmingly approve. "It arrived just this afternoon."

"Is that the gown you told me about?" Her mother came closer to feel the material. "Oh, how lavish."

The burnt gold silk very nearly glowed in the electric lighting of the room. Trimmed with hundreds if not thousands of sequins and pearls, it was a gown fit for a queen. Lenore had fallen in love with it almost upon first glance and had begged the dressmaker to sell it to her. Lucky for her, the gown had recently been rejected by the woman who'd originally ordered it, and the dressmaker was more than happy, if not relieved, to fit it for Lenore.

"I've never seen anything so regal. You were quite right to purchase it without consulting me." Mother seldom said such things, and Lenore was momentarily taken aback. "I must say for the price you quoted, this is more than worth the money paid."

"I thought so, too," Lenore replied, feeling a sense of pleasure in her mother's approval.

"Do you have shoes that will work?"

Lenore nodded. "They were made to match the gown. I even bought the proper undergarments."

"Wonderful. Your father likes to show us off, and this gown will please him."

Frowning, Lenore got a worried thought. "He's not going to try to marry me off to someone, is he?"

146

"Goodness, no. Mr. Montgomery's sons are grown and married with families of their own. They don't even live in the city. They handle Mr. Montgomery's holdings in San Diego." Mother headed for the door. "There's so much to do in order to be ready in time. I'll send that little Mexican maid up to do your hair and help you dress."

Lenore said nothing. She knew it would do no good to offer further protest about going to the dinner.

Mother turned and gave her a smile. "If things go well tonight, we can head home the day after tomorrow."

This brightened Lenore's outlook considerably. "Oh, Mother, I'm so glad to hear it. I've grown so bored in this place."

"Bored? With all the shopping and theatre, not to mention the incredible dining?" Mother shook her head. "I can't believe you're bored. I find this place so exhilarating. I told your father that if he was of a mind to spend out his old age anywhere but Seattle, I would want it to be here."

Lenore couldn't imagine her father would leave Seattle. At least not on a permanent basis. Mother exited without another word, and Lenore went immediately to place the gown on the bed. It was a beautiful dress, and it had seemed like providence that it should be such a perfect fit for her. The seamstress had to tighten the waist a bit and raise the hem a good deal, but otherwise it was as if the gown had been made for Lenore.

She tried to imagine what Kolbein might think of her in it. The absolute latest fashion, the gown made a beautiful contrast against her complexion and dark hair. The dressmaker had spared no expense in its creation. How awful it must have been to have the woman refuse to buy it, but how fortunate for Lenore that she had.

Pepita, the young Mexican maid, entered the room and immediately motioned for Lenore to take a seat. Lenore did as she was instructed. Pepita spoke only Spanish, which made conversation most taxing, as Lenore generally ended up failing to make her point. Tonight, however, when Lenore fashioned her hair atop her head to show the maid what she wanted, Pepita nodded with a smile and quickly went to work.

By the time her mother sent word for Lenore to join them for the carriage ride to the Montgomerys', Pepita had mastered the coiffure perfectly. Lenore stared at her reflection for one last check. Her hair had been teased and brushed back to create fullness and then pulled back into a most fashionable bun. Bangs were the rage right now, but Lenore preferred her hair swept back and up. The maid had artfully accomplished this, leaving just enough hair free to curl around Lenore's face and neck.

The gown picked up the light with every movement, and Lenore knew she had never looked so grand. If she had a chance to attend the bridal ball in June . . . with Kolbein . . . she would wear this gown for certain. Now, if she could just convince Kolbein that they belonged together.

A hired carriage took the Fulcher family to the Montgomerys' palatial mansion. Father rambled on and on about how successful he had been in negotiating the sale of his business and how tonight he and Mr. Montgomery would sign the final papers.

"Once they are witnessed and the money delivered to the bank, I will be a free man," he told the women.

Lenore had been quite concerned about how she would find excuses to visit with Abrianna once her father moved his business from the Madison Building. It seemed there were always hurdles to overcome in her life. Her surprise at finding out that her father had even intended such a move was almost more than Lenore could keep to herself. She wanted to ask a million questions, but her father was rarely around the hotel, and when he was, he wasn't in any mood to soothe her worries.

"Women don't need to bother themselves with such things," he would often say. Lenore, however, thought otherwise.

A butler in his stately uniform met the Fulchers at the door of the house and ushered them inside. Two additional servants awaited his instructions as wraps and hats, gloves, and Mr. Fulcher's outer coat were taken before the family was led into the drawing room.

"Glad you could come, Fulcher," Mr. Montgomery declared, giving Lenore's father a hearty slap on the back. "We've been quite anxious to conclude our business. Several of my associates are awaiting us in the billiards room."

He motioned to one of the awaiting maids. "Please let Mrs. Montgomery know that our guests have arrived." The woman curtsied and hurried to do her master's bidding. "Ladies, if you'll excuse us. Please make yourselves comfortable. I'm sure my wife and daughters will join you shortly."

Inside the drawing room, Lenore found herself more than a little shocked by the gold trim on the opulent furnishings. The paintings—and it seemed there were hundreds—were trimmed with thick ornate gilded frames. The trim on the fireplace and hearth, as well as the lamps and lighting fixtures, reflected the wealth of these people. Even some of the chairs and side tables were touched with gold.

"Oh, do forgive our tardy appearance," Mrs. Montgomery announced, coming into the room, followed by two younger women. "We were delayed by a mishap. However, that is behind us now. How very nice to see you again, Mrs. Fulcher."

"It's my pleasure, as well," Lenore's mother replied. "And this is my daughter, Lenore."

Lenore smiled but said nothing. Mrs. Montgomery turned to introduce her daughters.

The Montgomerys had two daughters slightly Lenore's junior. They seemed to look down their noses at her as they waved fans with bored expressions. Lenore hardly concerned herself with their behavior. The elder, Sabina Montgomery, was a striking beauty who bore her Spanish mother's black hair and dark eyes. The younger, Olivia Montgomery, was also quite lovely, although she seemed to follow in her sister's shadow, as if waiting for cues as to what she should do next. Despite being younger than Lenore, the Montgomery daughters appeared more sophisticated and experienced in socializing.

"Cook made us a special meal for this evening," Mrs. Montgomery told Lenore's mother. "We love to entertain."

"It won't be as grand as when we hosted the governor," Sabina interjected with a smirk.

Her mother looked displeased, but her expression quickly changed when the butler came to announce dinner was served.

The gentlemen rejoined the ladies just before they entered the dining room. Mr. Montgomery offered his arm to Lenore's mother, while her father graciously aided Mrs. Montgomery. The Montgomery girls were teamed up with two of their father's associates, while Lenore found herself escorted by an older gentleman who smelled of strong cologne and body odor. She could only hope he wouldn't be seated beside her at the table.

The dinner was laid out in a grand fashion at a huge table that could easily seat twenty, though there were only half that many tonight. In addition to the Fulchers, there were the three men who had been introduced as legal consultants for the sale of the business. Lenore's escort assisted her into a chair and then plopped down beside her. Lenore coughed into her scented handkerchief for relief from the excessive odors. It would be a challenge to eat seated next to the smelly man, but Lenore was determined she would not shame her family.

Course after course was served. Lenore thought the fish too heavily seasoned, while the soup was rather bland. The beef was disguised beneath a heavy cream sauce, and the bread was stale. She couldn't help but wonder if the governor had been served bread that was less than fresh.

Lenore received praise for her gown and questions from all three gentlemen as to how long her family intended to be in the area. Once she explained the possibility of going back to Seattle the day after next, they seemed disappointed. She couldn't help but wonder if they had thought to capture her attention. Even the older man seemed particularly eager to suggest they remain at least another week so that he might invite them to some musical event he was hosting. Her father, thankfully, declined, explaining he was eager to return to his final duties and oversee the transfer of the business to Montgomery.

After dinner, Sabina and Olivia were instructed to show Lenore around the estate while the men saw to business. The older women were to entertain themselves with viewing the grand salon, where Mrs. Montgomery announced there were over two hundred paintings. Many of these, she assured, revealed a long line of Spanish ancestors from which she had descended. The girls told Lenore that their mother's family had come from Spain in the early years before California became a part of the United States. Their holdings had been quite vast, but some had been stolen from them when America claimed the area. Sabina relayed the latter bit of information as though Lenore had personally had some hand in the matter.

Lenore found herself quite bored with the tour of the house. The Montgomery daughters were only concerned with what their family owned. Prized artifacts and antiques were all but worshiped by the young ladies, who appeared disappointed that Lenore was less than captivated. Trying her best to hide a yawn, Lenore hoped her father might conclude his business quickly and take them back to the hotel. There was packing to oversee.

"I'm to be married soon," Sabina announced without warning. "Would you care to see my gown?"

Lenore perked up at this and nodded. "I would like that very much. I hope to marry soon myself." At least that wasn't a lie, but should she say much more, she knew it might well develop into one.

Sabina looked at her as if surprised. "When do you plan to marry?"

"We've not set a date, but I would very much like it to be in June."

"June?" Sabina questioned in surprise. "But how will you arrange a wedding in such a short time? My gown alone has taken over a year to complete. First the fabrics had to be brought in from Spain and then the lace and beading had to be made—by hand, of course. It was just completed and delivered yesterday." She paused at a set of double doors and shook her head. "I don't know how you would ever marry in June."

Olivia pushed open the doors. "Isn't it grand?"

Ahead in a stately golden room a dressmaker's dummy stood gowned in ivory satin and lace. The gown was exquisite, and Lenore saw no need to hide her approval. "It is most grand. I don't think I've ever seen a wedding gown more lovely."

"Oh, how stupid!" Sabina hurried into the room and crossed to where a young maid was dusting. Without warning she began to hit the girl. "You fool. You'll get my dress dirty. Do you not know to cover it before dusting this room?"

Lenore watched in horror as Sabina beat the girl over and over about the head and shoulders. Had she not been so shocked she might have intervened. Instead, she stood frozen to the ground. Never in her life had she ever seen anyone treat someone, even a servant, so poorly.

The girl was kneeling on the floor sobbing before Sabina finally stopped. "Get out of here before I start in again. Don't ever come in here to dust unless that gown is first covered."

The girl nodded and gathered herself up. She hurried from the room, passing Lenore with a look of utter terror. Blood trickled from her lip, but there was no time to offer her assistance. The girl fled before Lenore could so much as offer a nod.

"You hurt her," Lenore said, looking at Sabina. "How could you just beat her like that? She made a mistake, but you acted as though it were intentionally done."

"It doesn't matter," Sabina said with a shrug. "She's just a servant and she must learn her place."

"She's a human being," Lenore insisted, ashamed that she hadn't done something to stop Sabina.

"I say she's nothing," Sabina replied. "My father can hire a hundred others just like her. She was not trained properly, and I shall dismiss her tomorrow."

"And your parents will have nothing to say about this?" Lenore asked.

Olivia spoke before Sabina could. "Mother says we must manage our staff if we're to learn to run a productive household of our own."

Lenore wanted to say much more but held her tongue. Obviously these young women had been brought up in ways that Lenore could not understand. Such cruelty for a mistake was abominable in her mind but evidently acceptable in the Montgomery household.

"Come get a closer look at my gown." Sabina walked to the dressmaker's dummy. "Do not touch the fabric lest you leave oil marks on the gown. Mama says that human fingers are always secreting oil, and it would stain the satin."

Lenore hadn't heard such a thing but nodded in agreement. She had no intention of touching the dress anyway, especially not after what she'd witnessed. Goodness only knew whether Sabina would start beating her about the head should she step out of line.

The wedding dress was beautiful. The bustled back flowed into a twenty-five-foot train that had been carefully stretched out to keep it from wrinkling. Beading had been sewn into the material to make the image of flowers. It must have cost a small fortune, Lenore surmised, feeling rather sick.

"The train is completely removable so that I may wear the gown again after the wedding," Sabina told her. "I think it would be most wonderful to wear it to the opera this fall."

"When is your wedding?" Lenore asked, feeling sicker by the minute. She longed to get away from the company of these young women who held life so cheaply.

"The marriage will take place on the twentieth of May. It is to be held in a grand cathedral, and I will have ten attendants."

"I am to be one of them," Olivia offered, appearing excited. Her sister gave her a harsh glare, and immediately the girl quieted and lowered her head.

"How exciting for all of you," Lenore said, smiling. For a moment she wondered what it would be like to have such a grand gown. However, as she looked around her and then back to the sisters, Lenore could think only of the young maid.

There had been a time when Lenore would have let the matter go. She hadn't been raised to be cruel or physical with servants. However, she had been told that servants were not on the same social level as she was; therefore their feelings and concerns weren't to be considered. Lenore was to be pampered and spoiled and to enjoy all the wealth her father's good investments and business could afford.

She had heard her mother say at least a hundred times that they were among the privileged who could live well, with great beauty around them. Now her words seemed hollow. What really mattered were people, Lenore realized.

Abrianna had helped her to see that. Lenore sighed. Abrianna, with her heart of gold—solid gold, not just gilding. Abrianna had taught Lenore to see the poor and their needs with the intention of offering help. She knew her father and mother gave generously to various charities, but Lenore also knew they would never dirty their hands by stopping to share food or clothing with those people. And they definitely wouldn't allow themselves to be found in some of the areas Abrianna visited.

Lenore looked down at her own gown and thought it all rather silly now. The gown's cost could have bought bread for a hundred people. Lenore suddenly felt ashamed. She longed more than ever for home. Why had she allowed herself to become so selfish?

"How is your intended employed?" Sabina asked, bringing Lenore out of her thoughts.

"He's a lawyer from Chicago, but presently he's in Seattle attending to his sister's needs," she replied without thinking.

Sabina smirked. "My fiancé is a highly respected man of personal wealth inherited from his family. He doesn't need to work." She sounded quite pleased with this announcement.

Lenore met the younger woman's expression. "He must get very bored."

"Ha!" Sabina shook her head and laughed. "When you are rich, you do not bore easily. My Stephen has many interests—the arts, the opera, and always his investments and holdings. But rather than have to see to these things himself, he has several men who do his bidding."

"How nice. You must be very proud."

Sabina looked momentarily confused, as if unsure whether Lenore had just insulted her or offered praise.

Lenore had little patience for her. "Does your fiancé do anything to assist those less fortunate?"

"But of course," Sabina replied, regaining her composure. "He donates to many foundations that help the poor and needy, but he also stresses that they must be willing to do for themselves. Too many are just lazy and refuse to help themselves. Stephen has made this a strong stand of his, and I am proud of him."

Lenore smiled sadly. "But of course . . . you would be."

The day that Wade and Thane came to install some much needed cabinets in the kitchen was also the day that a third man turned up dead. Aunt Miriam had ordered the cabinets to replace those damaged by the water leak, as well as to offer additional storage. Wade had made the cabinets in his spare time and now brought with him news of the murder. Again, the body was found in the alleyway behind the building, and once again Abrianna knew the man who'd been killed. At least this time she didn't have to identify the body. The police were well familiar with the old man and his panhandling ways. His name was William Elliot—most of his friends just called him Billy Boy. Abrianna had called him Bill. He was very fond of Aunt Miriam's bread pudding.

"The police say he was killed elsewhere and left here," Wade told them. "Even so, it would seem most dangerous for any of you to be out alone." He fixed his gaze on Abrianna. "Very dangerous."

"We had determined to hire someone to run errands and bring in groceries," Aunt Miriam admitted. "It seems a terrible thing to be a prisoner in our own home, but that is what we have become. Mr. Booth has agreed to help us, so along with your assistance, I'm sure we will not want."

Abrianna wasn't at all pleased with this turn of events. "I don't see why we need worry. The killer has only taken helpless men. Not that I don't miss them dearly and abhor what happened." She paused for breath and continued. "Still, we needn't be fretful. He hasn't gone after any women. Aunt Selma has always told us that in times of testing and trial, our calm spirit and willingness to endeavor are signs of our faith in God. I know my faith is strong enough to continue walking out when shopping needs to be done."

"I wouldn't want you to be alone," Wade said. "You may think you're capable of fending for yourself. You may even have made friends with the entire population of the friendless, but you are just one young woman."

Abrianna clenched her hands into fists but kept them hidden in the folds of her skirt. "I may be just one woman, but I am a woman of God, and as such, I must do what He would have me do."

Wade narrowed his eyes. "He would have you respect your elders and yield to their authority, as the Bible says we should."

"Yes, but Jesus separated from His parents when He was twelve and was later found in the temple. He told His authority that He had to be about His Father's business."

"Last time I checked . . . you weren't Jesus," Wade said seriously. He picked up several nails and went to where Thane was lining up a wood strip to hold the cabinets.

Abrianna wasn't about to let him get away with this. She was full of fight, and no one was going to lock her up in this building. "There were others who defied authority to serve God," she said, going after Wade.

Aunt Miriam took hold of her arm before she could cross the kitchen. Abrianna came to an abrupt stop, surprised at the old woman's strength. "You will not go out without an escort," Aunt Miriam declared. "I won't have it."

"I won't either," Aunt Selma threw in.

"Nor me," Aunt Poisie said, not to be left out.

"If I have to," Wade said, crossing to where Abrianna stood, "I'll nail your door and windows shut and lock you in your room."

Abrianna stomped her foot, something she had rarely done since her early teens. "You don't care at all about what's important to me. No one cares." She pulled away from her aunt's hold, embarrassed that tears were coming to her eyes.

"Without my help, many will go hungry or cold. Some might even die," she said, shaking her head. "And their blood will be on your hands, Wade Ackerman. All because you do not care."

"I care," Wade told her. "But I care more about your well-being than theirs. They survived life on the streets before you came, and I'm sure they will continue to do so when you are gone. But I would like to see that end not come for a very, very long time."

Abrianna looked to the others. Would no one champion her cause? Her shoulders slumped slightly, and her breath came out in a sigh. "I shall take the subject up with the Lord. He will show me what I am to do."

"Well, if He disagrees with me and your aunts," Wade said with a grin, "then I guess we'll have to have words."

Kolbein sat toying with his pencil and glancing up from time to time to check the clock. It seemed impossible to keep his mind on work. He had heard nothing more about Greta, and he feared the worst. She was naïve and unable to take care of herself. She needed him, and yet she had run away from home.

He leaned back in the leather chair. It was as if his sister had disappeared into thin air. No one had seen her. No one knew her. Since finding her gown at that secondhand store, Kolbein hadn't been able to find anything that would even hint at Greta still being in Seattle.

The clerk came to his door and knocked lightly before entering. "I have those papers you asked for, Mr. Booth."

Kobein sat up. "Just put them there." He pointed to the right side of his desk. "Thank you."

Once the young man was gone, Kolbein got to his feet and walked to the window. He looked out on the busy city street and wondered if his sister was among the pedestrians. She could be that close, he thought, and yet he'd never know it.

He caught sight of a redheaded woman and immediately thought of Abrianna Cunningham. A smile touched his lips. She was quite a rambunctious soul, but she had a heart of gold. Of course, thinking of Abrianna led his thoughts to the one place he'd avoided. Lenore.

Her image flooded his mind. It was really quite uncalled for. They didn't know each other at all, and yet Kolbein found himself longing for her as if they'd spent a lifetime together. He ached for her return. How could it be that he could have lost his heart to a woman he didn't even know? Worse yet, how could he put aside his true mission of finding Greta and allow Lenore to consume his time?

Abrianna had been good to tell him of Lenore's interests and even something of her past. Apparently the two had been longtime friends. Lenore, Abrianna had told him, was determined to make a proper lady out of her. He'd laughingly asked Abrianna what she did for Lenore in return.

"I doubt I do much for her at all, unless it's to encourage her to seek the Lord. Of course, I also encourage her to sneak out with me from time to time, which might suggest that my endeavors where the Lord are concerned are less than sincere."

Kolbein smiled and returned to his desk. He gathered his papers together and locked them in his desk. It was nearly five and he had no desire to give legal matters another thought. He had been invited to partake of supper with the Madison Bridal School residents, and that was what he intended to do. At least in being there, he could hear any news of Lenore. There might even be some talk of his sister—after all, Abrianna had friends searching the city for her.

He grabbed his hat and headed for the stairs with the trio of women vying for attention in his mind. He was most determined where each woman was concerned. He would find his sister. There was no other possibility. He would get Abrianna to relate all she knew about Lenore. And he would get Lenore to fall as deeply in love with him as he had done with her.

12

Priam Welby looked over the packages of brownish bricks. The opium now processed in morphine-based bricks would bring him a small fortune in cash. The country was hungry for the substance, and he was more than happy to act as its supplier. His attention to discretion and quality brought him a growing number of men who would otherwise not wish to be known for such use. The elite were no different from the poor in their desire to escape the burdens of the world. However, they didn't want anyone else to know that—especially their friends. Welby smiled. Their friends were buying just as much opium as the rest.

"This looks to be a very good quality," Welby said, handing the package back to one of his men. "Load it in the warehouse with the rest of the stuff." He dusted his hands and checked his pocket watch. It was nearly seven, and he was supposed to attend a play tonight with men who were soon to be business associates. They didn't realize that, of course, but they would eagerly join him once Priam told them what would happen to them if they didn't accept his proposal.

Turning to leave, Priam instructed his man, Carl Neely, as

to how he wanted the morphine bricks distributed. He had made contacts all through the North and even into Canada. The money he'd made so far had surpassed the import of Chinese pottery and art.

"You need to make certain the shipments go out immediately," he told the twenty-five-year-old. "Package them in the false-bottom wagons, as usual, lest anyone be tempted to rob us."

"I'll take care of it, Mr. Welby," the man assured. "You want me to get the other stuff sorted out?"

Welby nodded. "You might as well. It would be foolish to wait until morning and have to rush the job."

"That's fine. I have men to help me," Carl replied.

"Then go to it. I'm supposed to be attending a play tonight." He gave a yawn. "I don't know how I'll manage to stay awake, but the company I'm keeping is very important."

"Mr. Welby!" a voice called out from the wharf as Priam made his way to the awaiting carriage. "Mr. Welby, I have another matter to discuss."

Turning back, Priam waited until the ship's captain caught up with him. Priam had long worked with the man, and Welby knew he could trust him. "What seems to be wrong?"

The man shook his head. "Nothing is wrong. It's about that other matter we discussed several months back." He stopped and looked at Carl. "Perhaps we should talk in private."

"My man knows all about my dealings," Priam replied. "He can be trusted. What matter are you talking about?"

"The one that would involve bringing in . . . young women."

"Ah yes, the virgins." He looked to Carl. "You weren't there the day the captain and I discussed this venture. There are a great many clients of mine who would pay outrageous sums for virgins—particularly for Orientals. Some men have a fetish for such things and will pay any price. Afterwards they sell them to work in the brothels. For me, it poses a simple way to make easy money."

The captain motioned for one of his men to come forward. The man did so, keeping a tight hold on a cloaked figure at his side. When they reached Welby, the captain gave a quick look around and then yanked off the cloak.

A beautiful Oriental girl stood before them. Priam couldn't see her as well as he would have liked because the lighting was minimal, but he could see enough to offer the captain praise.

"Good job. How difficult will it be to get others?"

"I have a dozen," the captain told him. "Most of them were sold to me by their own families. Females aren't as valuable as males, and most of the families are too poor to buy food. They aren't all as pretty as this one, but they are young and are virgins." He gave a lecherous smile and added, "But it wasn't easy to keep 'em that way. My boys were more than a little desirous to make their acquaintance."

Priam scowled. "I'm sure. A dozen, you say? What will I have to pay for them?"

The captain smiled. "Twenty apiece. That way I'll make some money, too."

Welby didn't tell the man that he would have paid four times as much. He had buyers who were ready to pay almost any amount he asked. Reaching out to touch the girl, Priam wasn't surprised when she tried to back away.

"Does she speak English?" Priam asked, stroking the girl's soft cheek.

"Not a word. None of 'em do. I don't know if that makes things better or worse, but at least they won't be telling anyone what we're up to."

"That's very good. I'd hate for my reputation to be compromised," Welby said. "I have way too many irons in the fire to have to deal with that kind of trouble. Just bringing Chinese into the country creates an uproar. Every city seems to have its own law regarding the matter. I don't need folks questioning my loyalties."

The captain nodded. "Well, what do you say? I can certainly get some girls on each trip. I put word out among the farm families and poorer folk that I would be willing to buy the girls and take them for a good life in America. I figure they'll be lining up by the time I dock again." His eagerness was clear. "Can we strike a deal?"

Welby thought for a moment. The man's eagerness was clear, and his ability to purchase the girls and transport them was apparent. "We can, although I'm not sure where to put them. I had hoped to acquire a downtown building by this time, but that hasn't come through. Can they remain in the hold of your ship until morning? By then I should be able to find a small place to house them in secret."

"Most of the crew is on leave seeing to their needs, so I should be able to keep them safe." He gave his man a nod. "Cover her up and take her back to the ship."

The girl's eyes widened in fear as the cloak was repositioned on her shoulders. Welby held up his hand. "I think I'd like to better inspect this one. Carl, take her to my place and stay with her until I return tonight." His man smiled and stepped forward most eagerly, causing Priam to add, "And don't touch her. Understand?"

Carl nodded and took hold of the girl's arm while the captain's man pulled up the cloak's hood. "I'll keep her safe. How do you want me to get her there?"

"Take my carriage," Welby said. "I'll find my own way to the theatre and home. Make certain no one sees her. Take her in by the back way."

Pulling the girl to follow him, Carl seemed taken aback when the girl wrenched away from him and tried to run. The captain's man easily caught up to her, but the girl began yelling at him in such a way that none of them needed to know Chinese to understand the girl's anger.

"Shut her up," the captain told his man. The big man quickly clamped a hand over her mouth.

"She's a feisty one," Priam said, shaking his head. "Better make sure you have a better hold on her, Carl. And keep her quiet. You know how. I don't want any marks on her. I already have a customer in mind, and he won't want her banged up."

This time Carl gave the girl a withering stare. "I know exactly what to do if she gives me any more trouble."

The girl went silent, but her eyes never left Welby's. If she could have caused his death with a glare, Priam knew he'd be headed to the morgue. But it was of no matter. Right now he was late for his appointment at the theatre. "Captain, I'll see you in the morning and bring your money."

"Always a pleasure doing business with you, Mr. Welby."

From some distance, Wade watched the strange confrontation with the small figure and larger man. The smaller one took off running and the larger one quickly followed. The men who stood awaiting the return of the two seemed unconcerned with the situation. With the girl screaming unintelligibly, Wade wasn't at all sure what was going on as one of the men led the girl to an awaiting carriage. He thought to approach the men and see if they were taking advantage of the girl, but just then a policeman happened by. The officer chatted with the man for a moment and then took his leave. Apparently nothing was amiss, but still Wade didn't feel comfortable about the situation.

He recognized the man who'd talked to the officer as Priam Welby. At least he was pretty sure it was Welby. With only the glow of a few dock lights, it was impossible to tell for sure. It might just be that Welby was on his mind a lot and his mind had conjured up the image, but somehow Wade had a feeling his hunch was correct. The man had a certain bearing and a particular style of hat that he always seemed to wear.

Wade frowned at the scene he'd just witnessed. Even after the carriage drove away, he was tempted to confront Welby about what had just happened. He didn't like the man—not one bit. Wade had learned from Mrs. Madison that the man wanted to court Abrianna. He had to be nearly twice her age, and Wade had suggested the man was much too old for their ward. He didn't think the ladies would force Abrianna into courtship, much less marriage, but he did feel it important to share his opinion. He'd watched over Abrianna since they were children, and worrying about her well-being just came naturally.

Welby had first come to Wade to buy wagons with false bottoms. He had told Wade that it was for the purpose of protecting valuable imports, but that explanation never rang true. Wade had heard far too many stories to the contrary. The man was known to be seen with the socially elite and politically minded, but those on a lower rung spoke of him as a man without a conscience—a man who would do anything to make a dollar. He was definitely not the kind of man Wade wanted for Abrianna.

He saw Welby head up the street toward the better parts of

town. *What are you up to, and why must you involve the people I care about?* he wondered.

Wade squinted against the dark as the man disappeared into the night. The other men had gone, as well, and the police officer was nowhere in sight. Making his way home, Wade thought perhaps he should share what he'd seen with the ladies. Maybe Mrs. Madison would be less inclined to trust the man if she knew he was up to no good. Had he been up to no good? Perhaps the young woman was a runaway and Welby was only trying to see her returned to her parents. There was room for legitimate explanations, and Wade didn't want to falsely judge the man.

"I don't really know what he's doing," Wade reminded himself. "And appearances can be very deceiving." It might be that the girl had stolen from the men or had done something even worse. Perhaps Welby was seeing this person delivered to the authorities, though he doubted it. If that were the case, the officer would have taken her into custody.

Unlocking the door to his shop, Wade thought about all the trouble of late. The city's crimes were on the rise, and people were quite ruthless with one another. He had taken to locking his shop and even now felt for the revolver he'd begun to carry for his nighttime work. It gave him a bit of assurance that he could handle whatever came his way. An assailant would toy with him only once.

He was about to close the door behind him when someone called out his name. Wade jumped a foot in the air and then had to laugh at himself. No attacker was going to call him by name. He opened the door to find Thane grinning and holding up a sack. "I come bearing gifts."

"Oh really? Smells more like food—maybe Mr. Appleton's meat loaf."

Thane chuckled. "Meat loaf can be a gift. Appleton was just closing his restaurant as I happened by. He made me a good deal if I'd take it off his hands. I thought maybe we could eat and play some chess. Are you up for that?"

"I am. Come on. I've got some fresh bread from the Madison School and a pie. I'll gift you with that and you gift me with meat loaf."

"And pickles," Thane added. "I have also brought pickles."

Wade laughed. "By the way, what do you know about Priam Welby?" Since Thane worked around the docks as well as volunteered as a fireman, Wade figured he might know quite a bit. Talk ran rampant among the working men of the city. Sometimes they were worse than women with their gossip.

Wade turned on the light and pulled the revolver from his coat pocket. Placing it on the table, he noticed Thane's expression. "What? You think I'm wrong to carry a weapon?"

"No, I was just thinking about your question regarding Welby. I have to tell you I've heard some pretty ugly rumors about the man. There are a lot of folks who believe him to be involved in every kind of vice. Why do you ask?"

"Well, according to Mrs. Madison he wants to court Abrianna."

"Our Abrianna?"

Wade laughed. "I doubt there's more than one. I'm not sure the world could handle two Abriannas." He sobered. "I don't like the idea one bit. The man is a lot older than she, and now you tell me what I already suspected. I saw him tonight down at the wharf. It looked like he was up to something, but I couldn't tell what. I just got the feeling from the way the men in his company acted that it wasn't legal. But then a police officer came along, and nothing seemed to be wrong."

"Welby is known to have the police in his pocket," Thane replied. "Some of the firehouses, as well. It's said that he's committed arson on more than one occasion. Maybe not him personally, but his men."

"How is it he has so many politicians and authorities under his control?"

Thane shrugged. "My guess is blackmail. I'm sure a man like that gets the dirt on everyone else and isn't afraid to rub their faces in it unless they pay up."

Lenore paced her cabin, anxious to be home. They would arrive in Seattle at the top of the hour, and though that was only some forty minutes away, it might as well have been forty days. She felt her journey would never come to an end.

"You'll wear a hole in the rug," Mother chided. "Why not relax so you'll be rested when we arrive."

"I'm just afraid that we've been gone too long."

"Nonsense. If this young man you want to court is as worthy as you say, he'll be happily awaiting your return."

Lenore couldn't begin to explain that Kolbein didn't even know of her feelings. How could she expect her mother to understand that she had fallen in love the first time she'd glimpsed the man? How could she express her fears without Mother thinking her unbalanced in reason?

No, she could only pray that God and Abrianna had interceded on her behalf. God, she knew, was wholly reliable, but she worried about her friend. Abrianna could be rather open-minded at times. Unfortunately, that open mind often led to an open mouth. Lenore couldn't help but wonder if Abrianna might have slipped up and said something revealing. Lenore wanted Kolbein to realize her good qualities, but she feared Abrianna would just blurt out the truth that Lenore was love-sick for the man.

However, Lenore knew that the trip to San Francisco had helped her to realize one thing. She didn't want the life of opulence that her mother enjoyed. She didn't want the duties of a socialite wife. Seeing the way the Montgomery family lived and the things they valued, Lenore had been reminded that treasures on earth were fleeting. Seeing the things they didn't value, such as the people who worked for them, left her determined to be a better mistress of her own household one day.

Abrianna had long tried to encourage Lenore to be more mindful of those around them, and now she had plans to do just that. The only problem was, she really didn't know how. She could scarcely go out in the streets as Abrianna did.

"You aren't even listening to me, are you?" Mother said a little louder than usual.

Lenore realized she'd been completely rude. "I'm sorry, Mother. My mind is . . . well . . . it's elsewhere." She smiled and forced herself to take a seat beside her mother. "Are you glad to be almost home?"

"I am, but I will miss San Francisco. I love the climate. Mrs. Montgomery told me that farther south is much more desirable for its temperate climate and warmer temperatures. I will have to convince your father to journey there one day."

"I find I don't like the heat," Lenore said. "I prefer my life in Seattle. It's sometimes quite warm here, and we have some beautiful days." She paused and looked at her mother for a moment. "May I ask you a question?"

Her mother looked surprised. "Of course. What is it?"

"Before Father made his fortune, what was life like for the two of you?" She knew her mother had married against the wishes of her parents, and although capable of helping their daughter financially, they had cut her off. Punishment for refusing their counsel. In time they had changed their minds, but Lenore couldn't help but think her parents' start had been a difficult one.

Mother considered the question for a moment. She didn't seem upset by Lenore asking, but neither did she seem eager to reply. "It was quite difficult at times. I used to worry about everything. We rented a small house, and it was in very poor condition. I worried about having enough food to put on the table, and I hated that we were too poor for a carriage of our own. I had to walk most everywhere, and everyone looked down on us. That wasn't in Seattle, but rather Tacoma. We moved after your father's business began to bring a profit."

"But you remember how awful it was to do without?"

"I doubt one ever forgets such a horror."

"I know there are a great many people who do without in Seattle," Lenore said, trying not to sound overly interested.

"There are. Your father said that Skid Road is full of depravity and poverty. Your father believes it won't be long before folks get the situation under control, as they did with the Chinese problem."

Lenore frowned. She had never heard her mother speak out against the Chinese. She knew many of her mother's peers were given to such negativity, but it truly surprised Lenore that her mother would be one of them.

"But not everyone can be rich, Mother. There will always be folks poorer and less affluent. You can't get rid of them all."

"No, but I do believe we can get rid of the troublemakers and lawbreakers."

"Get rid of them, rather than try to help them reform?"

Mother nodded. "I think most of those people are beyond reform and don't deserve anything more. They are filled with evil intentions at worst and apathy at the least. They seem not to care for humanity and only for themselves. They do not deserve our mercy, much less our concern."

Lenore had never seen this side of her mother, and it troubled her deeply. Abrianna talked of showing kindness and love, reaching out to people who had nothing and no one helping them to overcome their downtrodden situation. Mother would have them all rounded up and sent away. But to where?

The door to the cabin opened, and Father made his way into the room. "We have finally arrived. It won't be long before we can depart the ship and make our way home. I've already arranged for our driver to meet us." He seemed quite pleased with himself.

Mother got to her feet and smiled down at Lenore. "I hope you won't trouble yourself with further concerns for the poor. There are fine organizations that take care of those matters, and you needn't let it bother you."

But it *did* bother her. And it bothered her even more that her mother would cast the problem off to someone else—to an organization. Was she completely without feeling? Lenore knew she herself had to be awakened to the problems, but that was due to her innocence and youth. Mother was not bound by either and surely should understand the need to show compassion and love to a world of hurting souls.

13

Wade listened as Abrianna's aunts chattered on about his concerns related to Mr. Welby. It seemed each woman had an opinion and was more than happy to share.

"I find him difficult," Miss Poisie admitted. "He's much too stern."

"Perhaps he needs a purgative," Mrs. Gibson suggested. "Mr. Gibson was often stern when his bowels were inclined to move slowly."

"God rest his soul," Miss Poisie declared.

"Amen," the ladies replied.

Nearly choking on his tea, Wade tried not to laugh out loud. Sometimes the ladies were so certain they had the answers for everyone's problems.

"I believe he's stern because of his business dealings," Mrs. Madison declared. "He has a great deal on his mind with his import business, as well as his desire to court Abrianna."

"But Abrianna has not shown any affection for him, Sister." Miss Poisie straightened her skirt.

"That's true enough. I think his biggest need at the moment is this building."

"The building? He's still after you to sell?" Wade asked.

"Oh, to be certain. He says he needs it most desperately, and what with the various murders practically at our doorstep, I'm inclined to sell."

Miss Poisie leaned forward. "He has in mind to pay her, as well as provide a grand house where we might continue teaching the young ladies. Isn't that something?"

"And is that what you want to do?" he asked Mrs. Madison. "I thought this place was dear to you."

"It is, but I would not see the lives of those I love endangered for the sake of a building." Mrs. Madison shook her head. "Mr. Welby has made me a solid offer, a most generous one. As Poisie said, he offered us a large house in a beautiful neighborhood as a part of the deal."

"Why does he want this building so much?" Wade asked. Surely there were other properties available if the man was inclined to be so generous.

"I do not know," Mrs. Madison replied. "Except that it is the perfect location for his import business, and nothing else similar is available for purchase. I suppose also the size is greater than anything else at hand."

"I would definitely be sure to review the contract with a lawyer," Wade said. "I would hate to see you go farther away, but I know this area isn't as safe as it once was. There is a ruthlessness among some of these people—they care nothing about life."

"So you believe we should sell?" Mrs. Madison asked.

Wade had given it quite a bit of thought. "I suppose it might be best. I wouldn't handle the arrangements yourselves, however."

"What about church on Sunday?" Mrs. Gibson asked. "We will still be close enough to walk, but without you as our escort,

I would not feel at ease. You never know when some rogue might seek to attack us."

Poisie nodded. "No woman is safe. I heard it said that there are men who give no thought to age and will take liberties with any unescorted woman."

"Let me put your minds at ease," Wade replied. "I will continue to walk you to church. I'm not sure where this house is located, but I promise you I will see to it."

"What a relief!" Mrs. Gibson declared, fanning herself. "I can't tell you how much this has weighed on my mind."

"It's weighed on mine, as well," Mrs. Madison admitted. "And were Mr. Welby less persistent, I would probably put the decision aside for a time."

"Don't let him push you to make a deal you aren't ready for," Wade said. "It's true this area of town is changing, and I would feel better having you ladies living in a respectable residential area, but Mr. Welby needn't be the one who makes up your minds."

"But he is persistent," Miss Poisie declared.

"And possibly constipated," Mrs. Gibson added in her sober fashion. "Not only that, but there is some concern about whether or not he's a brandy drinker."

"Brandy?" Wade asked, having no idea where that thought had come from.

Miss Poisie nodded. "Sister was certain she smelled it on his breath."

"Well, I suppose it wouldn't surprise me," Wade began, trying his best to remain serious, "that Mr. Welby imbibed from time to time. He is, after all, a businessman, and often those dealings are handled with a libation or two being shared."

"Mr. Madison, God rest his soul, was completely against

alcohol," Miss Poisie declared. "I don't think he would enjoy Glory knowing a brandy drinker had purchased his building."

Mrs. Gibson leaned forward. "First it's brandy, and the next thing you know, they're reading Darwin. That's how it was with Mr. Gibson." She gave a shudder, as if the shameful memory were too much.

Abrianna caught Wade just as he was about to leave. She knew by the look on his face that his time spent with her aunts had been trying. "Would you like to have some cookies and milk before you head out?"

"That sounds good. Your aunts were so upset that they didn't even offer me refreshments."

Abrianna frowned. "That certainly isn't like them, but I know they are seriously considering the possibility of moving. Aunt Miriam hasn't bothered to read her morning paper in the last week, and Aunt Selma put aside her embroidery and took up crocheting. She says that no woman can give her mind over to fancy work when there are heavy issues to consider."

Wade looked at her oddly for a moment. "And what about you? Your aunts told me that Mr. Welby has set his cap for you. Are you considering heavy issues such as courtship and marriage?"

Abrianna burst out laughing. "Oh, goodness no. I couldn't be less interested in Mr. Welby. I've done as my aunts suggested and visited with him at the receptions, but honestly, I find him to be something of a dullard. Not only that, but"—she lowered her voice—"I fear he might be a Democrat. Oh, he says he's a Republican, but I think he may have voted for Grover Cleveland, and that makes him a Mugwump at best. I doubt I could ever love a Mugwump." She paused a moment.

Not wishing to sound harsh, she added. "I could be wrong, but I doubt I am. I'm certain I heard him say that he voted for the president. He didn't tell me directly, so perhaps he was just saying so to impress the man to whom he said it, but if that's the case he's a liar, and that's worse than being a Mugwump. After all, the Lord doesn't say anything about Mugwumps in the Ten Commandments, but He does speak about bearing false witness."

Wade took hold of her shoulders. "Abrianna, just take a breath and listen to me. I think I witnessed Welby up to something down at the wharf. I don't know that it was illegal, but it looked underhanded. Not only that, but Thane said the man does not have a good reputation among the working class, and furthermore, his reputation with the elite might be out of a forced situation."

"Goodness," she said, shaking her head, "Mr. Welby seems to be a plethora of problems."

"But you aren't one of them—right?"

Abrianna found his question confusing. "What do you mean? The man said he wanted to court me, and I said no. Well, I told him that I wasn't interested in courting anyone. I didn't want to hurt his feelings just because of . . . well . . . his political alliance."

Wade let go his hold. "I'm glad."

"I take satisfaction in the fact that it pleases you," Abrianna said, still confused. "Now, do you want cookies and milk or not?"

He shook his head. "No, I'd best get going. I have to get back to work." He paused at the door. "You aren't sneaking out anymore, are you?"

Abrianna wrinkled up her nose. "Must you always think the worst of me?"

He smiled. "Sorry. I just thought I'd make sure you were staying safe."

She watched him walk away, thankful that he didn't press the matter. The truth was, she had continued her escapades, but she wasn't about to admit to it. He would only get upset and then relay the information to her aunts, and if she knew anything about Wade Ackerman, he would make good on nailing her door and windows shut to keep her inside.

Kolbein Booth sat in deep thought and enjoyed the sonata being played by one of Mrs. Madison's young ladies. He had determined to speak tonight to Abrianna about Lenore now that he had accepted the position with Heatherstone, Heatherstone, and Blunt. He'd also given serious consideration to finding a place to live but wanted to know first if he had any chance with the beautiful Miss Fulcher.

Miss Poisie had been hesitant to let him in. It wasn't a day that had been set aside for male visitors, but her sister quickly came to his defense and reminded Poisie that he was to be their lawyer if they decided to sell the building, and because of this they should visit with him even on days that were not set aside for receiving male visitors.

Her reasoning amused him, but Kolbein refrained from suggesting he was there for any other reason than to discuss business. He would bide his time, talking real estate and sales, and keep an eye open for an opportunity to speak with Abrianna alone.

After talking at length with Mrs. Madison and explaining to her the various nuances of real estate contracts, Kolbein accepted an invitation to stay for lunch. The meal hadn't afforded him a chance to speak to Abrianna, however, so now as he was listening to the young ladies practice for a piano recital, Kolbein found himself most desperate.

When Abrianna got up and left the room, Kolbein took the opportunity to do likewise. He followed her for a short distance and then called out her name. She turned in surprise.

"I'm sorry if I startled you," he told her, "but I had hoped to speak to you . . . in private."

"Of course," Abrianna said, smiling. "We can talk here or in the kitchen. That's where I was headed. I wanted to make sure that Liang didn't need help cleaning up. I'm still not that good at cooking, but I can clean."

He smiled. "I'm sure you're good at both." He followed her to the kitchen and was happy to find that Liang had already cleaned the room and departed for other duties. He motioned to the kitchen table. "Might you sit with me for a moment?"

"Of course." Abrianna took the chair he offered and waited for him to be seated. "But you mustn't be deceived by such thoughts that I can cook. I really am quite poor at preparing food."

Kolbein thought to stop her in that train of thought, but he found it unnecessary, for just as Abrianna was known to do, she changed the subject.

"You know, Lenore should be home any day now. I know she promised she would come see me as soon as possible, although I have no way of knowing when that will be."

"So you haven't heard from her recently?"

"No, but then I really didn't expect to get word. She sent me two letters while she was away, and neither gave me an idea of when we might expect her. She talked about the places her mother and father took her for dinners. Do you know they charge five dollars for a meal at some of the stuffy restaurants?

Five dollars! That's more than many people make in a week. It ought to be against the law."

"Abrianna, I appreciate your outrage at such pricing, but what were you saying about the Fulchers coming home?"

"Oh, I don't know, as far as Lenore's letters go. However, I heard the men downstairs saying that Mr. Fulcher had been in touch and planned to be back in the office tomorrow."

Kolbein relaxed. "I know you are good friends with Lenore," he began. "I . . . well . . . I wonder if you might tell me more about her."

Abrianna proved herself more than willing. "Lenore is a wonderful woman. She has been a good friend to me for ever so long." Abrianna leaned in, and Kolbein did likewise. When they were nearly nose to nose, Abrianna spoke again. "Lenore is always trying to make me into a proper lady. She has a way about her and knows how such things should be. My aunts do, as well, but they don't know about the latest fashions and entertainments like Lenore does. Frankly, I wouldn't know a thing about ladies tattooing their legs. . . ." She paused and giggled. "I'm sorry . . . limbs. That's another particular frustration Lenore has with me. I tend to forget the proper names for things, but she always remembers."

Kolbein leaned his head back and roared with laughter, which lifted his spirits considerably. Abrianna giggled and crooked her finger at him. Again they put their heads together in a most conspiratorial fashion.

"Apparently it was all the rage last year, along with blue stationery with gold monogramming. If you were any kind of lady at all, you had to have the stationery."

"But not the tattoo?" Kolbein asked, thoroughly amused with her.

"Apparently not. And an uproar was caused by it. Some thought it a sin, as the Bible speaks to not marking your body in such a way. Others said it was dangerous, and there were even those who suggested it was the mark of the beast spoken of in Revelation. Although I don't recall that the mark would be tattooed on legs . . . uh, limbs. For myself, I don't like tattoos. There's something about them that causes me discomfort, but I haven't quite yet figured out exactly why."

If she were to see how the tattoo was applied, she'd know even more about discomfort. He smiled but offered her no insight. "Lenore kept you apprised?"

"Indeed. She always does. She's like that. She cares about people, too. I'm not the only one to benefit from her—"

"I'm in love with her," Kolbein interrupted in a whisper.

Abrianna looked confused and leaned even closer. "What did you say?"

"I said that I'm in love with Lenore."

14

Lenore felt almost sick at the sight of her best friend and Kolbein with their heads together. They had apparently become quite comfortable with each other in her absence. Perhaps too comfortable. Why, they seemed almost . . . intimate. What if Abrianna had betrayed her? Seeing Militine coming down the hall as Lenore stepped away from the kitchen, she motioned to her.

"Would you go into the kitchen and ask Abrianna to come to the sitting room? Don't tell her that I'm here. I want to surprise her."

Militine grinned. "I know she'll be thrilled. She's done nothing but talk about your return. She heard from the men downstairs that it was to be soon."

"We just made it back. Father is downstairs checking on business, and I begged him for a moment to tell her that we're back. I'm afraid I was rather impatient." She smiled. "Now remember, do not tell Abrianna that I'm the one who wants to see her."

Militine hurried toward the kitchen while Lenore took a seat in the sitting room. She wondered if Abrianna had spent so much time with Kolbein that she'd lost her heart to him as

Lenore had. Whatever was she to do if that were the case? She loved Kolbein and couldn't bear the thought of losing him. Of course, Abrianna was her best friend, and she didn't wish to lose her, either. How was she to choose? Why did life seem a constant stream of difficult decisions?

The door opened and Abrianna poked her head in. At the sight of Lenore she gave a little squeal and rushed across the room. She didn't even give Lenore a chance to stand but bent to embrace her heartily.

"I thought you might never return. I have missed you so much. So many things have been happening. Oh, you have no idea. There has been one intrigue after another. I can't wait to fill you in on all the details. Things have definitely been changing around here."

"So I noticed," Lenore replied, rather coolly.

Abrianna straightened. "Well, wait until you hear what's going on with the building. Aunt Miriam is actually thinking about selling. Now that we've had a total of three murders in the neighborhood, she's inclined to think this area unsafe. She has even taken to insisting I remain inside." Abrianna paused and clasped her hands together. "My, but you are a blessed sight to behold. I feared you might not come home after enjoying the big city life of San Francisco."

Lenore knew she had to speak her mind. "I saw you with Kolbein."

Joining her on the settee, Abrianna turned with a shrug. "When?"

"Just now, in the kitchen."

"Oh, why didn't you declare yourself? We would have both welcomed you with open arms."

"You two looked awfully chummy," Lenore said, trying not

to cry. She didn't want to think badly of Abrianna, but the thought of losing Kolbein was almost more than she could bear. She knew it would be best to just speak her mind. "Are you in love with him?"

Abrianna's eyes widened and her face flushed. Lenore feared the worst, but when her friend began laughing, she wasn't at all sure what to think. It seemed the more Abrianna tried to sober and speak, the more hysterically she laughed.

Struggling to catch her breath, Abrianna waved her hand at Lenore and shook her head. "No!" she gasped. "No!" It seemed to be the only word she could get out for several minutes.

Lenore waited for her friend to calm but used the time to share her concern. "I can't bear the thought that you might have fallen in love with him while I was away. Grief would flood my soul if I thought I'd lost all chance of winning his love."

Abrianna finally settled down. "Oh, you are a goose." She panted for air. "I'm not in love with Kolbein. I was just telling him about you and . . . well . . ." She looked away and stopped talking—something most unusual where Abrianna was concerned. Her hesitancy caused Lenore to put her hand to her heart.

"But he doesn't care for me?" she asked, braving the question.

"Not at all," Abrianna declared. "I mean, he doesn't . . . he *does* care for you." She got to her feet and looked down at Lenore in frustration. "I can't bear for you to think these things of me. I would never interfere where true love is concerned. I know that you care about him, and I wouldn't betray you."

"Oh, I'm sorry, Abrianna. It's just that we've been gone for so long, and I couldn't bear it when I saw the two of you together. I suppose I was so jealous that I lost sight of our friendship. Please forgive me. Father has given me a deadline of one month to get Kolbein to ask him for our courtship. Or he'll make me marry James Rybus."

Abrianna smiled. "I do forgive you and hope you will forgive me for giving you any pain. I enjoy Kolbein's company, but like a brother. Like Wade. He's informative and pleasant to converse with, but otherwise my affection is purely that of a friend. Frankly, the biggest interest I've had has been in finding his sister. You know how I love a good intrigue. Mercy, but I've been all over asking about her."

Abrianna looked toward the still open door, as if fearful someone would overhear. Lowering her voice, she added, "I'm forbidden to leave on my own, but . . . well, it seems that finding Greta Booth is a higher calling. I know my aunts don't see it that way, but I do. Not only that, but I know how to take care of myself, and I have good friends out there. They would quickly come to my rescue."

As she chattered on about her mission to find Greta, Lenore lost patience and interrupted. "Abrianna! Please stop!" Lenore jumped to her feet.

Her friend's eyes widened and then a look of understanding crossed her expression. "I'm sorry, Lenore. You know how my thoughts tend to go rushing out like water over rocks. I didn't mean to babble. I have been trying hard not to go on and on about things, but it seems that I am a hopeless cause. Perhaps it's a curse, or maybe it's just the way God made me, but I know it's an irritation—"

Lenore put her finger to Abrianna's lips. "You're doing it again." She smiled. "Please understand. I don't usually mind, but right now I'm all done up in knots. I'm in love, Abrianna, and I need to know how Kolbein feels about me."

"Then why not ask me?" Kolbein asked from the doorway.

Lenore turned around to find him grinning at her like a ninny. She covered her mouth in horror and silently wished the floor might swallow her whole. Her mother would be absolutely mortified to know her daughter had made such an intimate declaration. And mortified didn't begin to cover all the emotions flooding through Lenore at the moment.

Kolbein stepped into the room and smiled at Abrianna. "You told me I could have hope of her affection. I just never knew she would be so forward about it."

This only served to deepen her embarrassment. Lenore lowered her head, wondering what she could possibly say that wouldn't worsen the situation. To her surprise, however, Kolbein came to where she stood and raised her heated face.

His blue eyes twinkled. "I had just told Abrianna the same thing. I'm in love with you, Lenore. I have been since I first set eyes on you. I thought it impossible to love someone so deeply at first glance, but you clearly affected me in a way I'd never known before."

Lenore felt her heart pounding and was certain that Kolbein and Abrianna could hear the drumming. Her mouth felt dry and her tongue stuck to the roof of her mouth. His declaration was more than she had hoped for, yet now that the words were spoken, Lenore felt all reasonable thought flee her mind.

Kolbein seemed to understand. He took hold of her hands and led her back to the settee. "It would seem we have much to discuss."

Just then, Lenore remembered her father downstairs. "I can't stay. My father only agreed to let me come here if I kept my visit brief. Why don't you come for dinner tomorrow evening? I'll let Mother know, and she'll be happy to plan something special."

"Special enough that I might ask your father for permission

to court you?" Kolbein asked. He grinned and added, "I would ask him for your hand, but I'm sure he would never approve, since we don't really know each other all that well."

Lenore shook her head. "I feel like I've always known you. Like I've just been waiting for you all this time. Since I was a little girl, I knew that I would one day find someone special." She got to her feet and Kolbein did likewise. "I have to go, but you will come tomorrow evening, won't you?"

"Of course. What time?"

"Come at six. That way you will have time to get to know my parents. Mother loves to have a time of visiting before the evening meal."

"Six it is," he said, lifting her hand to his lips.

His gaze never left her as he kissed her hand. The look on his face nearly caused Lenore to swoon. She pulled back her hand quickly and hurried for the door. Only then did she remember Abrianna. Lenore glanced back but saw that except for Kolbein, the room was empty. Apparently Abrianna had slipped away sometime during their declaration of love.

Fixing her gaze on Kolbein, Lenore drew a deep breath. "Until tomorrow."

He nodded. "Until then."

Abrianna could hear the clatter of heels on the wooden floor as Aunt Poisie led the girls in practice for the bridal ball that would be held in June—only about a month away. Only a few of the ladies knew how to dance when they'd arrived at the school, but now they were all becoming quite proficient. With exception to Militine, who seemed unable to learn the steps. Aunt Poisie constantly chided her that she would never get a husband until she could waltz properly. Aunt Selma in turn said that a woman wouldn't find a proper mate unless she could sew a straight line, and Aunt Miriam said it had to do with keeping an organized kitchen. Abrianna could see reason in sewing and kitchen work, but still had no idea why dancing was so important to marriage, and no one seemed inclined to explain it to her.

Abrianna shook the thought from her mind. She hadn't come here to think about dancing. Her encounter with Lenore and Kolbein had given her a great deal to consider. She felt a sense of emptiness that only came upon her when she allowed herself to dwell on the past. Moving from the window to the mirror, Abrianna allowed her thoughts to resurface.

She touched her red curls and once again thought of her mother. Aunt Miriam said that her mother had curly hair, but it wasn't red. The ladies had never known her father, but suspected he was the one who had contributed the color to Abrianna's curls.

Aunt Miriam had also told Abrianna that she bore a slight resemblance to her mother. Touching her cheek, thoughts poured through her mind. Had her mother ever touched Abrianna's cheek? Had she combed through the tangled hair?

"How is it that I can miss someone I've never known?" she asked. The longing went deep, and Abrianna could not ignore the pull of emotions that were associated with such memories. Or lack thereof.

I wish I could remember you. She gripped the back of the chair and stared hard into the mirror, as if it might allow her to somehow see the past. *I wish I could talk to you right now. If I could, I would tell you how much I miss knowing you, how I long to hear you speak.*

I can't remember anything about you.

That realization always hurt the most. It was one thing to have lost her mother but entirely another to have no memory of her whatsoever. There wasn't even so much as a single thought that Abrianna could associate with the past.

"If I just had a picture," she murmured. But of course there had been no money for such things. Her folks had been desperately poor. Aunt Miriam said that Abrianna's mother had related the sad facts of her life to the ladies one day after church. She told of her husband leaving to find better work and then the presumption that he had died. Abrianna had no memory of him, either.

Her mother had never been a strong person, Aunt Miriam had shared. This had come from the woman herself as she explained to the ladies that she was dying and desperate for them to take her young child to raise.

"We couldn't refuse her," Aunt Miriam had explained. "She wasn't long for this world, and we felt it our duty to ease her mind."

With a heavy sigh, Abrianna sat at the dressing table. No one understood her pain—the deep emptiness that threatened to swallow her whole. God had been her only solace. He alone could fill that emptiness, but only if Abrianna allowed Him to.

Most of the time she was strong enough not to let the sorrow consume her, but at times like this Abrianna couldn't help but cry. She wiped a tear away as it slid down her cheek and wondered if her mother had wept at the thought of leaving her child alone in the world.

"But I wasn't alone," Abrianna said with a sad smile. The ladies had been so good to her. They had mothered her and educated her, provided for her and directed her, and while Abrianna thought them rather overbearing at times, she loved them more dearly than any other souls on the earth. She would never reveal to them her secret sorrow. She would die before letting them feel that they had somehow failed her.

"Lord," she whispered, settling back against the wooden chair, "please bring me comfort. Please help me appreciate what I have and not long for what can never be. Let me be strong and face my life with determination to overcome."

Again she sighed and took long deep breaths to calm her spirit. She thought of Lenore and Kolbein. No doubt their love would grow deeper, and they would marry and have a family. It caused Abrianna only a moment of regret as she realized how their friendship would change. No doubt it was all for the best. It was the normal way of things for a man and woman in love.

"I doubt I'll ever know that kind of love," she said to her reflection. "I don't think I'm destined for it. My calling is too consuming." She smiled nevertheless. "But I do have love and will have it in the future. I can't help but have love because God has given it to me, and I must share it with others, no matter the cost."

15

Lenore waited until morning to speak to her mother about the dinner. She and Father had been so tired upon arriving home the previous evening that they had immediately sought solace in their adjoining bedrooms and ordered supper trays be brought to them. Now, however, as the servants cleared the breakfast dishes and her father read the paper, Lenore decided to spring the news on them.

"Mother, Father, I know this is rather last minute, but I've invited the man I hope to court, Kolbein Booth, to dine with us this evening. I ran into him last night at the Madison School. He was there because he's been searching for his sister and thought she might be there. It's a complicated tale but unnecessary to complete at this moment."

Father put down his paper, and Mother looked at Lenore as if she'd suddenly sprouted a third eye. She smiled apologetically at her parents. "I'm sorry, but I was so excited. He wants to meet you both and to ask you about our courtship. After all, Father, you told me I had only a month."

"Yes, but I didn't think you would arrange a meeting the day after we returned to Seattle." He drew a deep breath and looked to Lenore's mother. "I find it necessary myself to go and speak with Mrs. Madison about ending our lease, so I won't be in your hair today. Are you up to such an endeavor, my dear?"

"I suppose that I must be," Mother said, as though the very thought was exhausting. But then she flashed Lenore a smile and got up from the table. "Come, Lenore. We have plans to make and food to be selected. Mary!" She called for her personal maid.

The woman, a sturdy-looking homely sort, appeared at the doorway. "Yes, madam?"

"We are planning a dinner party for tonight. It will be an intimate affair for four. Please ready my mauve and silver gown. For Lenore, we should have the blue . . . no, the lavender Worth. The silk chiffon will give her an ethereal appearance of floating as she moves. Lay out the matching ostrich feather hair piece and lavender gloves."

"Yes, madam. Will there be anything else at present?"

Mother thought for a moment. "Not just yet. Later this afternoon, however, we will need to accomplish baths and hair, so you can prepare for those things."

"Yes, madam." Mary slipped from the room as quietly as she'd entered.

Lenore looked at her mother and smiled. "Thank you for doing this for me, Mother. You do not know what it means to me."

"Oh, I don't?" she asked. "I was a young girl with flights of fancy and love once. I want you to be happy, Lenore, and if this young man makes you thus, then I want to see things go well for the two of you. Now, come to my writing desk and we will figure what to plan for the meal and which china to use."

Lenore wanted so much to tell her mother everything that had transpired the evening before. It had been such a wonderful event—the happiest moment Lenore had ever known, and she longed to speak of it.

"I didn't have a chance to tell you, Mother, but Kolbein told me that he cares very deeply for me."

"And what did you tell him? You know it doesn't befit a properly brought up young lady to declare her feelings too early. You mustn't let him take you for granted."

Lenore smiled at the thought of anyone taking Kolbein Booth for granted. "I love him, Mother. I've loved him from first glance. I suppose that might sound silly to some, but it's the truth. I've even prayed about this. Abrianna told me that God would show me His direction for my life, and I believe that direction points to Kolbein."

"Goodness, now you're speaking for God?" Mother shook her head. "I appreciate that your friend is a woman of faith, but honestly, why would God spend time on such a thing when the entire world cries out for help?"

She supposed it didn't make sense, but Abrianna told her that was what was most important about faith. Having faith in God when you had only His Word and prayer wasn't easy. She could almost hear Abrianna going on and on about why such things were illogical yet vital to a Christian's walk. Just then Lenore remembered something they'd talked about in Sunday school.

"The Bible says that God has numbered the hairs on our head, Mother."

"Honestly, Lenore, you are full of surprises."

"Perhaps I am, but wouldn't such a Bible statement imply that God cares about the details of each person's life?"

Mother pulled out her china book and leafed through the pages. Lenore knew her mother was proud of her dozen sets of various dishes. Some had been given down from mother to daughter for generations, while others were later acquirements.

Mother looked up only briefly. "I suppose it could, but I certainly wouldn't venture to put words in God's mouth."

"I don't believe I'm doing that. Quoting a Bible truth merely asserts what God has already said. That's why I feel that this is a direction God has for me. I'm not trying to speak for Him, but rather to trust Him." For a moment Lenore thought her mother hadn't heard, but then she spoke.

"You sound so very grown-up. I suppose I must accept that you are a woman now." She smiled. "If you believe God is speaking to you in the Bible, then who am I to say otherwise?"

Lenore was surprised by this, but before she could say anything, her mother continued as if they hadn't had the discussion. "Let's use the blue and gold Coalport china. It dresses the table nicely and gives a refined elegance to the evening."

"I don't want to make him feel uncomfortable," Lenore said, uncertain as to how Kolbein might react to such grandeur. "We could use grandmother's Foley."

"Much too simple. It would be lovely if we were having an afternoon tea, but tonight we will need something that picks up the light. Oh dear. I completely forgot about flowers," she said, getting up to pull the cord for the housekeeper.

When the stocky woman appeared, she seemed out of breath. "Yes, madam?"

"We will need flowers for this evening." Mother tapped her chin. "A large center arrangement—something grand. Send someone to Matley's immediately and tell them to make it up right away." She continued to tap her chin several times as she considered the arrangement. "It should have roses. Tell them to use the Marchesa Boccella double pinks."

"Yes, madam."

"And tell them it needs to be delivered by three o'clock."

"Yes, madam."

Once the housekeeper set out on her task, Lenore looked to her mother, feeling an unexpected tenderness. "Thank you, Mother. I know this is taxing on your first day home, and I wouldn't have invited Kolbein, but . . . well . . . he's very important to me. I know he's the man I want for my husband."

Mother seemed perplexed and spoke with hesitation. "Lenore . . . I want you . . . to be happy . . . but you mustn't give yourself into marriage too easily. While your father is anxious that you should marry, I don't want you to rush into it. I married young and would have you wait . . . to be certain of your heart before you agree to wed."

"But I *am* certain," she countered, leaning forward as if to emphasize the truth. "You must trust me in this, Mother. We seem to think very much alike, and . . . well . . . I feel confident of his love."

For several long moments Mother said nothing. Finally she closed the china book with a snap. "Well, we shall see what your father thinks of him. I suppose love at first sight is possible, and if your father approves of this young man, then of course I give my blessing. Now, let's figure out a menu for our meal."

Lenore felt a moment of panic. "And if Father doesn't like him or thinks him too poor?"

Mother's expression was compassionate, but her words were firm. "You cannot go against your father, Lenore. It simply isn't done."

Wade waited patiently for his turn at the sale of baked goods being held by Mrs. Madison's students. The event took place every Friday during the warm months at a nearby park, and many a bachelor flocked to buy whatever he could and to speak with the pretty girls. Mrs. Madison had a strict rule for the receptions she held on Saturdays. The men had to pay to attend those affairs. This was in order to prove to Mrs. Madison's satisfaction that they had enough money that they could support a wife. But here at the bake sale, even the poorest man could seek the attention of the pretty maidens. When his turn finally came, Mrs. Madison spied him and pulled him aside.

"You know you needn't wait in line. I have a basket full of things for you."

"I'm happy to pay for my share," Wade said with a grin. "The food is always too good to pass up."

"Be that as it may," Mrs. Madison continued, "you work hard with all the help you give us. Giving you a basket of goodies is the least we can do. But that's not the only reason I took you away. We need to talk to you a moment about Mr. Welby."

Wade followed her to where Mrs. Gibson and Miss Poisie sat knitting. Their hands seemed to move in unison. "Ladies," he said, offering each a nod. "You look very lovely today, Miss Poisie . . . Mrs. Gibson. Are those new hats?"

The ladies stopped their knitting, and Mrs. Gibson actually touched her hand to the straw concoction on her head. "They are. We made hats last Tuesday." She seemed quite pleased that he had noticed.

"Well, actually we made over old hats," Miss Poisie corrected. "A lady can remake old styles over and over and save her husband a great deal of money. Isn't that so, Sister?"

"Indeed it is, but a discussion about hats is not the reason

I've invited Mr. Ackerman to join us. Put aside your knitting and let us discuss Mr. Welby and his offer to buy our building."

The ladies did as they were bid and devoted their attention to Mrs. Madison. She nodded in approval and took a seat while Wade continued to stand. "Mr. Welby continues to pursue this matter, and I am inclined to accept. Mr. Booth has looked over Mr. Welby's offer and believes it to be most generous."

"I'm glad, but I'm not sure how this involves me," Wade said, feeling rather confused.

"We trust your opinion," Mrs. Madison told him. "We have heard from several sources that Mr. Welby is highly regarded in some circles and despised in others."

"That's often the way with businessmen," Wade said. "For a variety of reasons, however, I do have some concerns about the man's transactions. I'm not trying to cast doubt on his business or this offer, but I wouldn't sign anything without Mr. Booth present. And I'd make sure that the money was on the table."

Mrs. Gibson nodded. "Mr. Gibson . . ."

"God rest his soul," Miss Poisie reminded. The ladies gave their usual response.

Mrs. Gibson continued. "He was of a mind that a man should prove himself able to deliver on his promises. He often said that he would demand this proof in whatever way seemed necessary. Of course he also drank brandy and read a great many books that no doubt displeased God."

Wade nodded. "No doubt." Poor Mr. Gibson. No matter his earthly flaws, Wade could only hope that God had indeed given his soul rest.

"Oh dear," Mrs. Madison said, glancing past Wade. "It would seem Mr. Welby has decided to visit us once again."

Wade glanced over his shoulder to find that the man was even now making his way across the park to join them.

"Perhaps he's here to see Abrianna," Miss Poisie suggested.

"Where is Abrianna?" Wade asked.

"She's helping Liang in the kitchen," Mrs. Madison replied. "Poor Abrianna. She is still quite insufficient in her baking, but I will say that she does try very hard to please."

Wade knew full well that Abrianna did what she could to satisfy her aunts. She loved those women more than life itself, but Wade also knew she was quite vexed with herself for being, as she put it, such a disappointment.

Nothing more was said on the topic, however, as Mr. Welby joined their number. He gave a sweeping bow toward the trio on the park bench. "Good day, ladies."

"It's late afternoon," Miss Poisie corrected.

"But I still hope that you had a good day," he replied.

Mrs. Madison patted her sister's arm. "What brings you to us today, Mr. Welby?"

"Well, of course, I came for the bake sale. I must say I've been pleased with the pies I've purchased in the past."

"It's the lard," Mrs. Gibson declared.

Poisie nodded and followed with her own comment. "We render our own."

Mr. Welby seemed rather confused, but Wade found it amusing. The man had no idea what he was up against. The trio was quite formidable when they chose to be.

"When I saw you over here, I thought I might inquire as to whether you had come to a decision on my offer to buy your building."

Mrs. Madison met his smiling face with a stern look. "I told you I would first have to speak with Mr. Fulcher on the matter, as well as our attorney. While I've done the latter, Mr. Fulcher only returned yesterday. I will no doubt have to wait until Monday to see him."

Wade saw Welby's jaw clench. He was clearly unhappy at the news. Why did he want that building so much? Was there something driving him besides the import business?

"I do apologize, ladies. My desire for a rapid conclusion to this business has to do with my receiving a rather large shipment of goods from China. I am quite desperate to find a place to house them."

"But why is the Madison Building so important?" Wade interrupted. "Surely there are other buildings available to you—warehouses that can be leased."

The older man was not pleased to have Wade's interference. Wade could see that much in the man's narrowing eyes as he turned. "I have my reasons. The location is perfectly located near my other holdings. It's close to the harbor, and I have it on good authority that the railroad will come through no more than a quarter mile away."

"But that may not be for years, Mr. Welby," Mrs. Madison said thoughtfully. "Therefore, I see no reason that you should rush into this decision. Surely there are other places you could store your imports in the meantime. Frankly, I need time to thoroughly consider it. And I need to speak to God on the matter."

"And Mr. Fulcher," Miss Poisie added.

Mrs. Madison nodded. "So you see, I am hardly in a place to give you an answer at this time."

"Very well," Welby said from clenched teeth. He squared his shoulders and smiled. "Since we cannot attend to that business, perhaps we might speak about my courtship of Abrianna."

"She doesn't desire to court you," Mrs. Gibson announced.

"Might I ask why?"

Mrs. Gibson looked to Poisie and then to Mrs. Madison. Upon the older woman's nod, she looked back to Welby. "She fears you are a Mugwump. She heard you mention that you were against the tariffs put in place by the Republicans. She was adamant that she couldn't love a Mugwump."

Welby laughed heartily. It wasn't at all what Wade had expected, and from the look on the faces of the ladies, neither had they.

"I am no Mugwump," Welby assured them. "I do protest the Republican tariffs, but as an import man I believe I'm entitled. In my business the evolution of government taxation has become a most desperate concern."

Mrs. Gibson poked Miss Poisie with her elbow but said nothing. Mrs. Madison, however, rose and extended her hand. "Mr. Welby, you were quite good to come to the sale today. I know you are disappointed that our niece has no desire to court you, but we are not in the business of forcing any woman to become a bride. We believe that love should come naturally through getting to know each other, and if that time spent together is displeasing to either party, we believe it should be terminated. You are, however, welcome to attend the receptions to search for another potential bride."

Welby shook his head. "Thank you, no. I do not believe my heart could be so easily manipulated." He took hold of her gloved hand and bowed. "I must attend to other business. If you'll excuse me." He released her and straightened to glare at Wade. "Good day, sir."

"Good afternoon," Miss Poisie corrected, but Welby was already stalking across the park lawn.

"Oh, Miriam, I'm not at all sure that we should further entertain Mr. Welby's offer. He's no doubt a Darwinist. You heard his mention of 'evolution.' No good Christian would put such a word in their vocabulary." She drew out a handkerchief and dabbed it to her neck. "Goodness, he talks just like Mr. Gibson did."

"God rest his soul," Poisie murmured.

"Amen."

16

Kolbein found the Fulchers to be rather superficial. Before they sat down to dine, Mrs. Fulcher made certain he admired her collection of various expensive objets d'art, and as they started in on the meal, Mr. Fulcher seemed interested only in knowing Kolbein's financial status. Kolbein felt sorry for Lenore. Her parents spoke of her as one might of a pampered and spoiled pet or a beloved painting.

"Lenore has known comfort all of her life," Mr. Fulcher said. "I'm not opposed to having a working man amidst us, but I would want to be assured that he could continue to support Lenore in a proper fashion."

"Oh, Father," Lenore said, shaking her head but smiling with a girlish kind of charm. "I thought we agreed to put that aside for now. Why don't you drill Mr. Booth on whether he can match you in croquet or tennis? You will have plenty of time to badger him about his earnings and net worth later."

Kolbein was surprised at her comment but couldn't help but feel proud. He liked that she could stand up to her father without resorting to belittling or rage. She had obviously learned the value of a sense of humor and of treading carefully where her father's worries were concerned.

"I do play a very good game of tennis," Kolbein said, looking back to Mr. Fulcher. "Do I dare hope we might have a match?"

"I would like that," the older man said with great enthusiasm. "I haven't had a worthy opponent in some time. Many of my associates don't even play the game. Their schedules will not allow for it. However, mine shall be considerably less filled in the days to come."

"And why is that?" Kolbein asked, nodding at the servant to remove his dinner plate.

"I have sold my freight brokerage to an acquaintance in San Francisco. The man has great plans for expansion. He intends to send his men up this summer to scout out a location that will best serve his needs. For the meanwhile, I am hopeful that I might persuade Mrs. Madison to continue renting the first floor of her building to Montgomery and Sons."

Kolbein realized that Fulcher knew nothing of Mrs. Madison's thoughts about selling her building. He kept the matter to himself, hoping that perhaps Lenore would introduce the subject, but she apparently knew nothing of it, either.

The servants cleared the table and then brought coffee and a tall coconut torte cake that beckoned Kolbein to find room in his already overstuffed stomach. He took a slice of the cake and waited until everyone else had been served before changing the subject.

"I am curious as to why you chose now to sell your business."

"It was for numerous reasons, the most important of which was that I have no son to pass it down to. When Montgomery approached me about buying it, it seemed a logical solution." Fulcher waited for the servants to leave the room before continuing. "I have done business with Montgomery for years. He runs his company headquarters from San Francisco, while his sons manage affairs in San Diego. His family has been involved with shipping for many generations and thought my brokerage business would come alongside quite nicely. I believe his biggest reason, however, was that he heard me mention selling and he desired a foothold in Seattle. I don't doubt that he'll one day run the entire West Coast of this country. At least where shipping and freighting are concerned."

Kolbein could see that Mrs. Fulcher was displeased that the conversation had turned to business, so he quickly posed a question to her. "And, Mrs. Fulcher, will you and your husband travel now that he's free?"

Lenore's mother perked up. "Oh, I do hope so. We have discussed a grand tour of Europe. I have wanted such a trip for a very long time, but Mr. Fulcher could not be parted from the business that long."

He smiled. Lenore's mother was a lovely woman, and he could easily see where Lenore took her looks. Turning to Lenore, he raised another question. "And what of you, Miss Fulcher? Are you hoping to accompany them on the grand tour?"

She met his gaze, and in her eyes Kolbein could see an impish twinkle. "That all depends, Mr. Kolbein."

"On what?" he teased, knowing that he was the reason she would stay.

"On whether or not I'm free to join them."

"And do you desire such a trip in your future?"

Lenore toyed with her fork. "I used to think I did."

"But of course she does," Mrs. Fulcher interjected. "She would love such a trip, wouldn't you, dear?"

"I believe," Lenore began thoughtfully, "that seeing the world would be a great pleasure. Abrianna has told me about many wonders that sound enticing."

"Goodness, child, a woman does not go to Europe for the enticing wonders. She goes to buy her wardrobe from Worth and to pick out the best china and crystal. And linens. Some of the most beautiful linens come from Ireland," her mother remarked.

Lenore rolled her eyes heavenward, which only served to endear her all the more to Kolbein.

"Mother," she said, "I believe seeing ancient castles, extensive gardens, and museums filled with artifacts and art would be preferable. Just imagine standing in the same place where Mozart created his music."

Her mother looked at her oddly for a moment and then smiled. "But of course, a person could purchase art and tapestries. I merely overlooked that thought."

Lenore met Kolbein's gaze. "And what of you, Mr. Booth? Would you care to take the grand tour?"

"I suppose it would be something to consider. My duties have not yet allowed me such a luxury."

"Lenore tells us that you are seeking to find your younger sister," Mr. Fulcher stated with a note of concern. "What can you tell me about the situation? Is there anything we might do to help?"

His offer surprised Kolbein. "I thank you for the offer. I'm not sure what is yet left undone. I have hired a man to search for her, and Abrianna—Miss Cunningham—put out word on the street amongst the shopkeepers and such." He didn't want to bring up the topic of Abrianna's homeless orphans and indigent seamen. "The police have also been made aware. They took her photograph and had an artist render a likeness. I am also having it published in the newspaper. I hope we will have better results in the near future."

"And if you do not?" Lenore's father asked.

"Goodness, Father, look at the time. We rarely sit around the table so long. Would it be acceptable for us—Mr. Booth and I—to take a brief walk in the garden before you have your discussion with him? I know that the lamps have been lit, so we would have plenty of light to see by."

Kolbein appreciated her redirection. He had stewed many hours over what might happen if he couldn't locate Greta. It troubled him more than he could bear to imagine she might have died before he could find her, or worse. Tonight, however, he wanted his full attention on Lenore.

"I suppose, if you do not stay outside too long," her father answered. "There is still a chill in the night air. I wouldn't want you coming down sick. Your mother would never let me hear the end of it," he mused with an affectionate glance toward his wife.

"You must wear a shawl," Mrs. Fulcher insisted. "And do keep the gown away from the damp ground."

Lenore scooted her chair back just a bit, and Kolbein jumped up to assist her. "I will see to it that we stay on the path."

He offered Lenore his hand and helped her to her feet. Her beauty put him in a state of awe. The lavender gown of costly silk chiffon draped her gracefully, and her beautiful cocoa-colored hair had been arranged in such a fashion to sweep all of the hair up and away from her face. He liked the effect. He liked it very much. But it was her eyes—the expression of contentment on her face—that truly captivated his attention.

"If you'll wait one moment, I'll fetch my wrap," she told him.

Kolbein hardly heard her for the pounding of his heart. He could only nod and watch her glide from the room. He felt as though he were in a dream. He thought of Abrianna's comment once about thanking God for his blessings, and Kolbein

209

realized he was very blessed to have Lenore's consideration and love.

I do thank you, Father God. I thank you for this young woman.

"Mr. Booth." Lenore's father interrupted his thoughts. "I hope that after your walk you will have the butler show you to my study. I believe we should talk in private."

Kolbein nodded. "I would like that very much." He gave a quick glance at the ceiling as Fulcher walked away. *And, Lord, if it's not too selfish of me to ask, please let Mr. Fulcher have no reservations regarding my courtship of Lenore. You know that my heart toward her is honorable. Please let Mr. Fulcher see that for himself.*

Lenore wrapped the wispy white silk around her shoulders and hurried back to where Kolbein awaited her in the hall. He smiled at her, and Lenore felt a shiver of pleasure run down her spine. He was clearly the most handsome man in all the world, and he desired to court her. The thought pleased and terrified Lenore all at the same time. What if she did something to betray his trust? What if upon closer inspection and getting to know each other, Kolbein found her to be boring or insipid? After all, she had hated school and was nowhere near the scholar that Abrianna was. What if Kolbein expected a smart wife—a wife with an interest in the world and all its affairs?

"You look troubled," Kolbein said, offering her his arm.

"No," she said, shaking her head. "I'm fine." She led the way to the French doors that opened onto the outdoor patio and gardens. "I hope you don't mind that most of the flowers are not yet in bloom."

"I really didn't come out here to see the flowers," he said in a low husky voice. He led her farther from the house and then stopped. "I wanted time with you . . . alone."

"I wanted the same," she replied. "I hope Father wasn't too overbearing this evening. He worries about whether my husband will provide riches and luxury for me all of my life, without consulting me about my desires."

"And what are those desires?" he asked, turning her to face him.

Lenore trembled. "You." Her voice could barely be heard.

"And you aren't worried about having less than you have now?"

She shook her head. "All of this used to be so important," she said, waving back toward the house. "I thought it was all that mattered, because it was all that mattered to my mother. Oh, I will say it's wonderful to have an easy life with servants and plenty, but I've had a change of heart regarding its importance."

"Because of me?"

"No, because of Abrianna. When I met her for the first time at church, I realized that she had a spirit of genuine joy and love to share. Even as a young girl, I envied her natural ability with others and her obvious concern for those less fortunate. Do you know that one of my first memories of Abrianna is of her dropping everything in her arms to assist an older congregant whose shawl had slipped to the ground? She has such a servant's heart and seems to find genuine joy in helping others. At first I didn't understand this. I'd been raised much too self-focused. I even tried to change her, to turn her into my mother's idea of a grand lady."

He chuckled. "I can't imagine that went well, although I have seen Abrianna dressed in some of the gowns you've given her."

"Mother only allows me to wear them five times before passing them along. I think it a waste, but Mother says that's what all ladies of society do." She shook her head. "But Abrianna is different. She's grand in her own way, but I failed to see that at first. I'm afraid I was quite firm with her regarding what her future should look like. I now realize I was wrong."

"And what brought you to this understanding?"

Lenore thought for a moment about the opulence of the Montgomery house. All the outward signs of beauty were there, but within the hearts of the people who lived there, Lenore saw only greed and haughtiness.

"I suppose I've simply had my eyes opened to the way upper society can be. Abrianna cares for the needy, and while I don't know if I would be able to do what she does, I don't want the trappings of my parents unless I'm able to use that wealth for helping others." She paused. "I hope that doesn't lower your opinion of me. I know you very well may be driven to higher society one day, and if that is where life takes us, then I shall be happy to do my duty."

"So you plan to spend your life with me?" he asked in an amused tone.

Lenore shrugged, more relaxed now. "I realize you haven't asked for my hand, but my heart tells me that it's implied."

He pulled her close and Lenore felt the warmth of his hands on her arms through the fine silk wrap. "It's more than implied. I want you for my wife, Lenore. I realize we've not had much time together, but my heart knows what it wants, and it wants you. Will you marry me?"

She gazed up into his eyes and nodded. "I will."

He lowered his mouth to hers for a brief but thoroughly enjoyable kiss. Lenore thought she might well faint, but when he raised his face and met her gaze with a mischievous grin, she changed her mind.

"You look rather proud of yourself, Mr. Booth," she said, pulling away from his hold.

He put his arm around her and drew her toward the house. "I am, actually. I have asked the love of my life to marry me, and I didn't stammer or . . . lose my supper."

She couldn't help but giggle. "Goodness, I didn't know I had that kind of effect on you."

Kolbein paused at the French doors. "You affect me in every way and always will." He straightened his tie. "But now I need to speak with your father. Otherwise we won't be able to court, much less marry."

The next morning, Lenore shared tea with Abrianna and relayed the events of the previous evening. "I'm so happy, I might very well cry," she declared.

"Please don't. I wouldn't want Aunt Miriam to question what's happening. She would never approve of your accepting Kolbein's proposal so quickly, although I don't know why not. Goodness, it seems to me if two people know that they're destined for each other, they needn't waste time with a set period of courtship. Although I will hate to see you go."

"What are you talking about? I'm not going anywhere."

"Kolbein is from Chicago, and while I know he's taken a position here, he will no doubt consider returning, although I don't know why anyone would choose to live there. The reports are always so negative. Not only that, but Chicago is so far away, and I would never see you again. Oh, that would be utter tragedy to our friendship." She paused for a moment to stand

and put her hand over her heart. "A devastation of the heart. I shall never recover losing your friendship. We shall be forever changed. You will be gone from me . . . never to return."

"Mercy sakes, Abrianna, you would think marriage and death were the same thing. I will still want to spend time with you. The only difference will be that now I will have a home of my own to invite you to. Perhaps I shall even have a carriage to send for you. I do not believe Kolbein wishes us to leave Seattle. From what he has said, I think he's grown accustomed to the rain." She couldn't help but smile. "He says he now sees things in cloudy days that he never saw before. I think he has a rather artistic soul, because he talked about shadows and hues." Lenore shrugged. "Nevertheless, my marriage won't come between us."

Abrianna sat back down beside Lenore, looking quite displaced. Slowly she shook her head. "It will be different. You will see. No, I shall prepare my heart for what is to come."

Her heavy sigh made it clear to Lenore that she would not be otherwise convinced at the moment. "Well then, we should endeavor to enjoy what time we have," Lenore said. "And I shall start by telling you that my days of trying to remake you are over. I no longer believe that you need to wear fine clothes and play the piano to be a good woman, Abrianna. I know that you are a better woman in your broadcloth and serge than I will ever be in my silks and velvets, and I hope you will forgive me."

Abrianna raised her hand. "Do not speak like that. You are the finest lady I have ever known. I will never be as charming or as lovely." She touched her hand to her hair. "Just as I can never change the color of my hair. I'm afraid that what you see is very much what you get."

Lenore laughed and reached over to hug Abrianna close. "And that is exactly what I want. While I was away I learned a very good lesson about appearances. An apple can be beautiful on the outside and yet rotten within. I met some young women who were very much that way. They were beautifully gowned and fashionable in every way, but inside they were ugly and spoiled. I realized that with very little trouble I could be the same."

Abrianna shook her head. "No. I do not accept that. You may have wealth and beautiful things, but your heart is more beautiful than anything money could buy. If you were a shallow or vapid woman, I could not confide in you as I do."

Smiling, Lenore patted Abrianna's hand. "And you, Abrianna, are the grandest lady I have ever known . . . or ever will. God has given you an incredible heart, a heart that is able to love in a far greater capacity than anyone I've ever known. I was wrong to try to keep you from your calling, and I pray you can forgive me."

Abrianna's brows came together as if she were thinking hard on the matter. "Upon reflection," she finally said, "I see nothing for which you need ask forgiveness. Nevertheless, I give it freely."

Lenore smiled. She had already known Abrianna would say as much.

17

Abrianna knew that Aunt Miriam would be horrified by her actions, but she couldn't help herself. There was a man lingering outside their building. She could see him in the dusky evening light, and more clearly each time he neared one of the streetlights. He seemed to be circling their building, because Abrianna observed that he would move down the alleyway and then turn to the right. After this he was gone for several minutes and finally would show up on the left reentering the alley.

Who was he and did he mean harm to them or others? She picked up the fireplace poker and gripped the cold iron in her hand. What should she do? If he was of a good nature, Abrianna felt it would be her duty to warn him about the murders that had taken place. If he was the murderer, however, she might put the fear of God into his soul. Maybe he would even confess and turn himself in to the police once she finished with him.

She took off her shoes to sneak down the stairs, hoping that no one would hear her exit. At the street entrance she slipped her feet back into the soft leather and reassessed her weapons. The boning knife was strapped to her right calf, and in her hands she held the rather intimidating fireplace poker. At least she hoped it would be intimidating. Otherwise, all she had was her wits and her ability to run very fast.

The air still bore the dampness of an earlier rain. Abrianna quietly picked her way between mud puddles and prayed that God would send legions of angels to protect her. She pondered only a moment whether He would give such an order to His heavenly host when Abrianna was clearly defying her authority, but she decided it was worth the risk. After all, she wasn't seeking to benefit herself so much as protect those she loved.

Drawing a deep breath, she waited as the man rounded the corner once again and headed into the alley. With only a moderate amount of fear, Abrianna jumped into the alleyway and held up the poker in confrontation. "Halt, in the name of the law."

The suit-clad man whirled around to face her. The lighting was poor, but Abrianna could see that he had an amused look on his face. "Ya hardly look like the law." His brogue was clearly Irish.

"I'm not, but I figured that would get your attention. I want to know who you are and why you are loitering here. Three men have died on this site, and if you are responsible, you should know that I intend to put a stop to your deeds. And if you aren't responsible, you should know what has happened here so that you can save yourself from possible harm."

The man snorted in seeming delight. Abrianna wasn't at all sure why he should act in such a manner. She meant business. "You are quite rude to laugh when I am completely devoted to seeing this through. Two of the dead were good friends of mine, and I will avenge their death if possible."

"Aye, I've no doubt ya'd be doin' just that. However, I'm not yar murderer. I was hired by a lawyer named Mr. Kolbein Booth to act as a night watchman for this building."

Abrianna lowered the poker and took a step forward. "Are you being truthful with me?"

He again chuckled. "Well, if I wasn't I wouldn't be admittin' it, now, would I?"

She nodded, pursing her lips together. He was, of course, right to point this out. She considered the man for a moment longer, then realized that a stranger would have no way of knowing about Kolbein Booth.

"You must be who you say you are," she said, relaxing a bit. "A murderer would have no knowledge of our good friend and lawyer. I must say it is a relief to have someone watching over us besides the Good Lord. Not that He doesn't have it well in His power."

"It looks to me," the older man said, stepping closer, "that ya had the situation completely under control."

"I couldn't help but be concerned." She extended her hand. "I'm Abrianna Cunningham and I live here. I do not like murders taking place near my home."

"I can well imagine that ya should feel that way. I would be feelin' the same about it happenin' near my home." He smiled and pushed back his hat. "Yar quite the woman to come out here and confront me yarself."

"Oh, I'm not really alone. God is watching over me," she replied. "Although I'm not supposed to endeavor on such escapades. My aunts would not be pleased to see me take matters in my own hands, and my dearest friend in the world, Mr. Wade Ackerman, would no doubt be very vexed with me."

"You've got that right." Wade surprised them both by stalking forward to take hold of Abrianna. "What in the world do you think you're doing out here?"

The guard narrowed his eyes and took a defensive stance. "Unhand the young lady."

"Oh, don't bother to order him around," Abrianna told him. "He does pretty much as he pleases. This is the man I was speaking of—Wade Ackerman. He thinks himself my big brother and guardian. Do you know he threatened to nail shut my windows and doors to keep me prisoner in my bedroom? Have you ever heard of such a thing?" She looked to Wade. "This is a night watchman hired by Kolbein. So you see there is no danger."

"Yes, I know all about him," Wade declared. "However, you should never have made his acquaintance. You should have remained inside the building as you were instructed."

Wade let go of her arm and extended his hand to the man. "I'm as she says—Wade Ackerman. Mr. Booth said he told you about me."

"Aye. He did." The man shook hands with Wade and grinned. "Malcolm Downy is my name. I'm the Irish middleweight champion of the Northwest."

"Glad to meet you. Now, if you'll excuse me, I will see to getting Miss Cunningham back to safety."

"She's a feisty one," Malcolm said, grinning all the more. "Must have a wee bit of the Irish in her."

"More than a wee bit, I'd say." Wade shook his head. "She's stubborn through and through, listens to no man, and believes herself invincible."

"Aye, she'd be of the Irish, all right. I should have known by that mop of red." He chuckled. "Good night to ya now, Miss Cunningham. May the Good Lord keep ya in His hand and ne'er close His fist too tight." He took his leave then, humming a song that Abrianna figured to be from his native home.

"What a nice man."

"Now I will know the meaning of this," Wade said, taking hold of her once again.

Abrianna tried to pull away to no avail. "I did nothing wrong, and you needn't treat me like a child. Goodness, Wade, I've been tolerant of your overbearing concerns for years now. At first they came as a welcome. I thought you quite the gallant knight to care so much about my well-being. Now, however, I feel less inclined to offer praise. You act as though I'm made of porcelain and have no knowledge of life on the streets." She looked down the alley as Mr. Downy disappeared around the corner. "That was so kind of Kolbein to send someone to watch over us."

Already Wade was dragging her back to the front of the building. Abrianna hurried to keep up for fear he would hoist her over his shoulder if she lagged.

"Truly, Wade, this is an embarrassment. I had taken precautions and everything was under control. You needn't have worried."

"It seems where you are concerned," Wade said, stopping at the front doors of the building, "worry is a natural state of our relationship. Honestly, Abrianna, whatever prompted you to take such a foolish risk? Do you suppose those three women could have borne the sorrow of losing you?"

Abrianna calmed. "I didn't think myself to be in danger. I suppose, upon reflection, that it wasn't my wisest choice. However, I didn't want to see harm come to anyone else."

"And what did you figure to do?" He let go of her arm and reached for the poker. "Would you have honestly struck the man? Don't you realize a strong man like Downy could easily knock this from your hands?"

"Well if he had, I would have had my boning knife," she said, thinking her plan quite reasonable.

"Like you did with me?"

"Well, I didn't really put up a fight with you, as I didn't wish to cause you harm."

"Oh, Abrianna," Wade said with a sigh. "Can't you see that times are different? You aren't a young girl able to slip unnoticed through the cracks and crevices of the city. You're a young woman now—a very pretty young woman." He held up his hand to still her. "I know you don't believe me, but it's the truth. There are indecent men who would think nothing of taking liberties with you."

She could see the fear in his expression. "I'm sorry to have caused you concern." She put her hand on his chest, realizing that he was more than a little fearful for her. "I can see that you are quite worried, and that wasn't my desire. I suppose sometimes it's just hard to be so limited because of one's gender. I only sought to protect the ones I love."

"And I feel the same," Wade replied. "You and the ladies are the only family I have around here. My own folks are far from this place, as you know. I've come to care very deeply about your safety."

"I know." She sighed. "I honestly do not strive to find trouble."

"I know that, Abrianna," he said finally, smiling. "Trouble just seems to naturally find you."

Wade was glad to see Thane leaning on the wall by his shop when he returned from the Madison Building. The diversion would help him put aside his thoughts of what might have happened to Abrianna that night. Mercy, but that girl could be an aggravation.

"Thought I'd come by for a game, if you have the time," Thane said, pushing off the building.

"Sounds good. Have you eaten?"

Thane grinned. "Yeah, but what's that got to do with it? I'm always ready for another meal."

Wade laughed and unlocked the door to his shop. He turned on the lights and waited for Thane to enter before relocking the door. He wasn't going to take any chance that someone would wander in to steal his tools.

Thane followed him back to his living space and then asked, "What have you been up to?"

Wade went to the stove and poked up the fire in order to re-heat the coffee. "I headed over to meet the new night watchman Kolbein Booth hired for the ladies. Unfortunately, I found one of them outside, trying to determine if the man was friend or foe."

Thane looked at him in understanding. "Abrianna?"

"Who else would be so foolish?" Wade shook his head. "Do you know she was standing there with a fireplace poker ready to bash the man's head in if he turned out to be the murderer?"

Thane laughed. "And she probably would have done it, too."

"Don't laugh. I was never so angry and scared in my life. I couldn't help but think her in danger. I swear that girl does everything she can to jeopardize her safety. I have never approved of all her sneaking around, but at least when she was younger, it didn't seem so bad. Especially when she dressed in a more boyish fashion." He sighed. "Now, however, there is nothing boyish about her."

"No, not a bit," Thane agreed. "But she is a redhead, and as such seems destined for conflict and disobedience."

Wade raised a brow. "You, sir, have a crown of red, as well."

"Exactly. So that makes me something of an authority on the subject. We are a stubborn lot. It's the way God made us. How else would we get as much done as we do? You have to admit that Abrianna is a most industrious young woman. And I'm not exactly idle myself. I work on repairing boats all day, volunteer for the fire department, help at the church, and play baseball for the annual fireman's tournament. And that doesn't begin to account for all of my activities. I'm also a master chess player, which you will experience in a moment."

Wade wanted to forget about Abrianna and the scare, but he couldn't seem to drop the matter. "I'm afraid she's going to get herself into trouble one of these days, and I won't be there to help get her out of it. If anything happened to her, I wouldn't be able to forgive myself."

"But you aren't her keeper, Wade. She's going to finish growing up and do as she pleases. She already pretty much does, and even her aunts can't keep her under watch. I think you might as well accept that Abrianna answers to God alone." Thane laughed, adding, "And I'll bet even He has trouble getting her to check in."

18

Kolbein arranged the paper work for the transfer of the lease from Mr. Fulcher to Mr. Montgomery. Designed as only a temporary situation with Montgomery, it was agreed that they would vacate the building by June fifteenth. This, in turn, allowed Mrs. Madison to sell out to Priam Welby. Of course, she hadn't had a chance to speak to Mr. Welby on the matter. Kolbein suggested she allow him to conduct the business of sale, and while she agreed in part, Mrs. Madison was quite firm that she would give Mr. Welby her answer in person. She thought it only polite.

Mr. Fulcher joined Kolbein upstairs at exactly one-thirty, just as they'd agreed upon. The school and home of the ladies seemed the easiest place to conduct business. There was no sense in forcing the ladies to break from their normal routines. From what Kolbein had learned, they hated this more than most anything else.

Kolbein gave a nod and smile when Mr. Fulcher entered the main sitting room. That smile broadened considerably when he saw Lenore appear in the doorway behind her father. Kolbein felt his heart beat a little faster just at the sight of her. She looked at him as if he were able to climb the highest mountain or fight off the fiercest foe. Her confidence in him only served to make Kolbein feel all the more capable.

He got to his feet quickly to shake hands with Mr. Fulcher and to offer Lenore a polite bow. "I appreciate that you would take time to meet me here," Kolbein said. "Mrs. Madison wanted to be present, and I knew it would be easier for you to come to her."

"I don't mind at all. I'm just relieved to get the matter settled. I find that idle afternoons agree with me. I've taken up an old hobby of mine, and the afternoons are perfect for such a thing."

"And what old hobby is that?" Kolbein asked.

Lenore interjected the answer. "Napping. Father seems to enjoy an afternoon nap."

Kolbein laughed. "I can't fault him for that. I rather enjoy the occasional afternoon slumber myself." He motioned to the table. "I have the papers ready, and Mrs. Madison will join us shortly."

"Good. I hope also to have a moment in private with her. I presume you and Lenore can occupy yourselves for a few moments."

"But of course," Kolbein replied with a wink at Lenore.

Mrs. Madison entered the room, dressed head to toe in a gray suit that made her look like a harsh governess. Kolbein liked the older woman despite her stern nature. She was by far the more serious of the trio and obviously the one who kept the others from attending to anything too outlandish. Even so, he'd seen a glimmer of amusement cross her expression from time to time.

Kolbein offered her his arm and led her to a chair at the table. "I have the papers ready for your signatures."

Mrs. Madison didn't hesitate to peruse the contract for herself. She studied the pages for several minutes, then looked up to nod at Kolbein. "It's just as I asked." She took pen in hand, dipped it in the inkwell, and signed her name.

Fulcher did likewise, having already seen a rough draft of the agreement. Mr. Montgomery had wired, giving him permission to act as his agent in the matter, so Fulcher signed, seeming relieved to have the deal settled.

"That's a weight off my chest," the man said as he returned the pen to the inkwell. "The last issue of my former business." He gave a sigh of relief. "I'm frankly happy to see it pass to another."

"I'm beginning to feel much the name," Mrs. Madison said. "I did not think I could ever part with this building, but with the help of Mr. Booth, my sister, and dear friend, I now see the sense of doing just that. Mr. Madison would want it that way, I'm sure. He wouldn't want our lives to be at risk."

"You will be safer moving away from the docks," Mr. Fulcher declared. "Do you yet know where you will go?"

"Mr. Welby said he has a house to include in our transaction. We will, of course, have to review and approve it, but he said it's in the Lower Queen Anne section with a view of the water. The house itself is quite large, with a great many bedrooms. He thought it perfect for our school. It stands on several acres and even has gardens to tend. We've never had the opportunity to work with the young ladies on gardening, although I believe it a sensible management of one's food needs."

Fulcher smiled. "Perhaps you will not live far from our home. I know Lenore would like that very much."

"I would," Lenore said. "I would enjoy being able to walk over for a visit."

"Well, we shall see. Mr. Welby agreed to show us on Sunday. He wanted to show us Saturday, but there was much too much to do, and our schedule would not allow for it."

Kolbein smiled, remembering the discussion. Welby couldn't see why the ladies' Saturday duties couldn't wait, but Mrs. Madison was firm. Kolbein almost felt sorry for Welby as he tried his best to convince her otherwise, but he finally relented and agreed to a Sunday afternoon viewing. Furthermore, he would send his carriage for the ladies. This met completely with Mrs. Madison's approval, as she had vocalized her concerns about how they would get to the house.

"Now, if you would allow us," Mr. Fulcher said, turning to Kolbein. "I'd like to speak a few moments alone with Mrs. Madison."

"Of course." Kolbein left the papers on the table and offered Lenore his arm. "Shall we go to the private sitting room?"

She smiled in that wonderful way that he had come to love. Her dark eyes seemed to shine as he squeezed her arm. Once they were safely alone, Kolbein pulled Lenore into his arms and kissed her gently. He felt her melt against him and sigh. Her action caused him to feel more certain than ever that they belonged together.

"I hope you don't think me too forward," he told her, setting her apart from himself. "I really don't see any reason to pretend that we aren't madly in love. When do you think I might ask your father for your hand in marriage?"

Lenore shrugged. "I've made it clear to Mother that I intend to marry you. I would think she would have told Father that, as well. If I had my way about it, you would have a wife today, but I'm uncertain we can convince Father of such a brief engagement. I suggest you ask him at dinner Friday night. That way at least we can be formally engaged, and it will be announced in the papers. That will please Mother."

"You don't think she'll be embarrassed by my being a lawyer?"

"I truly don't care," Lenore replied. "Does that sound harsh?" She didn't give him time to answer. "I hope not, but either way, I will choose my own husband, and I choose you."

"And I choose you, my dear." He glanced toward the clock on the mantel. Time was getting away from him, and he was to help with another business negotiation. "I will need to leave in a few minutes."

"Before you go, Kolbein, have you had any word on Greta?"

Kolbein frowned. He had mulled over the detective's latest report in his mind but had spoken of it to no one. "I had some rather unpleasant news."

"Unpleasant? She's not . . . she didn't . . ."

"She isn't dead, at least not that I know. However, the detective shared some very grave news. In his investigation he came upon a judge who remembers marrying a young woman who fits Greta's description. He was even certain her maiden name was Booth."

"Married? But that's wonderful, isn't it?" she said with such excitement that Kolbein hated to burst her bubble.

"She didn't know anyone long enough to marry them. Not only that, but she's a child. Just nineteen. Hardly an appropriate age to marry."

Lenore looked at him oddly. "I'm only a year her senior. What's wrong with marrying at nineteen?"

Kolbein felt as if Lenore had struck him. "You're only . . . twenty?"

"I'll be twenty-one in August. Not only that, you and I have known each other only a short time, and we're already speaking of marriage. Be happy for your sister. If she's found true love like we have, then all the better. She will be safe and cared for."

Lenore was only twenty. The idea of her being so young had

never really occurred to him. He had always presumed her to be closer to his own age of thirty. She certainly conducted herself as a mature woman. In fact, she was nothing like Greta, with her tantrums and girlish demands.

"Are you listening to me, Kolbein?" Lenore asked, touching his arm.

He pulled back as if she'd burned him. Looking into her beautiful face, Kolbein could not help but see the youth that his sister bore. "I thought you were older."

"I'm old enough," Lenore countered. "I'll come into a trust fund in August. So, you see, I shall come into this marriage with the promise of benefits from the start."

"I'm thirty years old, Lenore. I thought you to be closer to my age—at least twenty-five."

"Goodness. Girls marry much younger than twenty or even nineteen. I don't understand your concerns." She looked so innocent, so completely naïve of his worries.

"You are just coming of age. You haven't yet had a chance to really know anything other than being your father's daughter. I know that is the normal way of things, but as I told Greta, I would prefer that she attend school and expand her knowledge, have a chance to live life a bit, rather than marry at such a young age."

"Was that why she ran away?" Lenore's voice betrayed her growing distress.

Kolbein knew he had to be honest with her. "Yes. She had thought herself in love with a local young man—really a boy. They met at . . . oh, I don't know where they met. I tried to talk to Greta about the situation, tried to get her to see reason."

"Reason? You mean you tried to change her mind." Tears formed in Lenore's eyes. "Oh, please tell me you weren't that cruel."

"Lenore, the age and inexperience of my sister would make her a poor wife. She had been sheltered all of her life and knew nothing of the world. When my parents died she was ten and I was twenty-two—just out of school and already working to become a lawyer. I was hardly prepared to be a young girl's guardian, so I put her in boarding school—a strict religious boarding school."

"And you think that makes her unable to fall in love," Lenore said, sniffing back tears. "I was sheltered myself, Kolbein, but I found ways to expose myself to the world around me. Not only that, but I certainly know my own heart." She looked at him as if seeing a stranger. "I don't know what to say about this. It's breaking my heart that you should think me too young to know how I feel."

"I . . . I didn't say that," Kolbein replied, hesitating. What could he possibly say that would make this better? Lenore was only twenty and all she would hear is that he thought that too young to marry. The truth was, he still believed that, yet he wanted very much to make Lenore his wife.

Lenore shook her head. "You believe me too young to marry. Isn't that true?" The tears were streaming down her cheeks, but she held her head high.

"I suppose I do. But I—"

"Never mind. I don't need to hear anything more. Tell my father I shall wait for him in his office. Good day, Mr. Booth." She hurried from the room.

Kolbein followed her to the door, trying to get her to stay and talk about the matter, but she'd have no part of it. He could hear her sobs as she made her way down the stairs. What was he to do? He thought to follow her but held himself in check. What could he possibly say to make this better? He needed time to consider their relationship. Just then the large grandfather clock struck two. He shook his head, knowing it would have to wait. He had to be back in the office by two-thirty.

"Mr. Booth," Miss Poisie said, coming up beside him, "whatever are you doing staring out across the stairs?" She stretched a bit to peer beyond him. "Is something amiss?"

"I'm afraid so, Miss Poisie. I have hurt Lenore's feelings by suggesting she's too young for marriage." He looked at the older woman and shrugged. "I suppose I have lost the woman I love."

"Nonsense," Miss Poisie replied. "Have I ever told you about my beloved sea captain, Jonathan Richards? God rest his soul."

Kolbein restrained from adding an amen and instead shook his head. "I don't believe you have."

"Well, Jonathan was the love of my life and I of his." She clutched her hands together and drew them to her heart. "He was the captain of the *Sea Vixen*—a fishing vessel. He was a most amazing man, and we were to be married."

"What happened?" Kolbein asked, knowing that he really should put an end to the conversation and return to his office.

"He went north for fishing and never returned. The *Sea Vixen* was lost at sea. They found the wreckage a year later on the Canadian shores, but nothing of the men who served." Her face grew quite sad. "That was ten years ago, and I still mourn him. I will never stop loving him, just as I do not believe Miss Lenore will ever stop loving you. Lovers' quarrels are short-lived if sensible heads prevail."

"But I had always thought a woman should be older before marrying. Even here at the school most of your young ladies are older than twenty."

"It's true. Most of these women were unable to find love on their own. Goodness, some of them could barely boil water, and what man would want a wife who couldn't cook him a decent meal. I tell you, Mr. Booth, the stomach finds very little satisfaction on emotion alone."

Kolbein had never really heard Miss Poisie speak her mind. Usually her sister or Mrs. Gibson was quicker to share, and she often remained in the background, quiet and reserved.

"But Lenore is only twenty. My sister is but nineteen, and I thought her too young to marry. How am I to yield my viewpoint for the sake of my own happiness?"

"A wise man is willing to acknowledge when he has been foolish or . . ." Miss Poisie paused. "Dare I say . . . wrong? I was hardly young when I made the acquaintance of my beloved, but age had no bearing. I do not believe it will cause issue for your circumstance, either.

"Now, please understand, I would not have any young girl up and marrying the first man she meets. No, I am a firm believer in seeking the truth, and that truth can only come from God. You should pray about the matter, Mr. Booth. Pray and ask for God's guidance. He is always willing to offer wisdom to those who ask."

The quarter hour chimed, and Kolbein knew he would have to go. "Thank you for your advice, Miss Poisie." He gave a slight bow. "I will take this to the Lord, as you suggest."

Days after her encounter with Wade, Abrianna was still fuming. She'd never felt this much frustration with anyone. It was bad enough that he'd forced her back to the school as if she were a wayward child, but then he had done the unspeakable. Wade had told her aunts what she'd done. Now they were monitoring her every move. There was no chance for escape, and Abrianna's irritation was growing by the minute.

"He had no right," she told Militine as they washed windows. "He had no right to tattle on me. I was only looking out for the good of my loved ones."

"You are much braver than I would be." Militine picked up a piece of newspaper and began wiping the glass. "I would have been scared witless to even try such a thing. What if that man had been the killer? He might have killed you."

"The murders have only been of men. I doubt that the killer would attack me."

"But you don't know that," Militine countered. "I think you should be more careful. I would hate for you to be harmed. You're my only friend."

Abrianna sighed. "You are also dear to me, but there are matters that I need to be tending. One of the soiled doves recently had a baby. I promised to bring flannel for diapers. Then there was a fight several nights ago, and two of my good friends were injured."

"Sailors?"

"Yes, old sailors, men who have nothing but time on their hands. Goodness, Militine, you should see them. They have been healthy and hearty all of their lives, but now they are old and broken down. They are discarded by the world without regard. I would have that changed by law." She held up her hand. "I know I sound more Democrat than Republican in my thinking, but I'm really not either. Imagine, however, if we had a law that made it wrong to harm them. What if we were required to help those who were without work or unable to do for themselves?"

"That would be a huge task, Abrianna. Besides, there are already numerous laws. It's against the law to murder someone, yet we have a killer out there doing just that. Laws are only as good as they can be enforced."

"I suppose that's true. There are over six hundred laws in the

Bible," Abrianna said thoughtfully. "God couldn't get folks to obey those, either. That's why He had to sacrifice His Son on the cross." She shook her head. "With people no more appreciative than they were, I'm not even sure why God bothered. Sometimes I don't know why He bothers with us now."

Militine shrugged. "I'm the wrong person to ask. I've never been much for church. I usually doze off during the Sunday sermon. I get tired of being told how bad I am."

Abrianna hadn't realized Militine's feelings about church. "But without Jesus, we're all bad. We have all 'sinned and come short of the glory of God,'" she quoted from Romans. "And 'the wages of sin is death.'"

"I know. I've heard it all before. Like a parent, God will discipline us." Militine rubbed hard at a mark on the glass. "It's just that I believe God is a harsh Father."

"Harsh? Even loving parents have to discipline their children," Abrianna said, feeling sad that Militine didn't yet know the joy she had found in Jesus. "God wants us to put aside our sinful ways and seek Him. Then we can do good deeds for Him instead of wallowing in our sin."

"But I do good deeds. I'm always helping one person or another. I'm never cross or angry when people do me wrong, and I always forgive them. That's exactly what the preacher is always saying we need to do."

"But your good deeds won't save you from the fires of hell and eternal separation from God." Abrianna reached out and touched Militine's arm. "Only Jesus can do that. For certain God wants us to be forgiving, but—"

"Abrianna," Aunt Selma called from the doorway. "Mr. Ackerman is here to see you. It's not a proper visiting day, but he said it was important."

She frowned. The last person in the world she wanted to see right now was Wade. He had hurt her feelings, and she wasn't about to let him think the way he had treated her was acceptable.

"Please tell him I'm too busy and remind him again that it isn't a visiting day. I have much too much work to stop now and share conversation and gossip with Mr. Ackerman."

Aunt Selma didn't question her reply, much to Abrianna's relief. Once she was gone, Abrianna went back to work on the window. "He has some nerve showing up here to torment me."

"So," Militine said in a barely audible voice, "you don't intend to . . . forgive him?"

The word hit Abrianna right between the eyes. Here she had just been sharing God's directions for His children, including the need for forgiveness, yet she was unwilling to give the same to Wade for his transgressions.

"You have given me much to think on," Abrianna replied, meeting Militine's kind expression. "I shall have to ponder the matter for a time. Forgiveness will definitely be given, but I find that I must sort through my miseries in order to do so with a free heart."

Militine smiled. "I would imagine getting your own heart in order will give you great peace of mind."

Abrianna nodded. "Of course, you are right."

19

O h, Abrianna, it was just terrible," Lenore sobbed. "I can hardly believe this is happening."

Abrianna looked at her friend and felt great distress. The only problem was Lenore had been crying so much that these were the first actual words she'd understood.

"Drink your tea and then we can talk. I don't know what's happened, but I'm all ears and together we can figure it out. You know I'm good at figuring," Abrianna said, refilling her own cup. Seldom had she ever seen Lenore in such a state, and it troubled her deeply to see it now.

"You know, Aunt Miriam says there's nothing like a good cup of tea to ease your miseries. Aunt Selma, who, as you know is on the pudgy side, says that it's not actually the tea but the shortbread cookies that accompany it. She's convinced that sugar has a healing property when it comes to sorrow, although I haven't really noticed it as such. Still, I really haven't done much to prove it one way or another." She replaced the tea cozy over the pot to keep it warm and looked back to her friend. Lenore was now sipping her tea, and Abrianna breathed a sigh of relief. Goodness, but life could be complicated.

When Lenore finally put the china cup back on its saucer, Abrianna smiled. "I know that doesn't solve whatever is wrong, but I'm hopeful that it will allow you to speak about what's got you so upset."

Lenore nodded. "I'm sorry to be in such a state. I've hardly slept at all, and when I slipped out this morning, I didn't even tell Cook where I was going. I simply ordered the carriage and came here."

Abrianna smiled. "Just as you should when you are bearing overwhelming sorrow. Now, start from the beginning and tell me what's wrong. We shall resolve the matter before you know it."

"This has no solution. I can't change who I am or how old I am."

A frown came unbidden to Abrianna's face. Here she was trying her best to keep a smile, but confusion over Lenore's statement caused her great consternation. "What exactly are you saying? Who wants you to change?"

"Kolbein." Lenore looked very much like she might again burst into tears, so Abrianna reached for the teapot.

"More tea?"

Lenore shook her head. "No. I promise you I am more composed now."

Abrianna nodded. Apparently Aunt Miriam's assessment of tea was correct. "So please tell me what has distressed you so. I'm afraid you have me positively beside myself in worry."

"Kolbein thinks I'm too young to marry."

The statement was delivered in a matter-of-fact manner, leaving Abrianna to wonder what the real trouble might be. Surely her age wasn't the real problem. She looked to Lenore, waiting for more to follow. It didn't.

Hoping her words didn't sound callous, Abrianna shrugged.

"To one man a person is too young. To another, too old. Who can understand the mind of a man? Aunt Selma is convinced they cannot form what she calls 'reasonable living thought.' By that she means they can do all manner of intellectual reasoning and such, but when it comes to day-to-day living, they are often . . . well, these are her words, not mine: 'They are simpletons.'"

Lenore looked at her with a pained expression. "Kolbein is no simpleton, but he is . . . unreasonable. He thinks that just because I'm twenty, I am too young to know what my heart wants. He measures this by the fact that his sister is just nineteen. But honestly, Abrianna, there is a lot of growing up between nineteen and twenty. Not only that, but I'm soon to be twenty-one."

"It's true," Abrianna said, nodding. "I changed my opinions and views considerably between last year and this. I suppose someone Kolbein's age just can't appreciate what we women go through."

"I'm so afraid, Abrianna. What if I cannot convince him otherwise?"

"Perhaps you shouldn't try." Lenore looked at her as if she'd gone mad. Abrianna continued. "I only mean that perhaps you should isolate yourself from his company and give him time to reconsider. It's been my experience with men—I only have Wade to go on—that they need time to evaluate their mistakes. It seems to take them longer to realize the error of their ways, but with Wade, absence always seems to help."

Lenore nodded. "I suppose you're right. If I do nothing to reach him, then he will have to come to me. It's just that I cannot lose him, Abrianna. He is my heart and soul. My thoughts are centered around him these days, and I find I can scarce think about anything else."

To Abrianna this sounded like some sort of madness, but

she wasn't going to suggest such a thing. Obviously, her friend was in pain, so it stood to reason that she might say things that made no sense.

"I suppose," Lenore continued, "Kolbein believes me incapable of taking care of a household, a poor man's household." She grew thoughtful. "That's it, Abrianna. He's only worried because I've lived a life of ease and know very little about handling my own house. Goodness, I should have thought of this before." She perked up considerably. "Kolbein is simply concerned that I can't cook and clean for us. He mentioned his sister's naïveté and no doubt worries that I would be the same."

Abrianna had no idea if that was the real problem or not, but Lenore seemed at least partly recovered from her sorrows. "That's easily resolved," Abrianna said, realizing what needed to be done. "You must enroll in the school here. My aunts can teach you all you need to know."

"Mother would never approve," Lenore said, shaking her head. "Not if I were to enroll on a formal basis. Perhaps we could speak to Mrs. Madison and explain my dilemma. She might take pity on me and help us to figure another way."

"I suppose it's possible. Maybe she would allow you to simply come here every day and study with the other girls." Abrianna had a painful but acceptable thought—acceptable if it would help Lenore. "If I tell her that I, too, will study alongside you, she would be most encouraged to give it a try. She's always vexed that I manage to avoid her tutorage. I don't believe it to be without merit, but I do dread it." Abrianna touched her hands to her breast. "But for you, I would attempt most anything."

Lenore smiled for the first time since her arrival. "You are a dear, dear friend, Abrianna. If your aunts would help to train me in secret, I'm sure I could make some excuse for being here every day. Perhaps I could tell Mother that I'm giving you instruction." She frowned. "No, that won't work. Mother would ask why the ladies themselves weren't able to manage this."

"What if you were simply honest with her? The discussion might be uncomfortable," Abrianna said thoughtfully, "but the alternative might be even more so. You could explain to her that you will be twenty-one in August and that if you aren't allowed to train in secret, then you will enroll formally in the autumn. Since Aunt Miriam posts the names of the new young ladies in the newspaper, your mother might be willing to forgo what she would see as humiliation in order to keep things quiet."

Lenore nodded. "Abrianna, you are brilliant. And it wouldn't be a lie. If Mother and Father won't allow me to come here and train every day, I shall do exactly that."

"Of course," Abrianna said, fearing she'd gone too far, "you don't want to dishonor them. The Bible says you must honor them that your days would be long. I really want you to have many years of life. I couldn't bear to think of you dying young because I gave you bad advice."

"Oh goodness, Abrianna, you do go on. Don't you see? This would be a way of honoring them. By taking my courses in secret, they won't feel shamed by their peers. It's a perfect solution. I will train with your aunts—if they'll have me, and Kolbein will realize I'm more than capable of becoming his wife."

Abrianna hated that it was the perfect solution. She realized the sacrifice would force her to spend her days cooking and sewing rather than stealing out to seek aid for her friends. Maybe she could learn to sew well enough that she could make shirts for the old sailors. She frowned and shook her head. Maybe she could just learn to make them a handkerchief.

It wasn't easy to convince her parents that afternoon, but Lenore knew they saw the reason in her desire. They seldom denied her, and given she was willing to protect their reputation, Lenore knew they would acquiesce.

"I never thought to have a daughter of mine involved in such an arrangement," Mother said, looking a bit pale. "But if you are certain this is what you wish . . ."

"I am, Mother. I want very much to be a good wife for Kolbein. I've told you both how much I love him. He might not be wealthy now, but I know he will be one day. I feel confident of it, because he is so driven to work hard. Perhaps he will even go into politics. He has spoken about the possibility of getting involved. He has great experience with handling cases involving the government, and I believe he would make a wonderful senator." This caused her father to perk up.

"Having a son-in-law who is a senator would definitely be a great honor." He looked at Lenore. "Of course, he will first have to ask for your hand, and as of yet he hasn't done so."

Lenore ducked her head so they couldn't see her frown. She had no way of knowing if this plan of hers would convince Kolbein to move forward with their marriage plans, but she had to try. "I know he has planned to," she said softly. "He believes that courtship has no other end." Composing her expression, she looked up with a smile. "I know he will come to you very soon to ask for my hand. I feel certain of it."

She knew her parents had been completely surprised by her request, but now as they considered all that was involved, Lenore could also see them accepting the thought.

"But you would not live at the school as the other young ladies do," her mother said. "I couldn't bear that. Someone would be sure to find out."

"Of course not," Lenore replied. "I would simply go on the pretense of visiting Abrianna each day. No one"—she lowered her voice—"not even our servants need to know otherwise, and I'm certain the girls at the school can keep it a secret."

And with that the matter was resolved. Lenore couldn't wait to tell Abrianna that her parents had reluctantly agreed. Her father had even agreed to drive her to the school each day. It looked as if all of her problems would be resolved. Of course, she would still have to convince Kolbein.

Lenore smiled. She knew Kolbein loved her as dearly as she loved him. He wouldn't just walk away from this relationship, no matter how much he worried over her age. Once she helped him to see that his fears were for naught, they could get down to the business of planning their wedding.

~~~

The next day Lenore walked into the Madison Bridal School with a newfound determination. Abrianna's aunts had been more than willing to help her once they realized that it would also mean their ward's willingness to train. Lenore couldn't be certain, but she thought she'd seen Mrs. Madison gaze heavenward and mouth the words *Thank you.* She could be mistaken, but it did appear that way.

"First we will work in the kitchen," Mrs. Madison declared as Abrianna joined them. "Come now. I will show you first and foremost how to organize and stock a well-planned kitchen. This is important if you are to manage meals in a consistent and easy manner. Remember, having things in their place and ready at the hand will make all the difference in making a good meal and not feeling overstressed about the preparations."

Lenore took up the apron Abrianna offered at the door to the kitchen. She could see the resigned expression on her friend's face and couldn't help but smile. Abrianna seemed to believe domestic duties were akin to medieval torture, but Lenore hoped that with time her friend might believe otherwise. All she wanted for Abrianna was to see her settled with a husband of her own. Lenore knew this would keep her friend from sneaking around the streets of Seattle.

Mrs. Madison took them through detailed lists of the proper spices needed for the kitchen and then moved on to the basic ingredients that no kitchen should be without. Lenore made a list with the pencil and paper Mrs. Madison had given her. Flour, sugar, salt, soda, vinegar, baking powder, cornstarch, lard, eggs, butter, cream, and milk. Mrs. Madison assured them both that with these simple things a young woman could make a wide variety of foods. Lenore wasn't at all certain how that might work, but she was anxious to learn.

Next came information on fruits and vegetables and finally meats. Lenore took special note of Mrs. Madison's grave warnings concerning the latter.

"Spoilage has left many a man ill . . . some even dead," she declared. "Meat should be purchased sparingly. I do not allow for it to be bought more than a day before it is intended to be cooked. There are those who rely on ice to keep the meat fresh, but I know from experience that this is sometimes not as beneficial as one might think."

Lenore felt armed with knowledge by the time the day came to a close. She also realized as Father arrived to take her home that she hadn't once given in to her fears that Kolbein might never see her again. She was confident that he would think the matter through and realize his mistake. Not only that, but she and Abrianna had prayed about the entire situation and would continue to do so. With God on their side, there was nothing they couldn't accomplish. The only thing Lenore questioned was whether or not God was on their side. It was always possible that He didn't want Lenore and Kolbein to marry, but she found that most impractical. The Bible said in Psalms that God gave you the desires of your heart. If God indeed put the desire to marry Kolbein in her heart, then certainly He would see the marriage to completion.

Abrianna knew she had put Wade off long enough. She hadn't really intended her distance as a punishment—at least not at first. Now realizing that this was exactly her heart, Abrianna felt terrible. Wade had been her dearest friend for such a long time and to purposefully punish him for trying to keep her safe was not the heart of someone who cared as deeply for her friend as Abrianna did Wade.

She had never been one to balk at apologies, but trying to figure out what to say to Wade had been most difficult. She hadn't been sure he would feel much like forgiving her after Abrianna had kept him waiting. The clear snubbing might have caused him to forgo their friendship, and that grieved Abrianna in a way she couldn't bear.

When Aunt Miriam announced that Wade would be coming to the school on Friday evening to repair some loose spindles on the third-floor staircase, Abrianna felt confident it was God's way of telling her that the right time had come to apologize.

Wade arrived shortly before supper and enjoyed a meal with

the ladies and their students. Abrianna sat quietly in her regularly appointed place and focused on the food rather than the conversation. She knew her aunts would think her ill, but she felt her silence was a sort of penance for her heartless actions. Sharing in the discussion was one of Abrianna's favorite things, so fasting from this action seemed an appropriate way of proving her remorse.

After dinner she helped with the cleanup and then went in search of Wade. She found him working to glue a final spindle in place. The timing seemed given of God.

"Might I have a word with you?" she asked rather ceremonially.

Wade looked up and his expression was pained. Abrianna realized she'd caused him deep sorrow, and her heart grew heavy. "I want to apologize. I have been most grievously wrong and have caused you hurt. I know it was because of my own selfishness that I acted in such an abominable way. I assure you it was not my desire." She paused, relieved to see that he'd halted in his work to sit down on one of the steps and give her his full attention.

"I sometimes hate being a woman, as you well know," she continued. "I find it most difficult to do the things I feel God would have me do. It truly isn't to satisfy my own desires, I assure you. I want to be obedient to the tasks that He has given me. I know those tasks seem most unlikely for a woman, but I am not imagining that God has called me to help the indigent."

"I don't doubt it, either, Abrianna. What I do doubt is that you're supposed to do it alone. You used to let me help you. You didn't seem to resent my assistance then, so why now?"

Abrianna sighed. "I don't resent your assistance. I resent that I need to have it." She pursed her lips. "It isn't easy to be me."

He chuckled. "I don't imagine it is. Grief, Abrianna, you are more stubborn than anyone I know. Taking help from someone doesn't mean you are weak or a lesser person. I think God never intended for any of us to have to do things all alone."

"Of course you're right, and I deserve that correction," she said, humbling herself. She looked at him and smiled. "You are my best friend, and I do not wish to worry you or cause you concern. If you want to help me in my ministry, then why should I deny you?"

"I do want to help you. If only to keep you safe. You have no idea how desperate some men can be. When I saw you out there with the night watchman, I feared the worst. I can't bear the idea of anyone hurting you, Abrianna. You have been a part of my life for so long now that I can't imagine it without you."

She nodded at this. "And I feel the same. You have been a dear friend. No, you are a dear friend and brother to me, and I have ignored the value of that. I was wrong, and I hope you will forgive me." She extended her hand as if they were settling a contract.

Wade reached out and took hold of her hand. "Of course I forgive you. Will you forgive me for being so bossy and harsh?"

Abrianna squeezed his fingers. "Of course." She smiled, finally feeling at peace. "How could I do anything else?"

20

Lenore hadn't been home long when a maid came to fetch her. "Mr. Booth has come to pay you a visit, Miss Lenore. Should I tell him you are indisposed?" She glanced to the dressing table where Lenore sat working to rearrange her hair and then back to meet her mistress's face.

"No!" Lenore all but yelled. She hurriedly replaced her hairpins. "Tell him I'll be right down. But first, please do up the buttons on the back of my gown." Lenore turned to present the maid with her back.

The girl did as instructed, then headed for the door. Lenore stopped her. "Have him wait for me in the music room."

"Yes, Miss Lenore." With that, the girl curtsied and hurried from the room.

Lenore appraised her hair and gown. Her first desire upon returning home was to change from her rather soiled gown, and now she was very glad she hadn't taken the trouble to bathe first. The clock chimed four as Lenore made her way from the room and down the stairs. She could only pray that Kolbein had come to his senses and would offer her no further argument about her age.

"Please, God," she whispered, "let him see that I am not a child but a woman quite capable of being a wife to him." She paused, lifting a smile to the ceiling. "And please let me be a capable woman."

She made her way to the music room, stopping only long enough to order tea and refreshments. Sweeping into the room as though she hadn't a care in the world, Lenore found a most repentant Kolbein.

He held out a bouquet of flowers first and then spoke. "I've come to apologize for my beastly behavior."

She smiled and took the bouquet. Breathing in deeply of the various scents, she couldn't help but be pleased with his contrite spirit. God had surely answered her prayers.

"I knew you would," she finally said with more confidence than she'd originally felt. "You are a man of reason, after all. I knew that given a little time, you would clearly understand that your fears were for naught."

"Then you were much wiser than I," he said, hands held out in apology. "I am so sorry for my reaction to your age. I'm afraid I was terribly caught up in my worry over Greta. Your line of reasoning, however, helped me to better see what a tyrant I had become to my sister. I have to admit—that was hard for me."

"Why don't we sit and you can explain," Lenore said, moving to the settee.

Kolbein very properly pulled up a chair and sat directly opposite her. "I couldn't bear thinking that I might lose you. I realized that your physical age wasn't at all important, at least not in our case. I know that you're a responsible young woman with a good head on your shoulders. Greta too. I'm afraid I never gave her credit for having grown up."

"Is that why she ran away?" Lenore asked gently.

"Yes. She saw herself as full grown and capable, and I did not." He sighed. "Now she is lost to me. Maybe forever."

"You don't believe that," Lenore countered. "If you did, you wouldn't be here. I will not allow this apology to turn into a party of pity for all your regretful actions." She softened her words with a coy smile. "Besides, there are far more interesting things to discuss."

He returned her smile and leaned back into the chair. "Such as?"

"Such as . . ." She fell silent as the maid delivered the tea cart. Atop were several plates of cookies, cakes, and fruit. Cook had chosen her grandmother's Foley with its delicate floral pattern for the teapot and china. When the maid offered to pour, however, Lenore waved her away.

"I'll manage. Please leave us now and pull the doors closed."

Lenore reached for the pot. "As I recall, you drink it with one lump of sugar."

"I do. How very observant of you."

"A good wife needs to be observant. That's what I started to tell you, but I didn't want to be overheard. You see"—she leaned in and lowered her voice as Kolbein bent forward slightly—"I am taking classes on how to run a household."

"You?"

She poured the tea and laughed in a light lyrical manner. "Of course, me. I realized that you were right in the fact that I was immature when it came to running a household on my own. I have been trained to order servants around, but as far as being wife to a poorer man . . . well, there are a great many things I do not know." She saw him frown and shook her head. "Don't be like that. You probably worry about taking me away from a life of ease, but I assure you I can handle whatever comes my way. Especially after my classes are complete."

"Classes at Mrs. Madison's school?" he asked, taking the offered saucer and cup. He picked up the dainty silver spoon on the saucer and stirred the tea. "Are you now one of the bridal school students?"

"I am. Well, not exactly like the others," she said, pouring a cup of tea for herself. "I will be there only during the day. My father is taking me on the pretense of visiting Abrianna, who, by the way, is training with me."

"She must be overly excited about that," he teased.

"You know her well. Of course she wasn't excited, but she agreed for my sake. We are to receive private instruction from one of the aunts while the others take care of the students elsewhere. We are keeping it all very private, lest Mother and Father be shamed by their peers."

"I see. And when does this schooling begin?"

She offered him a plate with cakes, but he shook his head. Replacing it on the tray, Lenore picked up her cup and saucer. "It started today. I have learned all about stocking a proper kitchen. Tomorrow we are to learn about stoves—how to manage them, clean them, and build a perfect fire. I'm quite excited actually."

He roared with laughter, taking her completely by surprise. "Oh, Lenore. You do give me great delight. You have done this all to impress upon me that you are able to keep house for me, and I am deeply touched."

Shrugging, Lenore sipped the tea. What else could she do? After all, she would have to manage the house for herself on a lawyer's salary. Perhaps when she came into her trust, Kolbein would allow them to move to a bigger house and have a servant or two, but for now she was content to do what she could to serve him.

"I am hopeful that my studies will advance quickly, and by the time the bridal ball arrives, we can be married."

He all but choked on his tea. Hurrying to use his napkin to dab at splotches that had escaped to his clothes, Kolbein looked up to find Lenore grinning. She was pleased to have shocked him.

"Does that seem too soon to you?"

"It's less than a month, is it not?"

Lenore nodded. "Yes. The ball will take place Friday the fifteenth of June, and I would like to be married on the sixteenth."

"And you don't think it too soon to hold a wedding?"

"You do?"

Kolbein shook his head. "No. I would marry you today if I thought we could ever convince your parents."

Realizing she had him exactly where she wanted him, Lenore continued. "I will manage Mother and Father. What I need to know is if you intend to take the matter of matrimony seriously? After all, there are several things I need to plan out, and since I will be very busy with my training, I must know what your intentions are."

He put the cup down and stood. Without a word he joined her on the settee and took the tea from her hands and placed it on the table.

"I think you know what my intentions are," he said, turning to pull her into his arms.

Lenore didn't try to stop him. She rather liked that he was embracing her in such a possessive manner. She knew her heart and mind belonged to him, and one day soon her body would, as well.

He kissed her quite passionately. The depth of his devotion and adoration was completely conveyed in that kiss, and Lenore did indeed feel confident of his intentions.

Pulling away, Kolbein reached up to touch her cheek. "I hope I've made myself understood."

"Completely." She met his gaze—his face only inches from hers. His eyes seemed to pierce her heart. How easily she had fallen in love with this man.

"Then I will ask for your hand," Kolbein said, getting to his feet. "Where is your father?"

"In his study. It's the room just down the hall to the right." She smiled and picked up the tea cozy that had been placed on the tray. "I'll just wait here and keep the tea warm."

Kolbein grinned. "I doubt I'll care much about tea when I return."

Wade had just completed sanding the piece of lumber that would become a wagon seat when his shop door opened and to his surprise Priam Welby entered.

"Good day, Mr. Ackerman," Welby said, coming to where Wade worked.

"Mr. Welby," Wade replied with a nod. "What can I do for you today?"

"I need to order two wagons to be built."

Wade raised a brow in surprise. "Two?"

"Yes. You see, my import business is expanding. As you might also know, Mrs. Madison has finally agreed to allow me the purchase of her building."

"Yes, I knew that," Wade replied. "I'm actually glad she did. Those ladies need to be out of the area. It's just not safe this close to the wharf."

"I completely agree," Welby said, dusting his suit sleeve. "It took more work and negotiation than I've ever faced before. I swear, dealing with a woman is far more difficult than a man. With a man you know where you stand, and you aren't afraid to let him know what you want. With a lady you must be much more delicate and . . . creative."

"I can't see Mrs. Madison being all that delicate in negotiating much of anything," Wade said with a laugh. "That woman could run the city and make a profit."

"Indeed. Well, that's behind me now. I have agreed to allow the occupation of the building until after the annual ball. She said it would be too difficult to stage a ball at the new house so quickly after moving."

"And where is the new house?" Wade had been curious about this little detail since Mrs. Madison first mentioned it.

"In Lower Queen Anne. I purchased one of the grander homes some time back with the thought that it might one day be my residence. However, while I began immediate repairs and improvements, this opportunity was much too important to pass up. Since Mrs. Madison felt the house met all of their needs, including a third-floor ballroom and extensive outdoor lawns and gardens, I am quite content that it belong to her."

"Especially since it gets you what you want."

Welby nodded. "Exactly so, and isn't that what the art of negotiation is all about?"

"I suppose so," Wade replied. "It surprises me that you are so intent on that particular building."

"Well, if you've been keeping apprised of the real estate market, then you'll know that there is little available in this area. It suits my needs perfectly, since I already have space purchased near the docks."

"I'm just glad to see the women away from such a dangerous

location. Kolbein Booth arranged twenty-four-hour guard service, but I was never certain it would be enough."

"Yes, well, Mr. Booth is a man of many surprises," Welby replied, sounding none too happy. "I suppose he did as he felt necessary, but truly, if he would have just encouraged the ladies to move sooner, he wouldn't have had to bother."

"I don't think it was a bother to him." Wade wiped his hands on the leather apron. Walking over to a work desk, he took up a pad of paper and a pencil. "Now, why don't we get down to business. What kind of wagon do you have in mind?"

"I want two wagons, both with false bottoms like before. They must be large enough to hold valuable art but small enough not to attract attention. I believe the hidden enclosure should be a foot deep. I want the door in the wagon bed rather than on the end."

It seemed a strange order for a man who would soon have warehousing at the Madison Building. "I guess it's none of my business, but since you are buying Mrs. Madison's place, why are you so worried about hiding your pieces of art?" Wade couldn't help but think back to the night he'd seen Welby on the dock. "Are you up to something illegal?" he asked in a blunt fashion.

Laughing without any real amusement, Welby's eyes narrowed as he sobered. "Would I admit it to you if I was? It isn't any of your business. However, if you must know, I intend to transport goods from here to other cities. I won't have those treasures taken from me by underhanded thieves. You may not be aware of it, but some of the pieces I'm bringing into the country are priceless. I have customers who will pay a considerable fee for such things, and I intend to see that nothing goes wrong in the transactions."

Wade couldn't help but feel there was more to the story than the man was relaying, but there was little he could do to force Welby to admit to wrongdoing.

"What dimensions do you need and how much weight should they be able to haul?"

Taking down every bit of information provided him, Wade looked over the details. "This won't be cheap."

"I don't care." Welby reached into his coat and took out a wallet. He counted out five fifty-dollar bills. "I'm thinking this should handle the cost, but if not, you are more than welcome to furnish me with a bill for the remainder."

Two hundred fifty dollars was double what Wade had planned to ask. Even with the steel axles for the heavier weight, he would still make a hefty profit. But as much as he disliked Welby, he couldn't cheat him.

"This is double what they're worth," Wade said, pushing the money back.

Welby held his gaze and slid the money back to Wade. "This is what I'm willing and determined to pay. With it comes a fee for your silence. I don't want anyone to know about the wagons. It would, after all, defeat the purpose of secrecy."

Wade looked at the money and then returned his focus to the man before him. "All right. If that's the way you want it." He could think of no reason that it would be wrong to keep the matter between them. "When do you need them?"

"The sooner the better."

21

Abrianna knew better than to sneak out of the building and head to Wade's, but she was most desperate. For over a week she had been faithful to remain inside, busying herself by attending classes with Lenore and sewing diapers for the poor soiled dove who by now had probably despaired of Abrianna ever coming to her aid.

She wouldn't have broken her promise, but Wade hadn't bothered to show up in days, and getting a message to him was just as difficult as slipping out of the building. There was nothing she could do but hope that everything would work out.

"Besides, it's broad daylight. No one is going to bother me," she announced to no one. It was ridiculous the way everyone worried about her. "The biggest trouble I'll have is dealing with the mud and stench." She was glad she'd chosen to wear one of her older and shorter skirts. At least this way she wouldn't drag the hem through the mud and give herself away should Aunt Miriam see the results.

Making it to Wade's place without any problem, Abrianna smiled when she saw Thane approaching from the opposite direction. With this new male protection she felt confident Wade would be less inclined to scold her.

"Thane, you are a welcome sight," Abrianna declared.

"Give me that," he said, motioning to the heavy load Abrianna carried. She shifted the large basket of goods and happily handed it over. "This weighs a ton. What were you thinking? Is this food for Wade?"

"No. I need to get over to Washington Street and deliver these to a poor woman who had a baby a while back. She has no one to help her but her . . . her . . ." Abrianna frowned. What were they? Associates? Sisters of the night? "She hasn't anyone who cares for her. I'm hoping to talk Wade into accompanying me there."

She said the latter as they entered the shop. Thane came in behind her, both pausing to scan the room for Wade.

"Wade?" she called.

When he didn't reply, Thane put the basket on the nearby desk and went to search out Wade's private quarters. Returning, he shook his head. "He's not here."

"Well, if that doesn't just put a hole in the ice." She shook her head. "I haven't ever known him to be gone at this hour of the day. You would think the man might have the common decency to let folks know if he doesn't plan to keep regular hours. Not only that, but he left the shop door unlocked. What if I'd been here to rob the place?" Abrianna found the entire situation unacceptable. "I suppose we shall just have to go without him."

"We? You want me to take you to one of the worst neighborhoods in town? I didn't bargain for that," the redheaded man said, looking most apprehensive. "If I were to take you there, Wade would beat me and hang me off the pier. You know how protective he is of you, Abrianna."

"I do, but he trusts you. All I want to do is to take this basket to a mother in need. It's no fault of hers that she has no one. Poor girl fell into bad times and has supported herself the only way she thought available. I promised her this stuff more than a week ago, and I can't put it off any longer. If you won't come with me, I'll go by myself."

"No, you won't. I'll drag you back to the school, if need be," Thane threatened. He took a step toward Abrianna. "Or I'll tie you up in here, and we'll both wait for Wade's return. I have a feeling he might want to give you a good whipping just for sneaking down here without an escort."

Abrianna dodged around a wooden table. "You wouldn't. I'm just doing what God has called me to do. Grief and mercy, you would think you and Wade owned me."

Thane laughed at this. "You aren't a prized boat or horse, but you *are* a woman, and you need to conduct yourself as such."

"Well, you both make me feel like a helpless child. And I'd just made peace with Wade about all of this. He promised to help me with my endeavors. I've been nothing but patient, but he didn't come to see us two days ago as I expected."

Then, without so much as a greeting, Wade came in from the back way carrying several boards on one shoulder. He stacked the wood carefully before turning to question Thane. "What in the world is she doing here?"

"You might ask *me*. I'm standing right here. I don't know why you think acting in such a way is a gallant thing to do." Abrianna crossed her arms. "I'm quite dismayed."

"I wasn't trying to be gallant. How did you get here?" Wade asked. "I could hear you caterwauling clear out back."

"I wasn't caterwauling. I was trying to convince Thane to help me."

Wade studied her with a look that left Abrianna little doubt she had only just opened this Pandora's box. "Abrianna, what were you trying to get Thane to help you with?"

She knew Wade was already fearing the worst. "It's nothing bad. I just wanted to deliver some things to a poor woman who happens to be a new mother. I came here first because I told you I wouldn't go alone."

"So you left the safety of your home and ventured here to find me?"

"Well, yes. I knew you wouldn't approve, but this was a situation that demanded I risk your ire. Nevertheless, I came here rather than going to my friend alone."

"And just where is your friend?" Wade asked.

Abrianna looked at Thane, who just crossed his arms against his chest and made it clear he wasn't going to get in the middle of this mess. Glancing back at Wade, she could see he was reaching the end of his patience. "Washington Street." She held up her hands before Wade could protest. "She's alone in this world, forced to work the most depraved of jobs. She recently gave birth but she has no family and no friends. She's facing certain death, and we must help her. I have diapers and food for both her and the baby."

"So you just figured you'd risk everything to see to her needs?"

"I came here first," Abrianna protested. "Although now I'm not sure why I bothered. Goodness, but men can be so changeable. You told me you would help me."

Wade seemed to settle down at this, and Abrianna hoped he would remember his promise and stop chastising her. If not, she might not get back before Aunt Miriam realized she was missing.

"Please, Wade. You promised." She looked at him with all the hopefulness she could muster. "This woman has nothing. I just want to offer her some kindness. Imagine her and her baby lying there in the cold, hungry and out of food. She probably hasn't eaten in days and can't even nurse her babe. Oh, when I think of it, I imagine the baby Jesus and His mother." She paused to gauge the effect of her words.

"Of course, Mary wasn't a soiled dove, and Jesus is our Savior, but imagine them being without kith or kin in Bethlehem. It just pains me to imagine such a lonely existence, with no one there to dry a tear or offer a word of comfort. Oh, what must the Lord think of us who have so much and yet we give nothing?"

Wade pulled off his leather apron. "Well, I can see I'm not going to get anything else done unless I give in." He tossed the apron on the table. "You going to join this madness, Thane?"

"I suppose I might as well. Two bodyguards are better than one."

Shaking his head, Wade dug out the key so he could lock his door. "I'm not sure she even needs us. Frankly, Abrianna would most likely just talk her assailant to death."

Kolbein escorted Lenore from the party being held by the law firm he'd recently joined. It was, as Kolbein was told, a yearly event to celebrate their founder's birthday, and while he was all for the festivities, his heart wasn't in it. It had been over two months now, and still Greta was nowhere to be found.

"You are awfully quiet tonight," Lenore said once they were outside. "Did I do something wrong?"

He looked at her, not really understanding why she would ask such a question. "You've never done anything wrong. I've always been the one to cause you grief."

She smiled. "We have not had grief in our time together, just simple misunderstandings."

"I see your driver is just down the street. Shall I hail him or would you rather walk?"

"I'd like to walk. It's so nice to be on your arm, and I want it to last forever." She smiled up at him, making Kolbein momentarily forget his sorrow.

"You do remember that Father and Mother were hesitant about us marrying so quickly?" she asked, not waiting for an answer. "Well, when I suggested we could marry the day after the bridal ball, they agreed and will plan to host the wedding at our home on the morning of the sixteenth, just as I had hoped. Mother is already fast at work, demanding her friends repay favors given them.

"Mother wants to have a glorious garden wedding." Lenore paused and looked up at him. "She's certain that everything will be in full bloom—the azaleas and rhododendron should be glorious by that time and the roses, as well. Mother hopes to have roses everywhere, even if she has to bring them in from elsewhere."

"And if it rains?" Kolbein fell silent as he spied a theatre advertisement in the window of one of the businesses. The woman in the grainy image caused him to move away from Lenore momentarily.

"What is it, Kolbein?" Lenore asked, coming alongside. She looked at the poster. "Are you wanting to see this new troupe perform? I've heard that they're quite good. They have a wonderful actress in the lead. She's received great reviews. I can't remember her name just now."

"It's Greta." He reached out to touch the glass. Behind it the image left him certain that his sister was now this much-lauded leading lady.

Lenore bent forward to give a closer look. "Your sister? But it says the actress's name is Lavinia Longmont."

"Lavinia is her middle name, and I suppose Longmont is her married name. It's a poor photograph, but I'm certain it's her."

"That's wonderful. Then you'll know where to find her. Oh, Kolbein, I'm so happy for you—for us. She can be a part of our wedding."

He shook his head. "You don't understand. She's an actress." It sickened him to even say the word. He'd heard about the kind of debaucheries that took place in the world of theatre.

"But she's alive and well and, from what I hear, very talented."

"But an actress. I can't believe she'd stoop to that." He looked at Lenore with great sadness. "Our parents would be mortified."

"Well, since they aren't here to see her, perhaps you could refrain from doing the same. Honestly, Kolbein, I don't understand your distress. It might not be the best venue for your sister, but perhaps her husband brought her into the theatre. You did say that she'd recently married, so perhaps this is something they do together." She paused and looked closer at the poster. "She's beautiful and while I do understand that the theatre isn't the perfect place for anyone, she does seem to be talented. Perhaps you should be happy for her."

"Happy? My sister is living a life of . . . of . . ."

"It could be much worse, Kolbein. She might have . . . ended up . . . in other types . . . of work." Lenore stressed the words in her slow methodic delivery. "Things too shameful to even mention."

Kolbein let out a long breath. He knew Lenore was right. He had to look at this with different eyes. Life had changed so much for them both, and now Greta was living the way she wanted. At least he hoped so. There was always the possibility that she'd been forced into this position, although that hardly seemed likely.

"I need to see her." At least then he could ascertain for himself whether she was safe and happy.

"But of course. You could go to the theatre tonight. They might be rehearsing. They're having a performance tomorrow night."

"No. I wouldn't want to risk it. If she's not there and hears about me coming to find her, she'll flee."

Lenore took hold of his arm. "You don't know that. She has a means of support now and an audience that obviously adores her."

He looked to the picture but felt strangely numb. For so long he had feared the worst for her, never once imagining that she had ventured into the theatre. He tried to clear his thoughts. There had to be something he could do. Surely he could change her mind. Perhaps he could offer to release part of her inheritance early if she willingly came home. Maybe he could have her marriage annulled.

"Kolbein, what are you thinking? You seem so far away."

He blinked twice. "I have to get her away from this. I have to figure out how to save her."

"She doesn't exactly look like she needs saving." Lenore clasped his fingers in her gloved hand. "Darling, your sister has made her own choice. Will you take away her happiness?"

"What if she isn't happy?" That thought troubled him more than he could say. "What if this is all just something forced upon her because there was no other choice? She might have married only to keep from starving to death."

"As you said before, she most likely married the young man she'd fallen for back in Chicago. It sounds to me like your sister is as inclined toward love at first sight as you are."

Kolbein felt a sense of defeat. He knew Lenore was probably right. His sister had never been one to be backed into a corner. Her act of running away had proved that much. He forced his mind to calm.

He gazed back at the poster. "What should I do?"

"Why don't we attend the performance tomorrow night?"

"And do what?"

"Enjoy ourselves," Lenore said in her light and lyrical way. "We'll attend and enjoy the play, and then perhaps we can see your sister after it's over."

"Will they let us backstage without a scene?"

"If you offer money to the man guarding the way, he'll most likely give in. My father says there's little that money can't buy. I know that you probably haven't experienced as much, but—"

"Lenore, I'm not poor." He blurted out the truth before considering if it would offend her. She looked at him oddly, but Kolbein knew that since he'd opened this door, he would have to push them both through it.

"My sister and I received a large inheritance when our parents died. I put Greta's portion into a trust and mine into investments. I did very well and would venture to say that I probably have more than your father can claim."

Her mouth dropped, and for a moment she said nothing. Finally she shook her head. He didn't know if she would be angry or hurt, but when she began giggling, Kolbein was completely confused.

"Why are you laughing?"

Lenore looked at him with delight. "Father will be beside himself with joy, and Mother will no longer worry about me ending up in the streets selling violets."

He grinned. "Were they worried about that?"

"I think they feared I'd gone quite mad wanting to marry a poor lawyer. Goodness, Kolbein, but you might have told me sooner."

"I guess I liked knowing that you loved me for me and not my money." He shrugged. "I'm sorry if I hurt you."

"Not at all," she replied. "Just remember, I will always love you whether you have plenty or nothing at all. You are my heart, and I cannot imagine life without you."

He'd never known such a burning love for anyone in his life. Pulling her close, Kolbein smelled the scent of her hair as he turned her toward the carriage once again. "You won't have to," he breathed in a whisper. "I will always belong to you and you alone."

<hr />

"Oh, Abrianna, you look so pretty," Lenore declared. "I'm so glad you agreed to accompany us to the theatre. I think this will be a very hard time for Kolbein, and I know he can use our support."

Abrianna turned to inspect her gown in the cheval mirror. "I never thought I would like to wear pink with my red hair, but it's really quite pleasant."

"Your hair is a dark red, and that makes a big difference. It isn't that orange color that some redheads bear. Although that can also be lovely," Lenore said, reaching for a pair of gloves with delicate pink embroidery. "These are the gloves that go with your dress. I'm glad I remembered to bring them."

Abrianna turned once more to watch the gown swirl into place. The bustled back flowed in layers of lace and silk, much like a waterfall. The bodice, although cut low, had been reinforced to the neck with a beautiful cream-colored tulle that hid any hint of immodesty.

"I'm sure I've never worn anything more beautiful."

"I hope you'll wear it again for my wedding," Lenore said. "I want you to be my maid of honor."

Tears came to Abrianna's eyes, and she could only nod. Imagining Lenore married had once given her cause for sorrow, but now Abrianna couldn't help but see the happiness in her friend's face as she talked of the future.

"I will very happily stand with you. I can only imagine how beautiful you'll be. Oh, Lenore, I know I said some things in the past about how our friendship will change. Perhaps the change won't be so bad. After all, we all must change in one form or another."

"It won't be bad, I promise," Lenore replied. "Now, come along. We need to hurry. Kolbein is probably already here and waiting."

Abrianna took up the fan and small purse Lenore had suggested she bring. "I feel almost like a prize pig going off to market," she said with a laugh. "However, I must say it's rather fun to play the princess for a night."

"Of course it is," Lenore said. "I've tried to tell you that for many years."

"Though there won't be any Prince Charming awaiting me, it's still a very interesting way to spend an evening."

They started to head downstairs, but Lenore stopped on the top step. "I'll be right back. I was so worried about you having your gloves that I forgot mine," Lenore said as a knock sounded on the door. "Oh, that will probably be Kolbein now. Please let him know I'll be right back."

Abrianna smiled at her friend's excitement. Apparently love's happiness was contagious, for Abrianna felt she could very nearly fly. She opened the door with a confident greeting on her lips.

"Lenore said to tell you—"

Wade stared back at her with an open mouth and eyes so wide, Abrianna feared there might well be something wrong. "Wade, are you all right? What is it? Has something happened?"

He shook his head. "I . . . uh . . . you surprised me. That's all." He continued to look at her with an expression Abrianna had never seen. "I guess you're going out this evening."

"Yes. Lenore and Kolbein have asked me to accompany them to the theatre. Kolbein believes his sister is performing there, and we are acting as his support should things go wrong."

"Go . . . uh . . . wrong?" Wade shook his head again. "What do you mean?"

"He plans to see his sister after the play. Kolbein is afraid she will refuse to see him for fear that he will interfere in her choice of career, which, of course, he has no intention of doing. Well, at first he did. You know how terribly judgmental some people can be about theatre folk. I've never understood it myself. People are just people, and acting on the stage needn't be a terrible thing. I realize there are sometimes problems when women dress too scantily or as men, but honestly, I think it's wonderful when a person finds their calling."

Wade still looked at her as though she'd just slapped him. "Honestly, Wade, are you ill? You don't look so good. Is your stomach upset? I'm sure Aunt Miriam might have something to calm it. She's in the kitchen. Come along and we'll ask her." She reached out for Wade's arm, but he refused to budge.

"I'm not sick. I'm . . . I'm just surprised. I never figured to see you all dressed up like this."

Abrianna laughed. "It's my night to be a princess. Lenore insisted, although not in the same determined way she once did. She was quite reasonable and assured me that if I honestly couldn't abide the formal clothes, I could dress more simply."

"You look really nice, Abrianna. I guess I'd never realized just how nice you could look in the right dress." He shook his head. "I didn't mean that to sound like you don't look nice other times. I've told you before that you are quite an attractive young woman."

Abrianna smiled and shrugged. "Tonight, I could almost believe you."

22

Kolbein sat in the darkened theatre, all but holding his breath. When an amber-colored glow lit the stage and the curtain went up, he found himself leaning forward in his seat. Lenore patted his arm, but he couldn't help himself. He had worried so long about Greta, had feared the worst.

The play began and right away Greta made her appearance on stage to loud applause. She waited until the clapping died down, then turned to the woman who played her mother and began her part.

She was beautiful. Her long brown hair had been carefully arranged to flow around her shoulders and down her back. She was playing the part of an eighteen-year-old of means, and she did it well. Kolbein marveled at her acting ability. Where had this come from? Had she always been so capable of making believe she was someone else?

Gone was the child Kolbein believed her to be. She walked around the stage, toying with a bouquet of flowers and then with a stack of letters. Apparently in the envelopes were numerous proposals for her character's hand in marriage.

"Oh, Mama," she said, holding the letters close to her heart.

"Whatever shall I do now? There are no less than ten suitors who would have me wed to them, but none of the proposals are from my dear Albert."

Kolbein eased back in the seat and continued to study his sister. She seemed no worse for the time and distance that had separated them. Of course it was impossible to tell from his seat, and no doubt she was wearing heavy theatre makeup, but Kolbein assessed that she looked very well. Certainly better than he had imagined.

He found it impossible to keep his mind on the story of the play but instead watched each scene for Greta's appearance and lines. She delivered her memorized words with great passion, and Kolbein could see why the local papers had suggested her as the next Sarah Bernhardt. Throughout the various acts of the play, Kolbein felt a growing sense of peace. Greta seemed very happy, completely at ease in her role on stage. He couldn't help but wonder if she was content with her role offstage, as well.

Before he knew it, the lights came up and the play was concluded. The audience cheered and demanded that Greta and her fellow actors take several bows. She was presented with a bouquet of roses and smiled her appreciation, giving a delicate curtsy toward the crowd.

"She performs so well," Lenore declared.

"I was completely taken in," Abrianna replied. "She had me believing that she really was besotted with the penniless Albert. I was so glad that he turned out to be the long-lost son of the oil baron, and I have to say the actor who played Albert was quite dashing."

"That's her husband," Kolbein murmured. He'd noted from the play's program that the part of Albert was played by Simon Longmont.

"Truly?" Abrianna asked. Then, without waiting for a reply, as was her usual manner, she began going on and on about his acting abilities and handsome qualities.

Kolbein ignored her ramblings and looked at Lenore. He said nothing, but she seemed to understand. Putting her hand on Abrianna's gloved arm, she smiled.

"Perhaps we should make our way backstage," she suggested.

Abrianna nodded. "I think we should. In fact, I know I would love nothing more. Goodness, I had no idea I would enjoy this evening so much."

Kolbein took hold of each lady's arm. "I'll see what I can do to get us through this crowd." He maneuvered the ladies with great caution through the exiting mass. Going against the flow of people, Kolbein felt a growing urgency to see and speak with Greta. He had to know that she was well and that she was happy. He would never have chosen this life for her, but if she chose it for herself, he would, as Lenore had begged him to do, accept it.

When they approached the stage, a large man in a brown suit held out his arms to stop them. "No one's allowed backstage."

"But Mrs. Longmont is my sister, Greta." Kolbein reached into his vest pocket. "I have waited all evening to see her." He smiled and extended a five-dollar bill. "Perhaps this will allow us a moment to visit."

The man refused the money and shook his head. "We don't allow visitors, and as far as I know, Mrs. Longmont has no family other than her husband."

Kolbein grimaced at this. Greta had kept his existence a secret from her troupe. Perhaps out of shame. Or maybe in a desire to forget him. Either way, the truth of this cut Kolbein to the quick.

"Are you sure that we couldn't go back to see her for just a moment?" Lenore asked. "It really needn't take much time. I'm sure Greta . . . Mrs. Longmont would want to see her brother."

The man shook his head again. "I can't allow anyone backstage. I'll lose my position if I do."

Abrianna reached out to take hold of Lenore. "We can't have the man losing his job. Come on. I have a dear friend to whom I wish to say good-night."

She pulled on Lenore's arm and forced her to follow. Kolbein had no choice but to accompany them. As much as he wanted to see Greta, he couldn't leave his intended and her friend to suffer the crowds alone.

"What friend are you talking about?" Lenore asked.

"When we came in, I saw one of my orphan boys. This must be the theatre where they got jobs cleaning up. I'm thinking if we make our way to the workers' entrance, the boys will allow us entry."

Kolbein took hold of Abrianna and forced her to stop. "Do you really think they might? I don't want you ladies exposed to the riffraff of the alleys unless you are absolutely certain." He let go his hold, embarrassed at his impulsiveness. "Maybe you should stay here and let me go alone. The boys would surely recognize me after being with you and giving them money."

"Goodness, you worry too much." Abrianna elbowed him with a smile. "You really need to stop fretting and trust that God has brought us to this place for this time." She paused before continuing, "But I suppose there might be another guard on the back door."

"It's a chance we must take," Lenore said, looking at Kolbein. "It's worth the risk, and besides, Abrianna knows most every alley dweller in town." She touched her friend's arm. "I once thought her quite mad, but she helped me see that they, too, can be quite decent folk."

"I suppose if there's no other choice . . ." His words trailed off as Kolbein considered this madness. *I could insist on going alone, but then I would have to leave the ladies by themselves, and that would never do. Not that Abrianna would stay in one place even if ordered.* He glanced at the theatre. *If I take time to return them to their homes, Greta might well be gone by the time I get back to the theatre.* It was a most perplexing quandary. However, he didn't have to resolve it.

Lenore pulled at his sleeve. "Abrianna is leaving us." She motioned in the direction Abrianna had gone.

"That girl has no more sense than a cat," he said, taking hold of Lenore and following.

Outside, the carriages were quick to load up the theatregoers and whisk them away. Some of the homeless beggars had come to seek help from the patrons, and they quickly crowded round as the trio made their way to the alley.

"Hey, Miss Abrianna, is that really you?" one old man asked. He ran his hand down a scruffy beard. "Why, you're as pretty as a morning sunrise."

"Thank you, Shem. I see you managed to get the doctor to fix your leg." She looked back to Lenore. "Or should I have said *limb*?"

Lenore smiled and shook her head, but Kolbein marveled at Abrianna's lack of fear. She seemed perfectly at home among the street folk. It didn't matter to her that she was wearing a gown that cost enough to feed all of these people for a month. She simply loved them and moved among them as Kolbein imagined Jesus must have done with the beggars in His day.

"Now, you come to the back of the school tomorrow morning at exactly six forty-five," she told the old man. "I'll have some food you can distribute. Bring your little wagon."

"Don't got it no more, Miss Abrianna. Had to sell it," the man said apologetically.

"Not for liquor, I hope."

"No, ma'am. You had my promise not to drink again, and I'm holding firm to it. You've been too much of an angel to go back on my word. Nobody ever cared about me like you do 'cept for my mama."

Abrianna touched the old man's filthy coat sleeve. "And I'm sure she loved you dearly. Now, if you'll excuse us, we need to see someone in the theatre. Don't forget about tomorrow."

"I sure won't, Miss Abrianna. You have a good time with your friends." With that the old man scurried off to beg money from one of the well-dressed gentlemen.

Kolbein shook his head in amazement. He'd never met a woman like Abrianna. She was so rough at the edges yet so compassionate and kindhearted. As the man suggested, perhaps she was more angel than human.

Holding fast to Lenore, Kolbein followed quickly after Abrianna, who, despite the muddy alleyway, picked her way through without difficulty. Again, she approached the people gathered around the back stage door as if they were long-lost friends. He marveled at her ease with the actors who were smoking in the alley. She congratulated them on a wonderful performance and then explained her search for Toby.

"One of those cleanup boys is just inside," a tall, lean man told her. "Go ahead and see for yourself."

"Thank you so much," Abrianna said, beaming him a smile. At the back of the theatre she peeked inside the open door.

"Toby? Toby, are you in here?"

She stepped inside and Kolbein and Lenore followed her. The area was a madhouse of performers and stage crew, and the noise seemed to increase by the minute. As Abrianna led them through the onslaught, Kolbein thought it a most fascinating maze. The air smelled of cigarette smoke and body odor, but no one seemed to notice or mind.

"Toby!" Abrianna exclaimed, reaching out to hug the boy.

Kolbein saw the young man at nearly the same moment. He breathed a sigh of relief. He stood back for a moment while Abrianna conversed with him. No doubt she would have a better chance of gaining entrance than he would. Finally she motioned Kolbein and Lenore to join her.

"Toby will take us to your sister," she said. "Now, give him the five dollars that the big man wouldn't take."

Kolbein considered the demand for only a moment before reaching back into his pocket for the bill. "Thank you, Toby. I am most anxious to see my sister."

"Everybody wants to see her," Toby admitted. "She's got all sorts of folks trying to talk to her, but she don't talk to nobody. I reckon, though, she'll want to see her own brother, so I don't think anybody will get mad at me."

He led them through the back of the theatre, past the changing rooms, where most of the performers were in various stages of undress. They were laughing and chatting, as though being half clothed in the company of others was the most normal thing in the world. Toby looked over his shoulder, making certain he hadn't lost Abrianna, then paused at a door near the end of the hall.

"This is Mrs. Longmont's dressing room. She has a lady who helps her dress and fix her hair. Her name is Mabel, and she's always real nice to me." He knocked on the door, adding, "Sometimes she gives me her extra food."

"What a wonderful woman," Abrianna said. She stepped back so that Kolbein could move closer to the door.

Kolbein swallowed back his fear that he'd already missed seeing Greta. What would he do if he had? Try again tomorrow night? Send her a letter? Lenore gave his arm a squeeze as if she completely understood his fears. He placed his hand atop hers, only then realizing that he was trembling.

"Yes?" a middle-aged woman with coal-black hair said, answering the door. "Oh, Toby, what's this about?"

"Mr. Booth here is Mrs. Longmont's brother. He wants to see her."

"Ain't no one allowed to see Mrs. Longmont," she said, looking at Kolbein and the ladies as though she didn't believe their story.

"But you have to let him, Mabel. See, his sister left, and he thought she was dead. We been looking for her out on the streets for weeks now. Mr. Booth just wants to make sure she's doing all right. He won't stay long, and he don't mean her any harm."

Mabel looked skeptical. "Well, I don't know. I suppose I could ask. You wait here."

Kolbein didn't want to wait, but the woman was already closing the door. He could only pray that there wasn't another exit to the room. If Greta didn't want to see him, he knew she'd do most anything to escape.

However, it was only a moment before the door opened again and a robe-clad Greta stood in the entrance. "Kolbein! I can't believe you're here." She threw herself into his arms and hugged him. "Oh, please don't be mad at me. I didn't mean to worry you."

"Oh, Greta. I've been so afraid harm had come to you." He held her for a moment, thanking God in silence for her safety.

His little sister pulled away. "That's why I sent the letter. I didn't want you to fret. I sent it about two weeks ago. Didn't you receive it?"

"I've been in Seattle since you left. I followed you here but then lost track of where you had gone. I've had men—" he paused and looked back at Lenore and Abrianna—"and women searching all over town for you."

She looked completely dumbfounded. "Well, I never meant to cause you such worry. I know we parted on bad terms, but I've been so happy." She looked over her shoulder. "Come inside and we'll talk more." She led them into the small room. "Mabel, would you tell Mr. Longmont that I'd like him to join us here?"

"Of course, ma'am." The maid curtsied and hurried from the room through what appeared to be an adjoining door.

She gave Kolbein a sheepish smile that reminded him of when she was younger. "I suppose you must know that I've married."

"I had heard as much," Kolbein replied, uncertain what else he should say.

"I hope you will like him. He's the one I tried to tell you about. Simon and I first met when I was away at boarding school. His father and mother were administrators of the school. We became fast friends, even though the young ladies were not to have male friendships." She shrugged and smoothed down the collar of the silk wrap. "I guess I've always been good at going against the rules."

"Indeed," Kolbein said, smiling. He was so relieved to see her safe that he couldn't fault her for such behavior, much less chide her.

"I'd offer you a seat, but there's only one," Greta said.

"We don't need chairs," Abrianna said. "I'm Abrianna Cunningham. I'm a friend of your brother and his fiancée."

"Fiancée? Kolbein, are you really getting married?" Greta looked to Lenore. "Is this your bride-to-be? Oh, I thought he might never find true love."

Kolbein laughed. "I suppose I have no secrets where Abrianna is concerned. Yes, this is my intended. Lenore Fulcher, I would like you to meet my sister, Greta Lavinia Booth . . . Longmont."

"I'm so happy to meet you at last," Lenore declared. "You are a wonderful actress, and Kolbein has spoken about you with such fondness."

"I'm very glad to meet you, as well, and I thank you for the compliment. But you must forgive me for my shock. I can scarce believe my brother has proposed," Greta replied. "He's always been one to keep to himself. However did you meet?"

"We met at Abrianna's home," Lenore told her. "It's a long story but one that I hope we will have time to share in the near future."

"We'll have to," Kolbein said, "since we're to be married very soon."

Just then the dashing young actor who'd played the part of Albert joined them. He had a towel in hand and was in the middle of wiping makeup from his face. "Greta, are you all right?" He gave Kolbein a wary look.

"I'm perfectly fine, silly. Come meet my brother, Kolbein."

The man's expression grew more intent, and Kolbein couldn't help but wonder what his sister had told her husband. Kolbein sought to put the man at ease.

"I'm sure you were expecting a monster with three heads and horns, but I assure you I vanquished him before coming here and now stand before you quite at ease."

Simon gave a slight smile. "I am glad to know that he will no longer bother Greta."

Greta took hold of her brother's arm. "I hope you mean that, Kolbein. I want no trouble and desire only peace between us."

Kolbein looked at his sister with new eyes. When had she

grown up? When had she acquired a woman's heart and mind? "It seems just yesterday you were a little girl."

She let go of his arm to give a twirl. "And yesterday I was. But today I'm full grown. I love seeing new places and being on the stage." She stopped and looked toward Simon. "And I am most passionately in love with my husband."

Realizing there was little he could say, Kolbein only nodded. He loved Greta with all his heart. She was the only bit of family left to him. Lenore eased the awkwardness of the moment.

"Kolbein and I will be married soon. I would like very much for you to attend me in the wedding ceremony. Abrianna is my maid of honor, but I'd like you to be my bridesmaid."

"I would love to do that, Lenore. I have always wanted a sister, and now I shall have one." She looked to her brother. "We will be in town another month and then our troupe is traveling to California. Will the wedding occur before the end of June?"

Kolbein met Lenore's smiling face. Her eyes reflected the love he felt for her. "It will be perfect. I believe we have set the date for the sixteenth of June. It will be a late-morning wedding, so that shouldn't interfere with your performances."

Taking hold of her husband, Greta turned. "Could I have just a moment alone with Kolbein?"

"Of course." He looked to Lenore and Abrianna. "Why don't I show you ladies the prop room. I think you'll get a better idea of what we go through when preparing for our plays."

Lenore and Abrianna accompanied Simon from the room, leaving Kolbein and Greta alone. Kolbein had no idea what Greta wanted to say to him, but he hoped to interject his own thoughts beforehand.

"Greta, before you speak, I have to tell you how sorry I am for the way I behaved. You had every right to be angry—even to leave. I'm just sorry that I forced your hand in that way. You see, when Mother and Father died I felt so overwhelmed by my new responsibility. I knew I wasn't capable of being what you needed, so I sent you to the best schools, hoping someone there would be the one to meet your needs. I held you at arm's length, fearing that I would fail you. Therefore, I didn't want to be too near to you. I suppose I thought the distance would make it easier for us both. I know now that I was wrong. Seeing you tonight . . . well . . . I realize that I never allowed you to grow up—at least not in my mind's eye. I am sorry."

She put her finger to his lips. "I didn't ask to speak to you for an apology, Brother. I know how it was for us, and I always understood. It grieved me, but over time I came to realize that your love for me was just as strong as it had been, but there was the addition of responsibility for my well-being. That was a huge responsibility to put on your shoulders, but you handled it the best you could." She paused and smiled. "I wanted to speak to you alone to offer my own apology.

"I knew it was wrong to leave as I did. I was full of guilt and anguish in knowing that I had given you cause to worry and grieve. Oh, Kolbein, I never wanted to hurt you. Please forgive me."

Kolbein sighed. She truly had grown up. "It would seem we are both full of remorse and regret. Of course I forgive you, but I must know—are you truly happy?"

She laughed and tossed back her long brown hair. "I am. I have never been happier. I love acting, and while I know some think it scandalous, I find it the perfect way to share my heart with others. And Simon is the love of my life. I feel like we've known each other since the beginning of my days on earth. He is considerate and kind, and he wants only the best for me."

"I'm glad to hear it," Kolbein said. "All I want for you is that you have the life you desire. Which brings me to another topic. Your inheritance."

Greta's eyes widened. "You mean you will still allow me to have it?"

"How could I not?" Kolbein declared. "It's not my money. Even so, I hope you will be cautious. It is a great amount, and I would hate to see you swindled out of it."

She seemed to consider the matter for a moment. "Perhaps you could watch over it for me in Chicago, and when I need funds I could wire you. I know that Simon would agree that you are more knowledgeable about such things."

"I won't be in Chicago anymore, although our house there is still open to us. I haven't yet made up my mind about selling it. My life is here now in Seattle . . . with Lenore. I have taken a position at a law firm and am even now looking for a house to buy my bride. And if you wish for me to continue watching over your trust, I will happily do so from here."

"Wonderful. Then everything is resolved, and we can move forward the best of friends. Just as we should have always been."

Kolbein was humbled by her words. "You never gave up on me, and for that I'm grateful."

"Of course not, silly." Her smile broadened. "Just as you never gave up on me."

23

The planning of the bridal ball required a great deal of thought and attention to detail. For weeks, the entire school would be completely devoted to the preparations for the yearly dance. Abrianna's aunts were quite purposeful in their themes and decorations. They often spent most of their free time after Christmas each year searching through various magazines for ideas. This year had been no exception.

Aunt Poisie had talked her sister and Selma into a nautical theme in honor of her dearly departed sea captain. She reasoned that it had been ten years since he was lost at sea, and it would only be appropriate to remember him with the theme of the ball. Aunt Miriam and Aunt Selma had been hesitant at first but now agreed that it was a perfect idea.

The ladies of the school were deeply involved in the actual making and setup of the decorations. It gave the girls a creative outlet that seemed to ease the tension of wondering and fretting over whether or not they might find themselves receiving a proposal of marriage at the ball. Abrianna could only thank God that she wasn't among those young women.

Frankly, if I never marry, that will be just fine. But a longing fell upon her that she did her best to ward off. There was no sense in contemplating the matter now, with so much work to be done.

The ballroom was normally rather plain, but her aunts always managed to transform the space to a point where everyone forgot about the location and instead imagined themselves whisked away to a private retreat.

"I rather liked the Queen Victoria theme we had two years ago," Aunt Selma said, observing the progress her students had made.

"Well, we couldn't very well have it again so soon," Aunt Miriam chided. "Perhaps she will live a good many more years, and we can try it again at a later date."

"I suppose that is the sensible way to manage it," Selma replied.

Abrianna, dressed in serviceable work clothes, rolled up her sleeves and chuckled. "I wonder what the Queen of England would think to know we patterned our annual ball after her life in the palace. Goodness, but she would probably think us all mad. Imagine if she were to design her balls around a boarding school for brides."

"Oh my," Aunt Miriam said, shaking her head. "You do think of the strangest things."

"I suppose I can't help it," Abrianna said thoughtfully. "Perhaps my mother or father thought in such a manner. I wonder about it from time to time. After all, surely the actions and thoughts of one's parents would influence a child, at least in part. I mean, wouldn't it stand to reason that the blood in one's veins would give weight to one's behavior and thinking? Of course, I suppose where one lives might also conspire to sway one's temperament."

Aunt Miriam and Aunt Selma looked at her as if her words had proven their point. Abrianna could only smile. She knew that she could be quite the unusual dreamer, and that while her aunts were used to her comments and contemplations, they were also baffled by them.

"I do like those colors," Aunt Miriam said, moving the topic of conversation back to the ball. Across the room several of the young ladies were working together to hang swaths of crepe and tulle in violet gray, sea green, and turquoise blue—the latter of which did not resemble the waters of Puget Sound but rather those of the Caribbean Sea. This, Abrianna remembered, had been discussed at great length with the final verdict rendered that while the blue was unlike their own waterfront, it was indeed the color of seawater elsewhere. Aunt Poisie had this on good authority. It was exactly the color blue that her captain had described to her after one of his more lengthy voyages south. With that thought, the matter was settled.

"I believe adding the shells in our design was a stroke of genius, Sister," Aunt Poisie declared. "I'm so glad you thought to write to your friend in Florida to secure them."

Abrianna had been amazed that the shipment had arrived with most all of the shells intact. Had it not been for Aunt Miriam's specific details for packaging and shipping, they might have all been lost. With the fabric, seashells, papier-mâché, and real flowers, as well as netting, the room was taking on the appearance of a tropical paradise. At least what Abrianna imagined it might be.

Leaving her aunts to discuss what else needed attending, Abrianna slipped off to the kitchen, where Lenore was busy laboring over her most difficult project to date. A crown of lamb. Abrianna thought it looked very much like a battle had ensued between Lenore and the meat. She labored with two separate pieces to form them into a circle that could be sewn together. Just as she would have one piece in perfect order, however, the other would slouch to one side or fall over altogether.

"I don't know why you are bothering with this. Now that you know Kolbein is rich, you can hire a cook to do this for you," Abrianna declared from the door.

"If you are only here to criticize, then you may go. Otherwise, you might lend me a hand." Lenore's frustration was clear.

Crossing the room, Abrianna took up the string lying on the table. "Is this to tie it into place?"

"Yes," Lenore replied. "I never thought a little lamb could be such a devilish beast." She worked to form the ribs into a standing formation once again. "When I get this just so, you tie it together. Then I can get the ends sewn together and move forward in this process."

Abrianna did as instructed, all the while talking about Lenore's upcoming wedding. It was now just two weeks away, and already Abrianna was starting to feel the loneliness. "I shall miss you so dearly while you are away on your wedding trip. I hope you won't forget me. I just couldn't bear to think of you forgetting me. I know I shall never forget you."

"Oh, stuff and nonsense," Lenore replied. "I could never forget you. You are my dearest friend. Really more like a sister."

"And you are to me, as well," Abrianna said. "Even so, I can see how marriage will divide us. You will have your loyalties placed elsewhere while mine remain with you."

"Abrianna," Lenore said, finally managing to stitch one side of the crown together, "one day you will find true love yourself, and then you'll understand better. While I will give Kolbein my utmost devotion and loyalty, I will never stop caring for you.

To prove this to you, I will tell you a secret. I was going to wait, but I can see you need the information now."

"Do speak words of comfort," Abrianna said, knowing the words would sound overly dramatic. She smiled. "I so long to hear them."

Lenore giggled. "Well, the comfort I can offer you is this. Kolbein has found us a house. It is only a short walk from the one where you will live after the move. I specifically asked Kolbein to keep the new school's location in mind, and he quite neatly arranged to purchase a beautiful house at the end of the block."

Abrianna's mouth fell open. She couldn't help her surprise. She had never in her wildest imaginings thought such a thing possible. "Oh, that is wonderful! I am positively relieved of my grief. We shall not see our friendship fall into the vast void that might otherwise separate us."

"It's true," Lenore said, still smiling. She finished lacing the meat and then stood back to survey the little crown she'd created. "There, I think it looks fit for a king."

"King Kolbein, that is," Abrianna added.

Lenore ignored her and was already searching through the recipe for her next step. "I have already trimmed the bones to a uniform evenness," she commented while running her finger down the page of what Abrianna recognized as the *Mrs. Lincoln's Boston Cook Book*. Aunt Miriam swore complete devotion to this new cooking tool. Having only been published a few years earlier, her aunts had insisted on having several copies to use when teaching.

"It says here I'm to wrap each bone in salted pork to prevent burning." She looked up. "I suppose if the bones were blackened it would be far less appealing."

Abrianna nodded. "No doubt." Abrianna watched as Lenore wrapped each rib bone with the tenderness of a mother for her babe. She might have offered to help, but it seemed Lenore was quite caught up in her duties. With that finally managed, she wiped her hands on the apron and went back to consult the book.

"Then I'm to cover the bones with buttered paper and roast the entire thing for one and one-fourth hours."

"Sounds like your most arduous tasks are over," Abrianna said, smiling. "You will no doubt impress your king."

"Perhaps with the roast itself, but I still need to make the suggested chestnut puree to put in the middle." She shook her head. "We've only had mint sauce or jelly with lamb at home. I suppose, however, that Mrs. Lincoln knows how to prepare a proper crown of lamb."

"I would think so. After all, they took her word and created the book. Mercy, just imagine if she only made up the recipes and never tried them. We might well expect a most inedible dish of food. Aunt Miriam said it's always necessary to test out one's recipes before touting their quality."

"I'm sure Mrs. Lincoln would have done just that."

"Why, just last week I made the terrible mistake of putting in salt for sugar in my applesauce. The taste was unbearable. If I hadn't sampled it first, I might have given the entire school salt poisoning. Aunt Selma said that had we a garden, we might have used the applesauce for weed killer. Imagine that."

"Abrianna, I've been looking all over for you," Aunt Miriam interrupted, marching into the room like an agitated school-mistress. "This is the last place I would have thought to find you."

"I was helping Lenore. See here, her little crown is complete

292

with its pork covering and buttered paper. Now it is ready for the oven."

Aunt Miriam inspected the piece and nodded her approval. "You've performed the task perfectly."

"Thank you, but I doubt I could have done it without Abrianna's help. My little lamb was less than cooperative."

"They often are," Aunt Miriam agreed. She then turned to Abrianna. "I am hopeful that you managed to complete the hems for the tablecloths we'll be using at the ball."

"I did, Aunt Miriam, although I cannot say they are the best of my work. The thread kept puckering the material, and it caused me a great trial. Through prayer and considerable frustration, however, I did manage to complete the task. Although I will say I hope never again to be taxed with such a test."

Aunt Miriam rolled her eyes. "And where did you leave them?"

"In the sewing room after I pressed them. You'll find them hanging, just as you instructed."

"I shall go and inspect them and make sure your issues with the thread were completely resolved. I would appreciate it if you would go back to help the girls in making ready the ballroom. There is still a great deal of work to be done in the next two weeks."

Reluctantly Abrianna did as she was told. She would much rather have spent her time with Lenore. While it comforted her to know that Lenore and Kolbein would live nearby, the fact remained that a husband would take up a lot of Lenore's time. Abrianna knew this because Aunt Selma had often told her stories of her labors to keep Mr. Gibson happy. Apparently husbands were just as needy as children when it came to having their clothing laid out and their meals prepared. Aunt Selma had declared them to be most tiresome when seeking entertainment or consolation on long winter evenings. Of course, Lenore would have the added benefit of servants, but even then she would have to direct them and plan their duties.

The same gloom she had known earlier embraced her now. This really was to be the end of something quite precious. Their friendship would never stay the same. Not with one of them married and the other . . . well . . .

Abrianna couldn't understand the ache within her heart. She had always intended to spend her adult years working for the Lord. She had thought perhaps that someone would come alongside her, a man whom she could love. He would be completely invested in helping the poor and underprivileged. He would be kindhearted and soft-spoken. His very words would ease the worry of those around him.

She smiled to herself. Did such a man even exist?

On Sunday Wade joined the ladies for the noon meal, as he usually did. Today the fare was a delicious halibut with all manner of vegetables to accompany it. All in all, it was a very satisfying meal. Wade had been particularly surprised when Mrs. Madison announced that Abrianna had been responsible for making the dinner rolls. It would seem the hoyden was being tamed. He couldn't help but grin.

"What are you so happy about?" Abrianna asked. Several of the young ladies had already departed the table for an afternoon of leisure. On Sundays the rules were rather relaxed, and while some were off to tend to other things, there were often a half dozen or so who would linger over dessert. Today it was Mrs. Gibson's famous blackberry cobbler and homemade ice cream.

Wade shrugged. "I guess a good meal always puts me in a

mood of contentment. What about you? You seem awfully quiet today. Are you ill?"

"Abrianna is mourning her friend's upcoming marriage," Mrs. Madison declared. "Although I've assured her that Lenore will still find time for their friendship."

"Of course she will. Why would you think otherwise?" Wade asked.

Abrianna shifted in her seat and looked quite uncomfortable. "It cannot help but change everything. I'm encouraged to know they have chosen a house very close to the school's new location, but I fear there will be a substantial lessening of our time together. Kolbein will be her husband and require her full attention, and as Aunt Selma has said in the past, some husbands require a great deal of tending." She looked to her aunt with a nod.

Wade laughed out loud, receiving Mrs. Madison's frown and a startled look from Mrs. Gibson and Miss Poisie. It was Mrs. Madison who spoke, however. "As a former wife, I can vouch for this, Wade Ackerman. Men can be quite helpless at times."

"I've no doubt, but women can be just as much in need of . . . tending at times. However, my laugh was not to show disrespect. I am only amused at Abrianna's melodramatic mannerisms. One would think Kolbein intended to chain Lenore to the house. You do realize, don't you, Abrianna, that Kolbein will also be working a job—something, as I understand, he wouldn't necessarily have to do. You'll have all day to visit, if you'd like."

"It's true that Kolbein will work," Abrianna replied, "but Lenore will still need to manage her household and servants. She may have very little time to join me on my crusades or even to visit over tea."

"I seriously doubt Lenore will be interested in your crusades in the same way you are." Wade smiled sympathetically. "Few women could manage what you do."

"Speaking of which," Abrianna said, getting to her feet abruptly, "I wonder if you would accompany me to see a couple of my friends. Last we met, Barnabus had taken a summer cold, and old Mrs. Mannheim was suffering terribly from her rheumatism. I promised that I would help her clean her cupboards."

"On the Lord's day?" Aunt Selma asked in shock.

"Jesus cleansed the sick with healing on the Sabbath, and what with the restrictions you place upon me for my safety, I can hardly see to the task during the week. Sunday is one of the only days Wade has free to accompany me. Now, if you were to let me journey out on my own as I used to do—"

"No!" Wade declared in a firm tone. "I will go with you today and help you accomplish whatever is to be done." He got to his feet. "Thank you for a wonderful meal, ladies. I very much enjoyed your company and the food."

"Since you will be coming back with Abrianna when she returns home," Mrs. Madison said matter-of-factly, "I will have some food for you to take to your place then."

"Thank you. I'll never grow lean so long as I have your friendship."

"It'll be different once we move," Abrianna told him as they made their way from the dining room into the kitchen. She gathered several different things and put them in her basket. "You'll have a much longer walk."

"It's not that much farther for me. It's just a straight walk up the harbor, no more than a mile or so. Instead of walking into the heart of the city, I will simply take a different route. I'll manage it just fine."

Abrianna led the way from the kitchen and down the back stairs. "Still, it will be different. I will miss things the way they are."

"What do you mean?" Wade asked. She seemed much more serious than she'd been at dinner.

"I will miss this place and the ease with which I could slip down to your shop. I will miss the bustle of the city. We shall be on several acres and no doubt sheltered from the noise." She shrugged. "I'll miss it. I'll miss the vendors calling out their wares and the boys with the newspapers clamoring for business. I'll even miss the folks coming and going at all hours of the night."

"I can't imagine that being a loss in your life." He heard her heave a sigh and knew there was more. Something was troubling her. "What's this really about, Abrianna? You haven't been this miserable since you had to start pinning your hair up and wearing longer skirts." He grinned. "So tell me the truth. What has you so perplexed?"

She allowed him to lead her across the street before she attempted to answer. When she spoke it was in a hesitant manner that was most unlike the young woman.

"I know . . . that everything in life . . . changes. I suppose that Lenore and Kolbein's upcoming wedding has me realizing it more than ever before." Her brows knit and her face took on a worried expression. "I don't really understand what is wrong with me, but I feel . . . well . . . an empty place inside." She touched her hand to her heart. "I suppose that sounds strange, but it is a deep aching."

Wade shook his head. "It isn't all that strange. God made us to enjoy the company of other folks. Sounds to me like you're mourning a loss that hasn't happened. Lenore is just getting married. She hasn't died."

"But it's a sort of death to our friendship, don't you think? I suppose I just don't like change. Perhaps that is my greatest flaw."

He chuckled. "Abrianna, not liking change isn't your great flaw." He winked at the surprised look on her face. "In fact, I don't think you have any great flaws, unless it's taking too many chances. You are one of the most unflawed people I know. You have a heart bigger than the Pacific, and you genuinely care about what happens to the folks around you."

"But I suppose . . . oh, please don't say anything to my aunts, but I feel alone."

She looked to him with such a sorrowful expression that Wade couldn't help but stop walking. "You'll never be alone so long as I'm alive. Haven't we always had each other? Helped each other?"

He put his hand on her shoulder. "That won't change, Abrianna."

"It will one day . . . when you take a wife," she said sadly.

24

June had arrived in flourishes of flowers and greenery. The residential areas of Seattle seemed to explode in colorful gardens and beautiful lawns. The ballroom at the Madison Building was no different. Now complete in its tropical sea theme, Abrianna thought it perhaps the most beautiful ball they'd ever held.

For the sake of her aunts she had agreed to attend the ball itself rather than remain behind the scenes as a server. The young ladies who were deemed ready for marriage by the aunts were allowed to attend the dance and make permanent the relationships they'd formed with their suitors. However, those who were new to the school or less inclined to learn were assigned duties behind the refreshment tables and elsewhere.

Frankly, Abrianna had always preferred this station. Serving food to others and making light conversation about the party and weather suited her far better than trying to entertain lovesick young men. She'd been proposed to by no fewer than three complete strangers already and the evening had just started.

"You look amazing tonight," Thane told her. "You look good in that color."

He and Wade had been invited by the aunts to provide additional men for dancing. It wouldn't have been necessary, however.

The room was full of eager men who had paid to attend the yearly soirée. Many of them had regularly attended the bake sales and monthly receptions. But others in the collection were those who came annually. Abrianna thought they weren't half so interested in matrimony as they were in having a great evening of entertainment and the company of young women.

"Thank you," Abrianna said, suddenly feeling self-conscious. "Aunt Miriam chose it from the gowns Lenore had given me a while back. She's partial to lavender, so I suppose that is why this dress caught her attention."

"Well, it makes you look . . . well . . . real nice."

Abrianna knew better than to argue with Thane's assessment. Partly because she knew it wouldn't do any good, and partly because she actually felt rather pretty. Lenore's gown fit her like a glove after Aunt Selma had given it a slight alteration. Abrianna had been required to tighten her corset more than usual and was just as amazed as her aunts were at the tiny waist she'd revealed. Nevertheless, she didn't want to maintain a focus on herself.

"I'm glad you and Wade could come tonight. I fear I will die of frustration if one more man asks me to be his wife. You and Wade are the only men of whom I can be certain won't put that burden upon me."

Thane chuckled. "Well, I'd say it's a good thing we came, then. Someone needs to keep an eye on you. You've never looked more stunning. Say what you will about redheaded women not being considered beautiful, but looking at you proves it false."

"Thank you for your kindness." She looked past him to the dance floor, where couples were gliding in perfect step to the orchestra's waltz.

"I notice that you keep looking at the dancers. Are you wanting to join them? I'm not all that good at waltzing, but I'd give it a go with you."

Abrianna looked at him for a moment. His words almost didn't register. "No. I don't want to dance. I was just watching for Lenore and Kolbein. They haven't arrived yet."

"Are they still planning to attend? I thought the wedding was set for tomorrow morning."

"It is," Abrianna assured him. "But Lenore thought it would be great fun to come. She's gotten to know the girls and thought this would be a wonderful diversion from her fretting over wedding plans."

"I suppose that means everything is in order for tomorrow."

Abrianna shrugged. "I suppose it is. I wish it could be postponed for a time. Of course," she said, looking at him with a smile, "I know that Lenore and Kolbein are in love, and I wouldn't want to keep them from wedded bliss. I'm just being selfish. Lenore and Wade have been my dearest friends for most of my life. You are my friend, also, but they are the oldest. Well, their friendship has been the longest," she corrected.

"I've been quite dependent on Lenore for sharing confidences and the kind of things a young woman would share with her mother or sisters—if she had them."

"Wade told me you were worried that you were losing Lenore's friendship."

She looked at him in surprise. "He did? I wonder why. I can't imagine that he has given himself over to worry about such things. I mean, I know he cares about my feelings and well-being, but it surprises me that he would contemplate the matter of my friendship with Lenore."

"I suppose that's because it relates to those feelings you were saying he cared about. Wade is a good man with a big heart."

"Speaking of Wade, where is he?"

"Your aunt Miriam cornered him for a moment."

Abrianna shook her head and felt her long curls bounce around her shoulders. Aunt Selma had spent two hours working the mass into something presentable. "I hope she doesn't have a task for him. Poor Wade deserves to dance with the young ladies. Goodness, he might well find a bride. Now, wouldn't that be something? I've never really given it any thought until now. Imagine how that would be if you and Wade found brides here at the school. Wouldn't that be grand? You both are always here helping Aunt Miriam with one thing or another, not to mention you'll be responsible for getting us moved to the new house next week." She paused, realizing she'd never given the matter very much thought.

"Do you fancy any of the young ladies here?" she asked, looking to study his face in case he tried to deceive her. Men could be so funny about these things.

"I have noticed one or two. But one in particular. I had hoped to dance with her tonight, but apparently your aunts didn't feel she was yet ready to attend the ball." He glanced past Abrianna toward the refreshment tables.

She turned, wondering where his gaze would lead and found Militine serving punch to a couple of men. "Militine? You have feelings for her? Why, that's wonderful. She can be as clumsy as I am and just as poor of a cook, but Aunt Miriam says she's showing progress. Maybe next year she'll be able to dance with the others."

"I hope so. Of course, I hope to come more regularly to the receptions and bake sales."

Abrianna turned back to face him. "Have you told her that you're interested? I think it might give her the assurance she needs. Aunt Miriam says she's only clumsy because she lacks self-confidence. Perhaps if you shared that you were interested in courting her, then Militine would flourish like a summer flower."

"Maybe, but she also might refuse me."

"I have serious doubts about that."

"About what?" Wade asked from behind her.

His unexpected arrival took Abrianna aback for just a moment. She turned around once again as Wade joined the discussion. "Goodness, but you gave me a fright. You shouldn't sneak up on a person." She expected him to laugh and make sport at her comment, but instead he stared at her for several moments before speaking.

"You look truly beautiful, Abrianna. A fella would be proud to have you on his arm."

"I guess dressing up causes the fires of romance to stir in a man's heart. I've already been asked three times to marry and twice to court."

"Marry? Court? These buffoons?" Wade looked completely against the idea. "Most of these men wouldn't begin to know what to do with a woman like you. They wouldn't understand your desire to help the poor or to feed the orphans. They certainly wouldn't allow you to go about as you do on the docks and alleyways."

"Neither do you these days," she reminded him. "But never fear. I shall remain unmarried. I think perhaps forever. God has called me to serve Him, and marriage might well get in the way of His plans."

Wade shook his head. "God said in Genesis that it wasn't good for man to be alone. And in Ecclesiastes Solomon said that two were better than one."

"Yes," she agreed, "but Paul said it was better not to marry

303

if you were serving God. That way you wouldn't have to split up your serving. My aunts have told me on many occasions that once a woman marries, she has no time for anything but being a wife and eventually a mother. How would I serve God then?"

"Maybe as a wife and mother," Wade countered. "That's an admirable ministry in and of itself. Think of the encouragement and good you might have to offer a husband. Think of molding the young minds of your offspring and teaching them to have compassion on the poor."

"I suppose." She had considered this angle many times, but God had not sent a man into her life whom she considered worthy of her call. Maybe she was being prideful or wrong in her thinking, but any man she might consider for marriage would have to be completely devoted to God and willing to serve Him as Abrianna desired to serve.

"Oh, look. I believe Kolbein and Lenore have arrived," Thane said, pointing across the room.

Abrianna gasped. "Doesn't she look beautiful? I've never seen that golden gown before. Look at it shimmer. It's like starlight sewn into a dress."

The couple approached and Lenore quickly embraced Abrianna. "You look wonderful."

"So do you," Abrianna said. "That gown is lovely. It suits your complexion and hair perfectly. Why haven't I seen it before now?"

"I purchased it in San Francisco and only wore it once while we were there."

"So this is just the second time," Abrianna said with a grin. "I suppose that means you only have three more times to wear this queenly gown and then you'll be forced to pass it to me."

Lenore laughed. "So you are finally taking an interest in dressing in fine gowns?"

"Not really—no more than usual. I just happen to like that color, and I believe it would appear acceptable with my hair coloring and freckles."

"You're quite right it would. However, I plan to hang on to this gown for a bit. Marrying Kolbein means I will no longer be under the restrictions of my mother. I might break with all tradition and social decorum and wear it . . . six or seven times." They laughed over this and drew the attention of the men.

"What are you two hatching?" Kolbein asked. "It seems whenever these ladies get together, trouble soon follows."

"Don't I know it," Wade replied. "Keeping Abrianna out of trouble is a full-time job."

"Pity the man who marries her," Kolbein said, grinning. "She'll blind him with her beauty and then worry him to death with her antics."

"That's hardly fair," she protested.

"Maybe not, but it's true," Wade threw in. "Did I tell you about the knife she straps to her leg?"

"Better say *limb*," Abrianna corrected. "Lenore doesn't like anyone using the l-e-g word."

Lenore blushed. "Only when speaking about people. Legs are fine so long as they belong to a horse or a table."

The men laughed, but it was Wade who offered, "And limbs are on trees, so now what word shall we use?"

Abrianna grinned. "He's got you there, Lenore."

"And I have you for the next dance," Kolbein declared. He took hold of Lenore's elbow. "Shall we?"

She nodded and he led her out to join the other couples. Abrianna found Lenore's gown even more appealing in the ballroom light as she twirled in Kolbein's arms. It truly was an amazing gown, and Abrianna found it almost impossible to take her eyes off of the couple.

"Would you like to dance?" Wade asked her.

"Don't bother. I already tried that," Thane told him. "She doesn't want to dance. She just wants to stare at the people who are dancing."

"That's not exactly true," Abrianna said with a shrug. "I'd much rather be in my room reading a good book."

"And miss all of this?" Wade waved his arm toward the dancers. "You are a most unusual young woman, Miss Cunningham."

"Indeed she is," Priam Welby said, coming up from behind Abrianna. "And clearly the most beautiful woman in the room."

The interruption so startled her that Abrianna whirled on her heel to face him. She said nothing but looked upward to find the man smiling. "I have come to seek a dance," Welby continued. "In fact, I came to this affair solely with that in mind. Furthermore, I will be deeply wounded if you fail to accept a dance with me."

Abrianna drew in a long breath and let it out slowly. She knew Aunt Miriam expected her to join the others in merrymaking. "I suppose I can dance with you . . . once," she said, looking from Wade to Thane as if she hoped they might rescue her.

"She could," Wade said, taking the cue, "but she's already going to dance with me. I had just invited her to join me on the floor."

Welby frowned. "Then perhaps you will allow me the next dance." He bowed and walked away without another word.

Abrianna shook her head. "I don't know why I must dance at all. It's not like it serves any good purpose. I mean, look around you. Waltzing is nothing more than walking around the room to music." She took hold of Wade's arm. "But I know my aunts expect it of me, and if not with you, then it will just be someone else."

"Don't make it sound like you're being asked to give your life for the cause," Thane said, chuckling.

"She knows how to make a man feel special," Wade commented. "Special in a way I could do without."

"Oh, bother with the both of you." She pulled on Wade's arm and all but forced him to follow. "Let's get this over with."

Wade hadn't expected the strange feelings that seemed to grip his chest like a vise. What was happening to him, anyway? It seemed Abrianna had a way about her that could expose any and all emotions in him. The way she looked and her frank way of speaking were both things he had come to appreciate, but now with Abrianna in his arms, Wade found his thoughts to be more than appreciation.

"You dance like someone who really doesn't enjoy this any more than I do," Abrianna said.

"I'll admit it's not my favorite, either. Still, your aunts do expect it of both of us. When Mrs. Madison invited me, she explicitly told me I would have to dance no fewer than ten times."

"She told me the same thing," Abrianna said in a rather defeated way. "I've given serious thought to either lying about it and telling her I did so, or getting sick. Of course I'd have to do something quite bold to convince her that I'd fallen ill."

"Such as?" Wade was intrigued.

"Expel my supper or faint," Abrianna said matter-of-factly. "Neither really appeals to me, but they remain options, just in case."

He laughed. She could always find a way to amuse him with

her candid thoughts on everything from ways to escape her aunts' insistence that she learn to keep a household to her firm political beliefs that the Democrats had done a great deal to shake the foundations of the American Republic.

Perhaps it was her intellect that most amazed him. Wade knew her to be quite learned. She could hold her own in most any discussion, be it religion, social quandaries, or the price of fish. Once she had even given him a detailed account of how a particular piece of music had come to be. She never lacked for topics of conversation.

The music ended and Abrianna seemed most relieved. Wade understood. He gave her a wink. "Just nine more times," he told her.

Her shoulders slumped. "Nine. What a perfectly awful number."

Lenore had never known greater happiness than to be in the arms of the man she would marry on the morrow. Kolbein was an excellent dancer and a man of social etiquette, which would please her parents almost as much as his financial status did. He had won them over with his wit and intelligence, as well as his generosity. Twice he had taken her family out for expensive dinners, and both times her father had marveled at the money spent and the enjoyable company.

"You seem quite deep in thought, Miss Fulcher," Kolbein said. "Could it be that you are reconsidering our wedding tomorrow?"

"I am," she said with a most serious expression.

"What?"

She had taken him completely off guard, and the expression on his face was one of grave concern. "I'm thinking perhaps we should elope tonight." She grinned. "Of course Mother would take to her bed for a month, and Father would be beside himself over money already spent, so I suppose we shall have to wait until morning."

He gave her a wicked grin. "We could always marry with the justice tonight and then again in the morning. We could marry and then slip away for the evening—perhaps even the night. What scandal that would cause."

Lenore giggled. "Mother would never leave her bed again. She'd declare for all to hear that her social standing had been hopelessly altered by her daughter's thoughtlessness."

"I suppose we can't have that," Kolbein replied, leading Lenore from the dance floor. He maneuvered them through the open pocket doors into a small room where several couples were visiting before turning her to face him. "But I would do it in a minute if you told me that was what you wanted."

She sighed. "I want a great many things, but my wedding is the last thing I can truly give my mother. As an only child, I feel I am obligated. I wouldn't want to disappoint her after all the trouble she's gone to. My father would be disappointed, too. I don't want to hurt them after all they've done for me."

"Nothing is too good for you, Lenore. I intend to see you happy for the rest of your life. God had a plan in bringing the two of us together. I can see that now, where before I was blind to it and to God. Your influence has been good for me in more ways than I can tell."

She reached up to touch his cheek with her gloved hand. "And your influence has been good for me. I think I shall rather enjoy being Mrs. Kolbein Booth."

He laughed. "And I intend to see that you do."

25

I believe the ball is a great success," Miss Poisie declared.

"But of course it is," Wade said, smiling at the room of dancing couples. "Your dances are always successful."

The older woman nodded wistfully. "I do wish my Captain Jonathan could have lived to see this. I think he would have appreciated the nautical motif. He was always such a deep thinker when it came to the sea."

Wade felt sorry for the woman. Her ongoing love for the dead sea captain was something that he couldn't begin to understand, having never loved someone in such a manner, yet he held great tenderness for Miss Poisie. Even so, he didn't want her to dwell on her loss. Seeing Priam Welby had captured Abrianna for yet another dance, he turned to Miss Poisie. "What say we do something in honor of your captain. Would you care to dance?"

The woman's face lit up. "I would be delighted. I haven't danced at all this past year, and I believe Jonathan would heartily approve."

He led the old woman to the floor and swept her into a gentle waltz. They moved much slower than the others, but Miss Poisie didn't seem to notice. As she closed her eyes, the look on her face seemed more youthful. Perhaps in her thoughts she was young again and dancing with her beloved captain.

Wade kept his steps slow and steady, all the while keeping his eyes on Priam Welby. The man seemed far too familiar with Abrianna. He held her much too close, and the impropriety of it bothered him. Wade had certainly not been raised to concern himself with such rules, but his time spent at the school had taught him about the social etiquette of such affairs. Clearly Welby hadn't been taught or simply didn't care.

Welby momentarily let go his hold around Abrianna's waist and brushed back a stray curl. He let his fingers linger on her cheek longer than necessary before reclaiming his partner. Wade tried not to let his feelings control him. Making a scene was out of the question. Not only would it hurt the old ladies, but he'd promised himself he would allow Abrianna to manage her own affairs that evening. Still, it wasn't easy.

She can't understand that there are a great many people like Welby who seem destined to take advantage of others. Abrianna just assumes that everyone has goodness inside them, and no matter how deep that might be hidden, she is determined to find it. Even in the case of Mr. Welby.

The music ended and the orchestra took a brief intermission. Wade led Miss Poisie back to the refreshment table and gave her a slight bow. "Would you care for refreshments, Miss Poisie? Perhaps some punch?"

"Yes, that would be quite satisfying," she replied. Wade quickly took up a cup offered by one of the newer bridal students and handed it to Miss Poisie.

"Oh look," she declared, "Miss Fulcher's parents have arrived. I believe I will go and greet them." She padded off across the room, punch in hand, to welcome the newcomers.

Wade watched as Lenore quickly crossed the room to hug her mother. She beamed smiles upon each person as she introduced her parents to Kolbein's sister and brother-in-law.

"Doesn't she look absolutely radiant?" Abrianna asked, coming alongside him.

"She does, but then so do you."

For once Abrianna didn't correct him. "Thank you. You look nicely done up yourself."

Wade touched the collar of his suit coat. "Thanks to the secondhand store."

"You look quite fine," she said, turning her attention back to Lenore. "You will look perfect tomorrow at the wedding."

"I must say I didn't expect Kolbein to ask me to stand up with him."

"It isn't so strange," Abrianna countered. "You have been a good friend to him here in Seattle. I think he appreciates all you did to help look for Greta. I know I do. At first you feared he was a scallywag. It was a relief to see that even a man from Chicago could turn out to be an asset and a friend."

Wade started to comment, but just then Priam Welby interrupted their conversation. "I do hope you won't keep her all to yourself, Mr. Ackerman. I find that Miss Cunningham is the best dancer here."

"Oh, hardly that," Abrianna protested. "It's true I've had a great deal of practice in all my years of living in the bridal school. It would have been impossible to avoid dancing lessons. However, my skills are minimal, at best. There are far better dancers in this company. Not only that, but Mr. Ackerman is not keeping me. Keeping me would suggest I'm unable to keep myself, and that simply isn't the case. I am, of course, influenced by Mr. Ackerman's suggestions for my welfare, but no more so than I am of my aunts' directions."

"Which often is very little," Wade said with a chuckle. "I doubt anyone will ever 'keep' Abrianna."

"Perhaps she's not met the right man to do the job," Welby said, further irritating Wade with a suggestive smirk.

Wade wasn't to be outdone, however. He fixed Welby with a knowing look. "I don't believe Miss Cunningham has yet met a man who deserves her."

The musicians started tuning up again, and Wade offered Abrianna his hand. "Would you care to join me on the floor?"

She surprised him by refusing. "I believe I'm done with dancing." She fanned herself for a moment. "Oh, look. Lenore is going to dance with her father."

Wade heard something akin to longing, perhaps regret, in Abrianna's voice. Was she once again missing the father she'd never known? He wanted to say something to encourage her, but what could he offer as solace?

Miss Poisie rejoined them and offered her thoughts. "I find that it's always touching to watch a father and daughter share a dance. I remember once dancing with my beloved father." She didn't seem to notice the change in Abrianna's countenance, but Wade did.

Reaching over, Wade gave Abrianna's hand a squeeze. "Would you care for something to drink? You seem to have gotten overly warm."

She looked at him with an expression of appreciation. "Perhaps we could get some air."

Wade nodded. "I think I can arrange that." In that moment he would have done most anything Abrianna asked of him. He hated that she was once again reminded of all she did not have.

"I'm so glad that you and Mother came to the ball," Lenore told her father as they danced.

"Well, it hardly seemed I could refuse your request. After all, you will wed tomorrow and then be my little girl no longer."

"Oh, Father, I will always be your little girl," Lenore said, beaming at him. "Have you and Mother given any more thought to taking a trip to Europe?"

"We have discussed it at length," he replied, "but nothing will be decided until after we get you wed." He faltered in his step but corrected it before causing them both to misstep. "I'm afraid it's been a while since I danced."

"You're doing fine, Father." Lenore could see Kolbein dancing with her mother. "And Mother and Kolbein seem to be in perfect step."

Father smiled. "They do seem quite adept. It would seem your young man has won her over."

Lenore couldn't contain her glee. "Once Mother realized that I wouldn't live in poverty, she could find nothing with which to condemn him. Not that she would. Mother has always been very supportive of my finding true love just as she did."

"And of course she was right. I only wanted to see you safely cared for. The future isn't always something we can make plans for. I know . . ." He paused, panting. "I'm afraid I may not be up to this."

"We don't need to continue," Lenore told him. "It was wonderful that you could be here, and that we could share this moment." Her father slowed their steps and then without warning stopped altogether in the midst of the swirling dancers.

"Oh dear," he gasped.

"What's wrong?" Lenore could see the strange look on his face as his color drained. "Father?"

People around them slowed and then stopped as Lenore's father clutched his chest and collapsed on the floor.

"Father!" Even the music stopped when Lenore let out a scream.

Kolbein was at her side almost immediately, bringing Lenore's mother with him. "What happened?" He knelt beside the now unconscious man.

"He just stopped and then fell." She took hold of her mother's arm. "He just dropped to the floor."

Her mother nodded, fearful, but not looking overly shocked. "It's his heart," she said matter-of-factly.

Lenore looked at her in stunned confusion. "What are you saying?"

By now several people were attending her father. She looked to her mother for answers. "Mother, why do you say it's his heart? Is something wrong with Father's heart?"

"The doctor told him that his heart is weak."

"Then why . . . why did he dance with me?" Lenore looked back to her stricken father. "This is all my fault."

Her mother took hold of her. "No. It's not your fault. He knew the risk. He wanted very much to dance with you. It was all he could speak of prior to our arrival."

"Let me through," a man declared from the onlooking crowd. "I'm a physician."

It seemed to take forever, when in fact it was only minutes. The man spoke momentarily to Lenore's mother before kneeling beside the now still man. "We need to get him to the hospital. It would seem he's had some sort of attack." The doctor straightened and looked at the crowd. "I need some men to carry him downstairs to a carriage."

Wade, Thane, and Kolbein quickly stepped up, as well as several other men, and lifted Lenore's father. Nothing felt real and Lenore could only watch after them as they worked to maneuver out of the ballroom. Her mother trailed after them, but Lenore felt as if she were nailed to the floor.

Abrianna was quickly at her side, taking hold of her arm. "I heard you scream, and now I see that the reason was sound. How can I help you, my dear friend?"

Mrs. Madison took hold of her on one side, while Abrianna continued to support her on the other. "Help me walk her downstairs to join her mother," the older woman commanded.

Lenore looked to Mrs. Madison. "I . . . don't know what to do."

"Dear, you must not worry about anything. Your father is a sick man, and you must attend him."

"But the ball . . . our wedding . . ." She shook her head. "Someone will need to contact people . . . to cancel the wedding."

"You needn't worry about such things. We can take care of everything," Mrs. Madison soothed.

"I'm surprised you could even manage a rational thought about it," Abrianna offered. "In times of great stress one is often given over to a muddled mind." She looked at Lenore and nodded. "I can see that you are a much stronger woman than I gave you credit for."

"Abrianna, get the door," Mrs. Madison said as they reached the front room. "Now, Lenore, you do have one responsibility. You must see to your mother. She will need you at a time like this."

Lenore found rational thought difficult. Nothing seemed real, and for several minutes she wondered if this was a nightmare. Abrianna patted her arm, but Lenore felt no comfort. Her father might well die, and all from straining his heart by dancing.

"Might I go with them to the hospital, Aunt Miriam?" Abrianna asked. "In times like these, a trusted friend would surely be a fitting companion, even if one does have the support of a fiancé."

"I don't know," Mrs. Madison replied. "I suppose someone should."

Lenore heard the exchange but said nothing. When Mrs. Madison finally agreed to let Abrianna go with her, they had reached the bottom step. Just then Wade was making his way back into the building.

"Abrianna wishes to go with Lenore," Mrs. Madison declared. "Would you stay with her and see her home?"

Wade nodded. "Of course. I was just coming back to tell Lenore that her father is in his carriage. Her mother, too. I'm sure they have already left. One of the other men offered his carriage to transport you and Kolbein. I'm sure there's room for us all."

He led them outside, where Kolbein quickly joined them. "Oh, my darling, I'm so sorry." Lenore fell into his arms sobbing.

"Come on," Wade encouraged. "There will be time enough for that."

They climbed into the offered carriage, and Kolbein took the seat beside Lenore, while Wade and Abrianna sat opposite them. Kolbein drew her close and kept his arm around her, whispering words of comfort in her ear. Abrianna and Wade looked to be in prayer with heads bowed and hands folded. Lenore thought it all a strange sort of act—a tragedy—where each of them had a part to play.

Tears still flowed down her face, but a numbing sort of sensation was gradually sinking over her. She looked to Kolbein for answers, but his grave expression offered little consolation. No one said a word. Even Abrianna had nothing to say, and perhaps that worried Lenore most of all.

The ride to the hospital seemed to take forever, and all Lenore could imagine was a scene where her father lay dying in her mother's arms. Tomorrow she was to have married, but now she might well be burying her father instead.

When they arrived at the hospital, Lenore allowed Kolbein to help her from the carriage and lead her up the hospital steps. He held her tightly at the elbow and maneuvered them through the building to where her mother stood watching and waiting.

"Is he . . . has he . . ." Lenore sputtered the words and broke into sobs.

Her mother took hold of her. "He isn't dead, Lenore. You need to be strong now. I need you."

The tone of her mother's voice was one Lenore had never heard. She sounded frightened yet appeared so stoic. How long had she known of Father's illness? Why had they kept it from her?

Lenore forced her tears back and took a handkerchief that Kolbein offered. "Why didn't you tell me he was sick? I would never have let him dance."

"Which is why we didn't tell you. Your father didn't want people fussing over him. He wanted to live out his life without people fretting about his heart."

"But dancing with me caused him to have this attack. I may well have killed him."

"Lenore, you must stop this." Her mother reached out and took hold of her. Several nurses hurried past them, but Mother kept her gaze fixed on Lenore. "I can't bear to think of him dying. Oh, it's times like this that I wish I . . . well . . . I wish I knew God better. Perhaps then I would know what He has planned and what I should do."

The reality of the moment hit Lenore hard. Her mother had always been nominal in her spiritual beliefs. "We should pray," Lenore said, taking hold of her mother's hands. She glanced over her shoulder at Kolbein and her friends. "I'm not so very good at this myself. But maybe one of you might petition the Lord for us?"

"I'm not sure what to say," Kolbein admitted. "Perhaps Wade might lead us?"

Wade nodded. "Let's join hands." They did and bowed their heads. "Father, we ask your blessing on Mr. Fulcher. He has suffered this attack, as you know, and we ask that you would heal him and restore him to his family. We know that difficulties like this must plague us in this world because we are fallen from that perfection you once had for us. However, we also know that you are merciful and loving. So no matter the outcome . . ." He paused for a moment. "If you restore Mr. Fulcher here or in heaven, give us the strength to endure the circumstances. Help Mrs. Fulcher and Lenore to be strong and at peace, completely assured that you are with them and will never leave them to face such storms alone. In Jesus' name, amen."

"Amen," the others murmured.

Lenore felt a modicum of peace. How she wished her faith were stronger. She looked to Abrianna. "If only I had paid more attention to the sermons as you did and studied my Bible, I might be strong enough to bear this burden."

"You are stronger than you know, Lenore. And God knows your heart. Just trust Him."

"Trust is hard," Mrs. Fulcher interjected. "Like Lenore, I've not given much attention to things of spiritual depth. I suppose now I am paying the price."

"No," Kolbein said, putting his arm around his soon-to-be mother-in-law. "Situations like this draw a person closer to God or send them far away in anger. Even so, dying and living are all a part of our lives. But good friends recently taught me that there is always time while we have breath to make things right with God."

"I pray you're right," Mother declared. "Oh, I pray you are right."

The doctor who'd helped at the ball came from a room across the hall. "He's stable for now."

Mother dropped her hold on Lenore and turned to the doctor. "Can I see him?"

"Not just yet. The hospital physician gave him some medication to help his heart, and he must rest for the time. You should be able to see him in the morning. However, he will need to remain in the hospital for a time."

Lenore let out a long breath. She had fully expected the man to announce her father's death. She looked to Kolbein, who offered her a reassuring smile. It was the first moment since her father's collapse that she dared to hope.

"Will he be all right?" she asked.

"As right as a man with his condition can be," the doctor replied. "I presume you know that your father has a weak heart."

"We hadn't told her," Mother interjected, "but she knows now."

The doctor nodded. "Good. I would suggest you two return home and get some rest. He'll be ready to see you tomorrow."

"But if anything happens . . ." Mother let the words trail into silence.

The doctor understood and nodded. "We would send someone to let you know." Mother considered this for a moment and then nodded.

"Come, I'll take you both home," Kolbein announced.

Mother turned to him and surprised Lenore with a request

of Kolbein. "Would you please stay the night with us? I'd feel better if you were there, should something happen. And, perhaps we might . . . pray again?"

"Of course," Kolbein replied. "I would be honored to stay, and also to pray with you . . . both."

Abrianna watched the scene unfold, feeling ever so worried for her friend. Nothing like this had ever happened to Lenore. She wasn't accustomed to loss, and Abrianna worried that should her father die, she might not be able to bear the situation.

Wade led her from the hospital, following Lenore and Kolbein as they assisted Mrs. Fulcher into the carriage. Abrianna watched until the carriage had driven out of sight and then turned to Wade.

"Thank you for praying. It was a lovely prayer."

"I was happy to help. Now I need to get you back home."

"I suppose so," she murmured. "I suppose, too, that we must take the carriage back rather than walk. Although a good long walk is exactly what I need, it would hardly be appropriate in the gown and these shoes. Goodness, but I don't know how anyone wears shoes like this all the time." She lifted the hem of her skirt just enough to reveal a pair of lovely silver satin heels.

Wade shook his head. "I'm certain I don't know." He grinned. "They look rather like torture devices."

Abrianna nodded solemnly. "Indeed they are. I've never felt my little toe so pinched. I told Lenore they were too small, but she insisted they were the only thing for me to wear with this gown. So I was quite fashionable but in pain. Even so, what a positively terrible end to our evening."

Wade signaled the carriage driver and assisted Abrianna down the hospital steps. "At least Mr. Fulcher is stable, so it's not a complete tragedy."

"But it will alter everything for poor Lenore. Her wedding will be postponed, and her thoughts will be consumed with guilt. I know her. She will continue to blame herself for this mishap, even though she had no way of knowing that anything was wrong with her father."

Helping Abrianna into the carriage, Wade offered his thoughts. "Lenore will listen to you. If you tell her . . . better yet, if you show her through the Word that she can take comfort in God, perhaps she will be able to dwell on Him rather than her feelings of guilt."

Abrianna settled into her seat and waited until Wade took his place opposite her. Now that they were alone, there was no need to crowd together on one side. Even so, she missed his closeness.

"I have to admit, I have guilty feelings of my own."

Wade looked at her strangely. "But why?"

"I was feeling sorry for myself. I was quite immersed in envy, if the truth is told." She shook her head. "I found myself wishing that I might have known what it was like to have a father's love, to dance with him and know his pride in me."

"Abrianna, if your father were alive today, he would no doubt take great pride in you. You are a remarkable young woman, and I'm proud to call you friend."

She smiled, doing her best to put aside her feelings of sadness. "I'm proud to call you friend, as well, Mr. Ackerman. You have been quite tolerant and patient with me these many, many years. I thank you for enduring such difficulties."

He chuckled. "It wasn't so much of a chore, Abrianna. It

was worrisome at times, but our friendship was worth the endurance."

"I quite agree, even though you are often bossy and disparaging of my goals." She thought to go into more detail, then fell silent. "But those are better discussed another day. For now, I'm just thankful that you are here."

26

The doctor finally agreed to release Lenore's father from the hospital two weeks later and declared that he should be capable of attending a late August wedding at the earliest. To be certain her father would be well enough to walk her down the aisle, Lenore decided on a September wedding. And eager to keep her parents from worrying about any of the arrangements, she enlisted the help of the bridal school.

Now settled in their new extensive property in the Lower Queen Anne area just north of downtown, the old ladies were more than happy to direct their efforts to such a gay occasion. With the wedding in two days, Lenore was giving the gardens one final inspection.

"Everything looks lovely," she declared. "I'm blessed by all that you've done."

Mrs. Madison, accompanied by Abrianna, smiled and nodded. "The Lord has blessed us with an abundance of blossoms from the roses. Not only that, but the hydrangea are continuing to bloom quite late. Your wedding will not want for floral decoration. If you'll come this way, I'll show you where the tents have been arranged should it rain."

"You'll see that Aunt Miriam has made provision for most every possibility."

"Well," her aunt said, "we know that having a contingency for every situation makes for a more orderly event." She led the way to a massive pavilion of white canvas.

Lenore inspected the secondary site and gave it her approval. Mrs. Madison explained the plan to cut and arrange flowers from the garden and bring them into the tents should the weather turn bad.

"My sister has volunteered to finish decorating them and plans to use some of the silver, gold, and white materials we used last year for our annual ball. There will be bows and streamers of ribbon as well as green boughs and bouquets on every table. So you needn't worry come rain or shine."

"Well, I for one am praying for a beautiful day," Abrianna declared. "And you have picked a perfect time for the wedding. Eleven o'clock in the morning is perfect. It's not really morning, but definitely not yet afternoon. The sun can be quite warm but not too hot. At least that's been my experience. I wouldn't want the temperature to cause us discomfort."

Lenore smiled. "Oh, Abrianna, you do worry about the silliest things."

Her friend frowned. "But the temperature isn't at all silly. Goodness, we don't need you collapsing from the heat. And what of your father? We must consider his needs, as well."

Lenore put her finger to Abrianna's lips. "The Lord will take charge of the day. You needn't fret. After all, that's what you used to always tell me. So now I relay the same information. "'Do not fret, for the Lord is faithful.'"

Abrianna nodded and Lenore lowered her hand. "Of course

you are right to remind me." She gave a sigh. "Sometimes I fear I will never be as faithful as I should be."

In a gown of white satin and lace, Lenore walked down the garden path on her father's arm. Overhead, the skies were heavy with the promise of rain, but so far not a drop had fallen. True to her word, Mrs. Madison had created a beautiful, almost ethereal, setting for the garden wedding. Lenore tried to take in everything at once and memorize how each flower looked and how beautifully decorated the white wooden arbor stood.

Father was in fine spirits, teasing her prior to the start of their walk. He had jokingly said that now that she was an heiress and wealthy in her own right, she needn't marry Kolbein unless she truly wished to. He had laughed, knowing her answer, and Lenore felt reassured by his seeming strength. When he kissed her and handed her over to Kolbein, there was no sign of his being sick at all. For this, she praised God.

Kolbein flashed her a smile and held her hand most possessively. He was so handsome in his morning suit of gray, and his gaze made Lenore feel as if she were the most beautiful woman in the world.

Lenore couldn't help but smile behind her veil. Their romance had been a whirlwind, but their future lives would be fixed on a solid foundation of faith and love in God and for each other.

"Dearly beloved," the minister began, "we have gathered this day to witness the matrimony of Miss Lenore Fulcher and Mr. Kolbein Booth. Would the guests remain standing while we pray."

Lenore bowed her head and felt Kolbein tighten his hold on her hand. Was he worried that she might slip away before he reopened his eyes? Perhaps he felt as amazed as she and just wanted to hold on to every moment, every feeling and thought, lest anything be missed.

The minister finished his wedding blessing and bid the attendees to sit before continuing with the wedding service. Lenore lost track of the words and thought only of how much she had come to love this man who would soon be her husband. She had never imagined love could come so quickly to a heart, but God had definitely caused it to grow between the two of them. She prayed it would always continue to grow.

They exchanged their vows, and when Kolbein placed a beautiful ring of diamonds and sapphires on her finger, Lenore couldn't help but admire the piece. For a moment she wondered at the cost but just as quickly put aside her concern. She was marrying a man of means, and he was very generous. And, as her father had suggested, she was now quite well fixed herself. However, she had plans for a good portion of her money and knew that Kolbein wouldn't object. No doubt he would easily yield to her request that they help fund Abrianna's new exploits to see her street folk fed and clothed. Perhaps one day they would help shelter the poor, as well. She grinned, meeting her husband's curious expression. There would be time enough to explain later.

Lifting her veil at the minister's announcement that he could kiss his bride, Kolbein looked at her as if seeing her for the first time.

"I marvel to think you belong to me." He drew her into his arms. "My beloved Lenore."

After a kiss that didn't last nearly long enough for Lenore, Kolbein stepped back and turned to greet their audience of well-wishers. Abrianna handed Lenore her bouquet of flowers and kissed her cheek.

"I think that went beautifully," her friend murmured. "No one fainted or coughed during the recitation of your vows. And the rain held off." They both looked skyward at the growing heaviness of the clouds.

Then before she knew it, Kolbein was whisking her away into the crowd of people. Lenore longed for a quiet moment alone with her husband, but it was not to be. At least not just yet. By the time they shared a wedding brunch and received hundreds of toasts for their future, Lenore was exhausted.

When Kolbein leaned over to whisper in her ear, Lenore straightened in her chair and smiled. Standing, Kolbein helped her to her feet, and cheers sang out from the wedding guests.

"My friends, Lenore and I must leave your company now and prepare for our departure. Our ship sails at four and we must make ready. Thank you for your many blessings and prayers."

With that, he escorted Lenore rather hastily into the house, where the old ladies had prepared a room for them to change for their wedding trip. Lenore suddenly felt overcome by joy and burst into tears. She was married now. Married to the man of her dreams—dreams that she hadn't even fully known until Kolbein had come into her life.

Surprising her, Kolbein took her in his arms and kissed her passionately. Lenore felt breathless when he pulled away and gazed deeply into her damp eyes.

"I love you so completely, Lenore. I've never known such a thing, and I find that it consumes me. I thank God for bringing me to Seattle to find you."

"But you weren't looking for me," Lenore said with a tilt of the head.

"Wasn't I?" he asked and then kissed her again.

Tracie Peterson is the award-winning author of over a hundred novels, both historical and contemporary. Her avid research resonates in her stories, as seen in her bestselling HEIRS OF MONTANA and ALASKAN QUEST series. Tracie and her family make their home in Montana. Visit Tracie's website at www.tracie peterson.com.

More From Bestselling Author Tracie Peterson

To learn more about Tracie and her books, visit traciepeterson.com.

Three LONE STAR BRIDES seek out marriage for very different reasons. They each face difficult choices and obstacles on the road ahead. But they'll also find friendship and adventure, as well as romance and a place to call home.

LONE STAR BRIDES: *A Sensible Arrangement, A Moment in Time, A Matter of Heart*

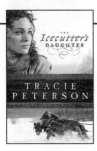

Three young women struggle to find love and a sense of belonging among the immigrant communities that first settled the harsh yet beautiful land of historic Minnesota.

LAND OF SHINING WATER: *The Icecutter's Daughter, The Quarryman's Bride, The Miner's Lady*

More Romance You May Enjoy

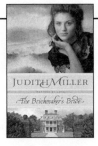